THE OMEGA CORPS II

The Giant and The Ghost

I0546437

KEITH HUNTSMAN

TREATY OAK PUBLISHERS

PUBLISHER'S NOTE

Copyright © 2020 by Keith Huntsman
Cover design by Kim McBride

**Printed and published in
the United States of America**

TREATY OAK PUBLISHERS

ISBN 978-1-943658-51-0

Cast of Characters

Senior Command of the Omega Corps

- **Jackson Alexander (Jander) Steele**, Lord Orion of the Omega Corps, Captain and Commander of the *Angel*; force projection and analysis, eidetics, second-level telepathy; husband of Vickie
- **Victoria Cunningham (Vickie) Steele**, Lady Alpha of the Omega Corps, First Officer and Chief of Staff of the *Angel*; telepathy, telekinesis, telehypnosis; wife of Jander
- **Denver (Denny) Connors**, Senior Commander Kodiak of the Omega Corps, Chief Engineer of the *Angel*; titanism
- **Theresa (Terry) Kirkland**, Senior Commander Chloe of the Omega Corps, Chief Science Officer and Chief Medical Officer of the *Angel*; transmutation/microvoyance
- **Jacob (Jake) Anson**, Lord Commander Binary of the Omega Corps, Director of Gaean Operations; telepathy, radiopathy; Arden's brother
- **Arden Anson**, Senior Commander Mercury of the Omega Corps, Master Engineer; teleportation; Jake's brother
- **Richard Ford**, Corpsman Hermes, teleportation; Jander's adjutant

Bridge Crew of the *Angel*

- **Pavel Kalanev**, Commander Cobra of the Omega Corps, Armaments Officer, telepathy; Jander's most trusted advisor

- **Nwoye Lam**, Corpsman Scatter, Helmsman, telekinesis
- **Alexiy Pashkov**, Corpsman Seshat, Navigator, computopathy
- **Tsin Li-san**, Corpsman Jinwu, Communications Officer, telepathy
- **Kurino Yukio**, Corpsman Kitsune, Sensors Officer, spectrality/clairvoyance
- **Geraldo (Aldo) Belocci**, Corpsman Portunes, Analytics Officer, computopathy
- **Mealla O'Hearne**, Corpsman Neamhain, backup Armaments Officer, clairvoyance/clairaudience

CREW OF THE *ANGEL*

- **Chelsea Winschell**, Corpsman Nebula, med tech, spectrality/clairvoyance
- **William (Bill) Wize**, Corpsman Kohana, engineer, eidetics
- **Simon (Slim) Crawley**, Corpsman Pecos, comm tech, telepathy
- **Elga Mançon**, Corpsman Dominique, coder, computopathy
- **Zachariah (Zach) Whitney**, Corpsman Peregrine, Banshee pilot, telekinesis; husband of Ann
- **Frederic (Freddie) Soames**, Corpsman Jumbuck, Banshee gunner, teleportation
- **Sharon Gibson**, Corpsman Harmonia, zoologist, zootelepathy
- **Walter Rosenberg**, Corpsman Doppelwulf, special ops/vet tech, metamorphism
- **Cielo Kiaga**, Corpsman Raankhak, special ops/pulse gunner, metamorphism
- **Ann Whitney**, Corpsman Sabrina, lab tech, transmutation/microvoyance, wife of Zach

- **Arai Osamu**, Corpsman Tenome, teleport engineer, clairvoyance/clairaudience
- **David Malloye**, Corpsman Clarion, special ops/beam gunner, teleportation
- **Harold (Hal) Summers**, Commander Surrey of the Omega Corps, Second Engineer of the *Angel*, telekinesis

THE STELLAR CONFEDERATION

- **Nil Spart**, of Sabar, Admiral of the Confederation Fleet
- **Tondo Lim**, of Sabar, Director of the Confederation
- **Ghgundh**, of Hasgonde, Captain of a merchant ship

THE TWIN PLANETS

- **The Head of Ertain**, the absolute despot of the Twin Planets
- **Z'zschou**, of Ertain, Captain of the cruiser *Rannz*
- **Meshzner**, of Liev, bodyguard to Z'zschou
- **Schaus**, of Ertain, *Rannz* crewman
- **Gazenhout**, of Ertain, *Rannz* crewman

The Giant and The Ghost

PROLOGUE

The double pocket hatch at the rear of the Bridge slid aside, and Jander Steele ushered his ash-blonde wife, Vickie, ahead of him onto the elevated command platform. The courtesy was to allow her to enter first and be announced in the order of arrival rather than rank.

"FIRST OFFICER ON THE BRIDGE! CAPTAIN ON THE BRIDGE!" The voice of Angela, the *Angel*'s quantum plasma persona, announced them in her near-human contralto. The crew at their stations straightened a bit but did not waver in their attention to duty. Aboard the *Angel*, "as you were" was a given.

Armaments officer Pavel Kalanev rose from the command chair, faced the pair and bowed his head in greeting. He and about half the others were dressed in the silvery blue shirt and slacks of the service uniform of the Corps; the rest were in casual or native dress of their choosing. The Omega Corps was an international cartel of many cultures; only on formal or public occasions was any kind of military dress code enforced. Vickie was in a flowing mauve summer dress while Jander wore an untucked green guayabera shirt and well-worn jeans.

"We are steady on course, Captain," the Ukrainian told them in his usual precise English. "Since we are well within Confederation territory our baffle screen is at maximum and our warp sphere and defensive shields are at minimum. Our footprint is therefore less than thirty thousand kilometers and undetectable. We are cruising at eight point six gravities squared and shall reach our intercept point in the Gramb to Larkant trade route in approximately fifty hours, with midpoint at twelve hours."

"Very good, Cobra. I have the con." Kalanev bowed again and turned to resume his armaments station on the foredeck below them. Steele slid into the command chair and scanned his console to check the general status of his ship. Pavel's report was, of course, dead on.

Vickie took the First Officer's seat behind his left shoulder. "Any sign of alerts from the Confederation, Li-san?"

"No, Milady," Tsin Li-san answered from the communications console a few meters in front of the command seat. "I expect Admiral Spart is still digesting our visit."

"I expect," Jander agreed. "I'd think he'd have spread the word of our existence by now if he was going to. He's had almost two days to work up another temper."

"Well, if that happens you can't blame him for it." Vickie's voice was its usual sweet music. It matched her face and form to perfection. "You've really got to stop sneaking up on the poor man." She sent an impulse that combined her telepathic, telehypnotic and telekinetic talents to give him a teasing caress.

"I'd be happy to, but since the rest of the Stellar Confederation doesn't know we exist yet we can't just knock on his door." Although his impenetrable mental shield made him immune to Vickie's hypnotic influence, he felt her embrace and returned it with a hug from a molecular cohesion forcefield.

He looked around the Bridge to see who was on duty. Since he was usually present for the forenoon watch, he was not surprised to see the first team manning the five consoles arranged on the lower level like five pips on a die: the telekinetic Nigerian, Nwoye Lam, at the helm forward to his left; Alexiy Pashkov, computopath, at navigation to the right of Lam; spectralist Kurino Yukio at sensors forward of Pashkov; the telepathic Kalanev at armaments to her left; and Tsin, also a telepath, dead center at communications. The computopathic Italian, Geraldo Belocci, was at his analytics station on the bulkhead to the left of Lam, but since they were at blue alert and expected no trouble the backup stations around the perimeter of the Bridge were mostly vacant.

Jander gazed at one of his readouts. "Yukio. What's the status of that set of bogeys off seven?" In practical usage, directions were indicated by which of the spherical *Angel*'s twenty convex hull sections was toward the object of interest. Seven was the rearward section above the *Angel*'s equatorial plane in relation to the Bridge.

Kurino Yukio flashed her radiant smile over her shoulder as her tiny fingers tickled her keyboard to send her sensors data to the big monitor on the front bulkhead. "We have a squadron of six warships, Orion-sama, a little smaller than Sabarian cruisers. They may be Dwatan." The Dwatans, a luxuriously furred species with prehensile tails, were of shorter stature than Gaeans or the hominin Sabarians. "Their heading is no threat to our stealth run."

Tsin interjected, "My passive scan shows they're running silent, but that's common on long trips. I don't think they're the guys we're looking for, this far off the major trade routes. I can breathe in their ear if you want me to."

Jander barely noticed the familiarity of the remark, much less did he give any thought to how unmilitary it was. Li-San was well known for his droll humor and, being an open-minded telepath, he was never hesitant to display it.

"Let's not," he answered just as casually. "Friendly or not, we don't want them to know we're sneaking around out here. Alexiy, where are they headed?"

Pashkov integrated Kurino's sensor data into his navigation matrix. "It would appear they're headed to intercept same trade route we are, sir." As many Russians did, he had a habit of dropping articles from his speech. "They're decelerating in curve that will get them there a day ahead of us, but on heading toward Gramb." The lanky Russian spun his chair to look up at his captain. "By then we'll be traveling in opposite directions. If they're the hijackers we are hunting for, we wouldn't be in position to intercept."

Tsin added, "The last success call we picked up from the pirates was a tachyon spurt from the direction of the trade route, sir. Too far away to be from these guys. That was an echo, though, so we can't be certain of the origin."

Kalanev too turned in his chair. "That is a point for investigating them now, as Mr. Tsin suggested. If they are indeed our piratical persons of interest, we will not have them this close at hand in the near future."

Vickie chipped in, "And if they're not, we'll expose ourselves and have every ship in the Confederation looking for us." She smoothly crossed her splendid legs, a gesture she often used as a debating tool. "Given that we're only a few parsecs from Falgum and the home base of the whole Confederation fleet, the chances are pretty overwhelming they're friendlies." Falgum was the star around which orbited Dephlet, the governmental seat of the Stellar Confederation.

Something nagged at Steele's subconscious, some tidbit of free association, but try as he might with his eidetic memory and analytical gifts, it refused to surface. He tabled it in his mind and decided to bow to the logic of his brilliant wife.

"Okay, we'll let them go. The last thing we need right now is a couple thousand ships looking for us while we're trying to do them a favor. Let's maintain course and speed, but stay alert for any more spurts. I want these murderous bastards in the worst way."

A murmur of agreement came from the Bridge crew, whose dedication to the cause of justice was as absolute as their commander's.

Jander sat back in his chair and closed his eyes, letting the second-level thoughts of his team wash over his mind. Since they were on blue alert he did not need to be there, but he felt an almost hypnotic pleasure in watching his Corpsmen work. They were the best, the very best. They were family.

CHAPTER 1

The fat, egg-shaped merchant ship sailed through space at its cruising speed of four and a half gravities squared, safe from the ravages of space-time distortion within its one point six million-kilometer warp infusion sphere common to commercial craft. The Hasgondi captain lounged on his command couch with only the communications operator to keep him company. The Gramb-Larkant trade route was a long one and most of his small crew took turns on watch. The kinetic collision shields of his unnamed command kept them safe from any deep-space debris that might enter the sphere.

The deep hum of the hyperspace proximity alarm forced Captain Ghgundh to open his eyes. His thick fingers touched a key, and his couch shifted to more of a sitting position so he could read the tachyon particle sensors that allowed him to see the universe outside his warp sphere. The proximity coding of the ship's unsophisticated computer sent the sensor image of the intruders to his forward monitor, with the relative course, speed and shield data displayed on the smaller monitor beneath it. Six twelve-gun cruisers approached from astern of his ship like a shiver of sharks, penetrated the merchant's warp sphere and blended their own with it, locking them all in the same bubble of sub-light protection.

Captain Ghgundh called the bridge crew to their stations and asked the com operator to send a short-range tachyon broadcast requesting the squadron's identity. It was met with silence. He was neither surprised nor annoyed by the lack of response; that was common during flybys within the more heavily traveled trade routes. Nor was he surprised when the cruisers split from their tight formation into a circle to skirt by with the much larger cargo ship in the center.

The Hasgondi, a peaceful ursid species from a peaceful planet and its colonies, were very forgiving when it came to protocols. The captain assumed the cruisers, their Confederation-standard ovoid profiles sleeker and faster than his fat command, would simply pass him and be on their way in no time.

The three other Bridge crew, coarse-haired pelts unbrushed, lumbered in and took their couches with only a few low greetings in their deep-throated language.

Ghgundh acknowledged them with a wave as he shifted his chocolate eyes from one monitor showing the approaching squadron to the other. He began to feel concerned when the six warships retroed back to his pace and ran parallel, encircling him like spokes on a hub. Even as he patiently waited for what he expected to be a brief greeting or perhaps an inquiry, he nonetheless called to his pilot to strengthen their energy defense shield.

It was too little, too late. The speakers on his console erupted in tachyon interference, causing the com operator to tear herself away from her console with a startled bawl.

With that as the only warning, the midships batteries of three of the encircling cruisers opened fire!

Ghgundh roared in distress as the nucleonic pulse bolts tore through his weak commercial energy shields and struck at the bow, stern and single gun port of his ship. The gun was obliterated with a single shot, leaving a gaping, air-venting hole in the broadest part of the hull. Two shots struck the bow, knocking out the quantum entanglement communications array and sending them into a yawing spin.

The stern took the greatest punishment. Pulse after pulse slammed into his drive engines and exploded their reactors, leaving the merchant drifting on momentum alone with a quarter of its length vaporized. Inertia pushed the blast energy and globules of melted nanosteel backward from the ship, exposing a white-hot and sparking crater. The engine room was destroyed with its crew, and both the energy shield and the kinetic shield flared and died. The warp sphere also failed, leaving their survival at the squadron's mercy. The mortal wounds rapidly cooled in the vacuum as the airtight doors slammed shut to seal off what remained of the ship.

Half his crew already killed, Ghgundh ordered his

Bridge personnel to suit up. He rolled off his couch and tore open the small-arms locker to arm them as soon as they scrambled into their environmental suits. Only then did he pull on his own. He stared grimly at his few remaining monitors as he sealed his helmet. From each of the six cruisers, a short-range armed shuttle emerged and closed the gap to his ship. One held back in reserve as two shuttles went to the stern, two to the bow, and a fifth to the gutted gun port.

Captain Ghgundh knew the cause was lost. His four remaining crew were no match for the boarders already setting up tactical airlocks at the breaches. Resigned to defeat, he ordered his two men and two women to lay down their arms. With no other choice, they waited for the invaders with the fatalistic patience for which their species was renowned.

The hatch to the Bridge slid open, and four slim bipeds a full meter shorter than the towering Hasgondi competed with each other to be the first through. Ghgundh pushed his big empty paws toward them to express his surrender.

It made no difference. The pirates leveled their short rifles and stroked the triggers. The lasers sent their searing red needles deep into the hapless citizens of the most nonviolent species in the Confederation, murdering them with no thought of mercy.

CAPTAIN Z'ZSCHOU OF THE BATTLE CRUISER *Rannz* settled back in his command chair and nodded complacently. A good job of cleanup. No remnant of the gutted merchantman larger than a few meters across could be detected. He would not make the fatal mistake of other captains, that of leaving detectable traces of his activity. Except for the cargo that now filled the holds of his squadron, the merchant ship had ceased to exist.

"Communications, send the spurt." The com officer barked acknowledgement and touched a key on his console. A split-second tachyon message sped through mobile relays toward their home world encoded with their identity and position, and a summary of their success. Normal procedure now called for the six ships under his command to rendezvous with a fast cargo vessel that would take the contraband off their hands...

"We have a response, Captain!" the communications officer rapped.

The commander straightened in his chair, a chill traveling up his spine. A reply to a success call was very much out of the ordinary. Success was always assumed; only failure would bring reaction, and his squadron had done nothing wrong. He straightened the snap front and cuffs of his maroon tunic as a familiar yellow-skinned face flashed onto the forward screen. "Your Excellency!"

The communication was by quantum entanglement rather than tachyon broadcast, so there was no delay in response. "Please remain seated, Captain. I understand you must be fatigued after your battle." The Admiral's pinched face stretched out of its accustomed shape under the force of a flat smile.

Z'zschou smiled in exactly the same way, his mind whirling. With some misgivings he decided to take the irony in the statement at face value. "It was not much of a battle, Excellency. The Confederation is still unaware that we are hurting them."

"So it appears. What is your prize?"

"Machine tools for working the harder alloys, sir. Top-quality Hasgondi manufacture, built of Nokilonian alloys and powered by Squn electronics."

"Prisoners?"

"None, Excellency. According to recent directives, no more merchant crews are to be taken alive. In any case, the Hasgondi make poor slaves."

"By whose opinion?" The Admiral's bland sneer did not change, but his voice was a bit too mild. The Captain felt his face turn a creamier shade of yellow. He was a good task force commander; he was not a xenopsychologist. He had stepped out of his station.

To his infinite relief, the Admiral waved it aside. "Be that as it may. What is your present location?"

"Seventy-four percent along the trade route between Larkant and Gramb, Excellency." He hoped the twitching of the black fur covering his forehead did not betray his nervousness.

"Good. About fifteen percent behind you there is a merchant vessel of a different type than we are accustomed to. We have intercepted a few fragmentary signals indicating that this ship is an experimental model of a size and type heretofore unknown. You are to investigate, and if you have any difficulty you are to call the Fourth Fleet for aid. Questions?"

The Captain pondered the scanty information. "I am flattered by the trust, Excellency. Have you anything on their course and speed?"

The Admiral glanced down at something out of the monitor's view. "Course is the reverse of yours. Speed is four Confederation gravities per second squared. One of the pieces we picked up indicates that that speed is considered 'excellent' by the crew."

"Easily caught, then." He paused, sucking one of his broad teeth. "Do I have your leave to attempt capture?"

"You do, but damage is to be kept to a minimum, and the crew taken intact. It might be correct to waive communication and fire immediately; we have no idea how or even if the ship is armed. You should strike to cripple, just in case."

Captain Z'zschou interpreted that as an order. "A sound suggestion, Excellency. I shall do so."

"Very well. I shall await your report." With no pause and no courtesy, the Admiral cut the communication.

The Captain snapped out the necessary orders and, holds still full, the six ships side-retroed to turn their momentum toward the new target. He leaned back and absently stroked his naturally unfurred chin, staring at the star-filled hologram in the center of the ring of command stations on his Bridge. After long minutes of mulling the conversation he arrived at the assumption that the Admiral was not expecting complete success from his initial contact. He was relieved by that conclusion; failure did not necessarily mean personal disaster. On the other hand, complete success could mean rich reward.

He let his thoughts drift in that happy direction. As he sat watching the stars in the hologram spring into being and flash toward him, fading at the back edge of the projection in seconds, he lost himself in visions of a great mansion and rich clothing, fine foods and a docile assortment of tall, long-haired and pale-skinned Sabarian females...

CHAPTER 2

Vice Admiral Nil Spart tried to settle his nerves as he waited in the outer office of the Director of the Confederation. Not that he had been sitting there forever; Director Lim appreciated that other people had schedules, too, and was meticulous in keeping his appointments. No, Spart was simply very anxious. The interview to come was certain to be the most difficult of his life. His fingers traced the circumference of the small data disk in an interior pocket of his insignia-covered forest green vest and for the thousandth time damned Lord Orion for putting him in this position.

His feelings for Lord Orion—that was the only name he knew the Gaean by—were an odd mixture of admiration and antipathy. The maddening barbarian had played him like a Dwatan tripleflute, shamelessly toying with his mind and rubbing his nose in the result. The fact that the result was unquestionably noble and admirable was the basis of Spart's respect. But that did not disguise the fact that Orion quite possibly had ruined his career with his impudent manipulations.

The door to the anteroom opened. The Director's

corpulent Leosan personal aide stepped out, raised her four-nostriled vocal and respiration organ in impartial greeting and tootled in her own language, "Director Lim will see you now."

"Thank you." Spart lifted to his feet, ran a hand over his short-cropped graying blond hair and followed her through the door into her electronics-filled inner office. The two shoulder-armed Fthlonian guards scrutinized their security scanners and saluted him through the nanosteel-reinforced inner door and into the Presence.

He had seen recordings of the office, but they did not do it justice. The light streaming through the atrium-style windows and skylights illuminated representative artwork from all eleven species of the Confederation. Scattered around the huge room were ornately carved wooden sculptures and dioramas from Dwat, multicolored Fthlonian blown crystal, fine Leosan porcelains, almost unfathomable steampunk metalwork from Nokilo, the ethereal laser holograms of the Squns, abstracts from Sabar cast from many materials, beautifully wrought if deadly Eleakan war blades, stone bas-reliefs from Kanitak, Ygun fluorescent paintings, intricate beadwork tapestries from the Karani and, taking up half a wall and filling the air with fragrance, a florid living wall from Hasgonde. It was a stunning display of the diverse cultures of the Stellar Confederation and created a breathtaking backdrop for the man who governed it all.

Director Tondo Lim was, like Spart, a Sabarian, of the same near-century age as Spart but with a body more suited to desk work than the Admiral's active lifestyle. He looked up from the console on his centuries-old desk centered amid the artwork and focused his blue-green eyes on his guest. Spart stretched to attention and clapped his left palm to the Stellar Confederation coat of arms embroidered below his right shoulder in sharp salute.

The Director rose with a smile, tapped his hand to his own chest and waved the Admiral to a chair as elaborately as only the Sabarian double-jointed wrist could allow. "Good to see you again, Nil. It's been a very long time."

"Yes, it has, sir. I was hoping you'd remember." Spart took the chair, sitting halfway to its edge.

Lim's smile faded a bit as the implications of that greeting sank in. He sat down behind his desk. "Let's get right to the point. You're here to ask a favor of me, and I know what it is. But I'm afraid I can't give you back your *Kaltim*. Your present assignment is far more important than exploration. We have to find the home world of that hostile fleet that chased you halfway across the galaxy, and try to get a line on the big stranger that destroyed it. You are the only one with any real acquaintance with either."

"You've got me wrong, sir. It hurts that I was 'promoted' out of my starship, but I know there's no going back—though I could argue that the way to find someone is to grab a ship and go looking. But that's moot, I'm afraid. The favor I'm asking is that you... well, that you trust me." Spart sought the Director's eyes and bored into them with his own.

Lim studied him with pursed lips for a long moment before replying. "We spent six years together in the academy on Sabar, Nil. I remember you as one of the most responsible of my classmates. And from what I've heard since, you've improved."

"I'm glad you think so, sir. I'm about to test your trust to the limit." He pulled the data disk from his pocket and pushed it onto the Director's desk. "Mission accomplished."

Lim sat back in surprise. He glanced at the disk but did not touch it. "So soon? How did you do it?"

Spart's own eyes dropped to the disk and he took a deep breath. Here we go, he thought. "I didn't. The stranger did." He looked up to gauge the reaction.

The Director stared back at him in hard silence. With a hesitation that would have surprised billions of Confederation citizens, he picked up the disk and slid it into the console on his desk. He eyes started to glaze as he speedballed through the files. After several silent minutes he clamped his teeth together, shut his eyes and sighed.

"Written in Sabarian, yet, with maps and graphics." He glared at Spart with hooded eyes. "I assume there's a good story behind this."

Spart sighed heavily. "I can't tell you everything. The stranger swore me to secrecy as to himself and his species, and I'm honor-bound by his saving my life to keep that oath. But I can describe the recent events from his point of view and add a few things from my own observations." He waited for permission to continue.

Lim took a deep breath and stared up at a skylight before answering. "All right," he said, "It disturbs me that you would take a binding to an alien above your oath as a defender of the Confederation, but we can discuss that after you elaborate. On the other hand, I can imagine that he wants to maintain a certain amount of security. That much power could disrupt the entire galaxy. By presuming trust in you, however, I don't mean to imply that I trust him."

"You can, I assure you. He uses his obvious strength very judiciously, knowing full well that it can be misused. Lord Orion is quite possibly the most intelligent being in the known galaxy."

Lin raised an eyebrow, then decided to pass over the praise. "Lord Orion?"

Spart sat back and chose his words with care. "They use code names to protect their origin. As you may be aware, I recently spent some time on a backwater planet named Gaea, tracking down some experimental quantum emissions the *Kaltim* caught in passing. It's in the Kitaote system—they call it Sol—a bit deeper in the spiral arm and quite a few parsecs outside our direct jurisdiction. I may now be the most learned in Gaea's history and current affairs of all the Confederation's contact explorers. Orion is a name from Gaea's extensive mythology, an

extraordinary hunter who cleared the land of dangerous beasts and became one of the most recognizable
constellations in the Gaean sky upon his death. The
man we're talking about may have picked the story
out of my mind somehow and liked the sound of it. In
fact, he's pretty much embraced the whole mythology
of Gaea, and uses it as camouflage since it's so evident that Gaea couldn't possibly be the home planet
of such an advanced intelligence." A plausible theory,
he thought to himself. Just don't ask me to prove it.

Lim swallowed it whole. "All right, let's call him
Orion. And what is so special about him?"

Spart sighed lightly, trying to hide his relief. "It
is both mental and mechanical. Orion and his company—he calls them the Omega Corps, another
Gaean concept implying the ultimate force—are a
step above us in evolution. They possess powers of
mind and body that are fantastic or even mythical to
us. They break down into four categories of ability.
The first is purely mental, including telepaths, eidetics, radiopaths and other wave sensors, zootelepaths,
telehypnotists, and maybe a few others. The second
is metamorphic: mimicry, transmutation, spectrality, zoocanthropy and the like. Third are the sensory
talents: clairvoyance, clairaudience, microvoyance,
force analysis and so forth. And then there are the
physical powers: force projection, teleportation, telekinesis, levitation, or pure titanic strength. This
is all on the disk. Orion wanted me to know pretty much what he had to work with in that regard.

Mechanically—"

"Hold it: question. Why you?"

"Well, remember, I was the first Confederation officer to come into contact with Orion. He saved my life and those of my crew by devastating the Sforan fleet. He chose me for his contact—"

"Wait. Sforan?"

"Oh, sorry. As you recall, this started with me running for my life with an unknown but very hostile fleet trying to blow up my drive pipes. The fleet that attacked *Kaltim* and chased us when we escaped was from a planet called Sfor, the primary race of which is a furred species who have a violent aversion to us hairless types. That's all on the disk."

"All right, let's save them for later, though I'm interested in their motivation. You're not all that ugly to me. Let's go back to the 'why you'."

Spart twitched a tentative smile at the attempt at levity. "Orion contacted me for the same reason you took my cruiser. I have first-hand proof of their ability."

The Director smiled wryly. "You'll never forgive me for taking you out of space, will you? And how did he contact you?"

Spart dropped his eyes and leaned back in the chair. "He showed up in my office. In person." He waved a hand at the scanner on the desk. "He sat in a chair in my new office and handed me that disk."

Lim blanched and his jaw dropped in shock. "He was here? A totally unknown and unvetted species made it through all our security?"

Spart shrugged. "I told you he was good. He was here, on Dephlet, in my office, in person, without triggering an alarm anywhere through several light years of the best security we've ever devised."

"How?"

"No idea," Spart shook his head. "They do bear a close resemblance to Sabarians, except that they have wrists that aren't nearly as flexible as ours. He could have sneaked through. But then again, they have mental and technological advantages that are superior to ours, any combination of which could have gotten him here with no interaction whatsoever." He flicked a wrist. "All I know is, he materialized out of thin air, and after a brief chat he vanished as abruptly as he appeared."

Lim looked again at his console display and nodded. "Teleportation. Telepathy. Clairvoyance. Friva crap, he could be right here, right now and we wouldn't know it."

"True, but not likely, sir. I got the distinct impression that he intends to stay below the sensor scan unless we contact him."

"Do you really think that big ship of his can hide from us? Or the news services?"

"It wouldn't surprise me. I have no reason to think their stealth technology isn't as advanced as their propulsion. He got through two light years of security, remember, and you know he'd never tell us how. He gave us a list of his mental resources because he knows we'd never be able to copy them. For the opposite reason he refuses to divulge his mechanical assets. If we got hold of them, you know what we'd do with them."

"Sure—start a war, whether we wanted to or not. It's always the same with the ultimate weapon. But surely you have some clues?"

"I do. His power supply is much the same as ours, stellar accumulation, but with the added twist of being able to absorb energy from any radiant source. His motive power, I believe, is gravitic."

The Director tensed and leaned forward. "Superconduction? How?"

"Now, you know he didn't tell me that. But I know from experience that it gives him a speed well over twice that possible with our nucleonic drive, and allows him a maneuverability far beyond what our nucleonic retros provide. It's his second greatest asset."

Lim settled back with a grimace. "Here I am, lusting after things I just said I didn't want. So what's his greatest asset?"

"His armament, both offensive and defensive. Remember, one of the mental powers he lists is force projection. From what I've seen his offensive weapons work on that principle, blasting out spherical shells or continuous rods of coherent force. Those fields will punch through anything, to a distance six or eight times the range of our guns."

"And how many does he have?"

"Well, the ship is nearly spherical but has three

rings of convex rectangular hull sections tapering to hexagonal poles, twenty sections in all. That computes to eighty-four motive engines and eighty-four guns."

Lim's jaw dropped. "That's ridiculous!"

"But true. And his targeting system makes them effective to the limit of his range. The defensive screens are just as tough. I saw him take thirty or more Sforan blasts and those screens barely even rippled—in fact, the visible frequencies appeared to be accumulated for fuel. I think he could run through a sun without getting singed."

The Director whistled through his teeth. "And he'd leave a nova behind him. Hot jumping figgabeans, what power!"

Spart nodded solemnly. "And he wants to use it to help us. Correction—not only us, but anyone who needs it. Call him a galactic guardian, totally unfettered, willing and able to use his time and his assets in the service of justice."

"And what does he want in return?"

"Nothing," Spart shrugged, "nothing but the right to use his own judgment. I know it's hard to believe, but he's basically an adventurer, in it for the challenge, and willing to help anyone who needs help. He's not after power or glory or wealth—in fact, he has enough of those things already to give them away, and that's what he's doing."

"That is pretty hard to believe." The silence grew as Lim stared out the window. "I'd have a real problem with allowing a self-appointed vigilante carte blanche in galactic affairs. The next thing you know we'll have more superheroes than we know what to do with—and super-villains."

"That's was my initial worry, too. But Orion has told me he wants as little publicity as possible, and he'll step on anyone outside his Omega Corps who tries to grab any of his turf. He's really sincere in his principles."

Lim shook his head. "I still can't allow it."

Spart sighed and flicked his double-jointed wrists expansively. "So get together a fleet of about four thousand capital ships and hope he doesn't just run away from the fifteen he leaves intact."

Lim chuckled. "I see your point, subtle as it is. What do you suggest?"

"We have to work with the guy; if we don't, he'll just ignore us. We can try to manage him, but don't expect that to succeed, either. If we try, he'll go where he wants to go and do whatever he damned well pleases anyway."

He shifted forward in his chair, planting his hands on his knees. "Now, I do have quantum frequencies through which I can reach him. In his words, we might find some situations we can't handle that he won't even notice, so he made it possible for us to inform him and request his assistance. But he doesn't guarantee he'll take any case we ask him to. All he guarantees is success in anything he does start— which isn't a bad guarantee."

"I'll agree with that, though I have no proof he can actually deliver." The Director sat back and again stared out the window, searching as he often did for answers in the amber clouds scudding through the blue-green sky. Spart, barely breathing, waited with as much patience as he could muster.

Finally Lim shifted uncomfortably and muttered the Sabarian equivalent of, "Son of a bitch."

Spart chuckled. "That's what I call him, too, with plenty of embellishments. You've got to admire the guy, but he's damned uncomfortable to have around. But you must admit he handled the Sforan problem rather decisively."

Lim looked at him inquiringly, seeming to appreciate the change in subject. "That's right, what's the story behind that?"

"It's on the disk, sir. Sfor was attacked by bareskinned hominids way back in their history, and they've had a fanatical hatred of anything remotely like them ever since. When I tried to contact their fleet, they took one look at my clean face and opened fire without parley. I got pretty scorched trying to get away.

"Orion's method of defusing the situation was to zip in, thrash the hell out of them and show mercy to the remnants. You remember the conditions in that battle sphere—we couldn't find enough left to give our follow-up investigators anything to work with. But Orion actually found a crewman who survived the destruction of his ship. He rescued and made friends with him, then went straight to the home world. He dropped in on the Sforan Sovereign and convinced them that there was more than one hairless bipedal species, and that an irrational war would harm too many innocents. The Sovereign is right now campaigning to wipe out centuries of prejudice, but I'd still recommend that the first Confederation visitors not be hominin. I'd think that Grauphe, the former Councilman from Hasgondi, might be a good first ambassador."

The Director has returned to the data console and was scanning intently. "I think I'll take you up on that. Maybe felids and ursids can get along. But this is a tough assignment; in the normal run of things the Sforans wouldn't have space travel for fifty generations. I wish I knew who it was that gave them that knowledge."

"Someone broke the First Law and landed on Sfor fifty years ago. The natives slaughtered them and duplicated the ship. That's something we'll have to look into." He considered, then added, "If Orion isn't already on to it."

Lim looked up. "That's a thought. Can you contact him any time?"

"Hm. I want to save him for emergencies. But I suppose I could..." He shook his head. "No. Orion specified that he would take on only those problems we couldn't handle, and this one we can handle. It wouldn't surprise me if he's ignored it completely."

Lim nodded slowly in thought. "Now I see what

he's about. He has no intention of being used as an operative."

"Right. He is completely nonpartisan, using his strength where needed for whomever needs it. If it were a Confederation fleet attacking a Sforan vessel instead of the other way around, he'd have sided with them—provided they were the aggrieved party. He's on the side of justice, not the Confederation."

"I see. I've been known to bend a few rules in that direction myself..." His voice trailed away, lost in thought as he gazed in Spart's direction as if the Admiral wasn't there. Spart remained still, sensing that anything more he could say or do would only complicate things. Tondo Lim was Director of the Confederation through no accident; selected by examination from hundreds of candidates, he was truly capable of wielding that awesome guardianship with the studied dedication of a crusader.

Lim rose from behind his desk and focused his eyes on those of his subordinate, who quickly found his own feet. "Vice Admiral Nil Spart of Sabar, you are, as of this moment, carrying the rank and privileges of Admiral of the Stellar Confederation Fleet."

Spart's eyes widened, then he snapped to attention. "Sir!"

"As you were, Nil. We can deal with the formalities later."

"Thank you, sir." He waited until the Director returned to his chair, then followed suit. "What are your orders, sir?"

"I'm putting you in charge of Operation Orion. Yours will be the responsibility for the Confederation's dealings with your magic man. You will organize a force of researchers to seek out and study any problems that might fall into Orion's province, both inside and outside the Confederation. You will be given access to Special Service records and personnel as needed, and the use of any military forces you may require." He thought a moment. "The Council and Fleet Services might have a thing or two to say about that, so be sure to run anything military through me. If I agree with you, which isn't a guarantee, I'll convey any military allocations."

He worked over his console as he spoke, then popped out a data disk and tossed it to the Admiral. "I would suggest as the first object of study, the recent disappearance of merchant vessels in interstellar space. The consensus is that there is some kind of organized hijacking operation in existence, but so far, we have no real clues as to the origin of the hijackers. Find out whatever you can about the problem, then hand it over to Orion. I know this is something we might be able to take care of ourselves, but not soon enough to prevent further losses, which have already been considerable. This will be a test of Orion's effectiveness, to see how he handles something of this magnitude, and how well. If he objects to the assignment, please inform him that if he wants information from us, he must first prove himself worthy of the trust."

He saw the guarded look on Spart's face. "Opinion?"

"Observation." Spart dropped his eyes. "If Orion wants information he'll get it, help or no help. With the kind of operatives he's got he doesn't really need us. We'd be useful to him, no more. Yet he refuses to be used himself, even while using us shamelessly. You cannot dictate to him or try to threaten him. If you do, he'll just go his own way."

He took a shaky breath and rubbed his damp forehead. "As I told you, I have information related to Lord Orion and the Omega Corps which I have been forbidden by him to reveal. You must take my word for this: if you intend to charge me with this organization you will have to recognize the fact that I would be working as much for him as for you and the Confederation. While my loyalties are absolutely with the Confederation, I could not accept your regulation any more than he would. As Orion uses me, I will use you."

He looked up, a haunted yet defiant look in every line of his face. "If this makes me a traitor, so be it. I believe in the man and what he wants to do, so much that I would resign my commission and go underground if it were the only way I could continue to support him."

The Director stared at him narrow-eyed, profoundly shocked. He knew Nil Spart as a die-hard, almost fanatic champion of the Confederation, one whose integrity and veracity were legend; a conservative dreamer who could well have had the Directorship if he wanted it. Who was this Orion, that he could entwine such a man so completely? Lim had thought that Spart had told him everything of importance, despite his sworn secrecy to Orion; but he now realized he knew next to nothing. Orion had a hold over him so powerful that nothing could break it. Whatever that hold was, whether it be awe, respect, or something more sinister, it was frightening.

What he could not know, what Spart could not tell him, was that the Omega Corps already had made a tremendous difference in their home planet of Gaea. In the short time they had been in existence, the political, economic and law enforcement conditions there had improved markedly. Spart himself had seen the results of their efforts and was impressed enough to want to see them take an equivalent role in the Confederation.

Spart went on in a broken voice, "Don't ask me to say anything more, and don't ask me to try to control Orion. I owe him my life and the lives of my crew. I'm his man, and I wouldn't have it any other way. If you can't reconcile that with my record, with my service, you'll have to do without me."

He lowered his head, lips set and tight. "You know, I hope you know, that I would never, ever betray the Confederation or cause shame to the uniform I'm so deeply honored to wear. But this assignment calls me to a higher purpose, and I in turn trust Orion never to put me in a position where you would have cause to question my allegiance. My service to him is based completely in that trust."

Lim stared at him, then rose and plodded to the window. The sight of the magnificent gardens of the Capitol complex did nothing to soothe his agitated mind. He swayed and started pacing, weaving through the art exhibits but not seeing them, seeking a solution to this impossible situation. In essence, Spart was asking him, the Director of the Confederation and the most powerful entity in known space, to give tacit control of his office and his forces to one man, a stranger whose origin no one knew and whose goals were a mystery. Why, he could become ruler of the galaxy!

But would he? Spart did not seem to think so; if he did, he would be Orion's greatest enemy. Spart was nobody's fool. If he had any doubts as to Orion's integrity, he would never propose such complete cooperation with the man. So the question was, did Spart himself harbor any doubts?

He turned to the Admiral. "Will you take a veracitor test?"

Spart's face cleared magically. He knew that the worst was past. "As long as it is the same test you yourself take. I will allow a mechanical examination of my motivations and integrity, but straight information will not be requested. I will divulge no secrets. Will that do?"

Lim sighed. The agreement was almost as valuable as the test itself. "I will be content with that." He returned to his desk and sat down, much relieved. "As for Operation Orion, I'll have to give it more thought. But I will put a few wheels in motion, including your new rank, Nil. The basic idea still holds true—and I still want to get him on that hijacking problem. Will you do that?"

"I can't guarantee anything, but yes, I'll get in touch with him." Spart leaned forward and put his head in his hands. "Thank you, sir. You can't imagine the burden I've had to bear."

Lim came around the desk and put a hand on the Admiral's shoulder. "I don't have to imagine it. I'm sharing it." He turned away and let out a nervous snort. "And I'll probably hate myself in the morning."

Spart laughed. "You've got it, exactly. But if I may say so, I don't like the name Operation Orion. We can't have a government agency with the same name as the hero who will be tearing this galaxy apart."

"I suppose not. What do you suggest?"

Spart thought through his encyclopedic knowledge of Gaean mythology. "Let's go with… Operation Messiah."

CHAPTER 3

Jackson Alexander Steele, PhD, Lord of the Omega Corps, Captain and Commander of the starship *Angel*, was lying on the grass under the Captain's tree, engaged in a staring match with the Captain's squirrel. Rufus, a tuft-eared Eurasian red, sat on Orion's upturned knee returning the human's stare with unwavering interest.

Many of the crew speculated as to why Rufus tolerated Steele more than anyone else who used the park. Wags put forth the opinion that the squirrel knew where the power was and wanted to curry favor; others resolved that Rufus used Jander as a method of getting close to his ravishing wife, Vickie.

Sharon Gibson, the zootelepath responsible for the control of the squirrel population, of course had the correct solution: Captain's favorite tree, squirrel's favorite tree, therefore squirrel's favorite Captain.

Steele caught movement in the corner of his eye and turned his head away.

Rufus, surprised at his easy victory, chipped with glee and sprang for the spreading oak. As his notoriously incontinent family tended to do, he deposited a wet spot on the knee as he left. Jander flagged a hand at him and grimaced.

The movement was the opening of the hatch concealed in a vine-covered arbor, which slid aside to reveal Victoria Steele. Jander was not the only one watching; to say that Lady Alpha's beauty was proverbial would be hopelessly inadequate. Every male eye in the place watched appreciatively as she glided over the thick grass and settled with consummate grace beside her husband. Every female eye clouded with both envy and relief; it was well known that the exquisite goddess was wholly devoted to her man and was therefore out of the competition.

She greeted Jander with a telekinetic kiss on the cheek. "It might interest you to know that, while you lounge here in indolent sloth, the stars still gleam, the planets still revolve, and life still beats strongly in the hearts of men." She curled up beside him like a kitten, floating her ash-blonde hair over his chest.

He gave her an amused look and wrapped his arm around her supple back. "Are you trying to tell me something?"

"Oh, no, no. I'm merely pointing out that the stars still gleam, the planets…"

"I get the message. There's something I ought to be doing."

She chuckled richly. "Well, Spart called. And we're being followed."

He sat up. "Why didn't you say so? Spill it."

He watched in appreciation as she rolled onto her back and stretched. "We have six ships in our wake," she said, "almost out of sensor range…"

"Six?" Something clicked in Jander's brain, the detail that had eluded him days earlier. "The Confederation fields squadrons of five."

"Well, this one has six. So far, they've made no demonstration—they're just sitting there, wondering what in the universe this gigantic hunk of metal might be doing here. As for the Admiral, we just got a one-way signal saying that he'll instigate full contact in…" her eyes lost focus for a second as she telepathically picked the time from someone's mind, "…fifty-five minutes, give or take. That's all that was in the message."

Jander grunted, "He'll be disappointed this time. Until we clear up this little thing we're working on he can hop." He stood up, carrying her with him by way of a forcefield. "But I guess I can talk to him, at least. Fifty-five?"

"Time enough for you to shave and change, slob. Oh, and Denny wants to talk to you. He says he has a new wrinkle for the pulse projectors."

"You're just a bundle of old rumors. Anything else you've been holding from me?" He built an energy screen flush with the skin of his face and neck, shifted it just a bit, and allowed his day's growth of beard to fall into the grass.

"Well, I'm having an affair with a werewolf, but that wouldn't interest you." She grinned and ran a fingertip over his smoothed jawline. "All this has come up in the past fifteen minutes. I can't do everything at once."

"The First Officer of a starship should be able to do just that. I'd be interested to know how you talked to Denny and started an affair in fifteen minutes. Denny doesn't get to the point that fast."

She chuckled in her lilting tone and patted him on the chest. "Let's go, boss."

They left the park through the familiar tingle of the scanner that kept the resident critters confined to their habitat and crossed the lightly populated crew's lounge to the null gravity shaft. The shaft was another innovation of the giant engineer, Denver Connors; ship's transportation was something the titan could not leave alone. He assisted in developing the telebooth, a mechanical manifestation of the variant power of teleportation; one could trip instantly from one booth to another, or even to a remote location, with the press of a button. He also fitted the conventional elevators with gravity plates that allowed them to reach fantastic speeds with no discomfort. His latest brainchild was to rip out one of the central elevators and bring the shaft to zero gravity, leaving a gaping, gut-wrenching vertical corridor for the full length of the ship. With the stairways and maintenance ladders hidden in the bulkheads, that provided four methods of movement within the ship: one could ride, jump, climb or swim.

Steele chose to swim. He stepped into the empty air of the grav shaft and pushed off against a bar mounted next to the hatch, propelling himself downward at an easy pace. Vickie used her telekinetic ability to accomplish the same result, and they floated together to the Bridge Deck. A quick pullover on the bar, and they were striding toward the Bridge itself.

"CAPTAIN ON THE BRIDGE!" Angela announced as Steele entered through the sliding double pocket hatch. Since he entered first, the outranked Vickie was not announced.

"Hi, Cobra. Where's Denny?"

Pavel Kalanev was again on duty in the command chair. The sandy-haired Ukrainian telepath rose to his feet. "The chief engineer is in his office, devising some new infernal machine. I understand that it will make our pulse spheres more effective, although I cannot imagine how he could accomplish such a task." He indicated the forward center monitor with a flick of his icy gray eyes. "We have visitors."

"So I see. Thank you, I have the con." Kalanev stepped aside and Steele settled into the center seat, studying the images on the big monitor. A digital readout in its corner told him that it was a port diagonal image. Dozens of smaller monitors to its left and right, their different color-coded borders indicating the direction of their view relative to their line of flight, displayed the full global scene. "Six of them. Is that the greatest magnification we can get?"

Kurino Yukio answered from her sensors console, "We have them in sight, Milord, but no more. They've penetrated and matched our warp sphere so they can keep station, but just barely. It's like peeking through the union of a Venn diagram. We're much bigger than they are, so they're correspondingly smaller to us." No longer in stealth mode, the *Angel*'s baffle screen was disengaged and the warp sphere was at its full two million-kilometer diameter. The tiny Japanese leaned over her big board and fiddled with a pair of speedballs. The monitor showed no change. "That's all, Orion-sama. I can't even determine their exact size at this range."

Steele pursed his lips. "Thank you, Kitsune. Keep a sharp eye on them. Have they tried communication, Jinwu?"

"No, sir." Tsin Li-san responded much more formally than usual since his captain was using their Corps names. "Shall I try to reach them?"

"Negative. If I read these guys right, we'll hear from them soon—violently. Stay at blue alert and let me know if there's any change. First Officer has the con. I'm going to change before Spart calls." He plucked at his patterned polo shirt. "I don't think the Confederation has weekends."

STEELE RETURNED BEFORE THE HOUR passed, now clad in the nanosteel-colored silver-blue shirt and slacks of the Corps' service uniform. He saw to it that the communications pickup would not show anything of the *Angel*'s Bridge instrumentation; he knew that Spart would be all eyes. He took his chair from

Vickie, who returned to her accustomed seat behind his left shoulder.

Denny Connors entered and settled his seven-foot-plus frame into the chair to her right. "Hi, chief. You hear about my new gizmo?"

"Several times. I hope it can wait until I'm through with the Admiral."

"Well, it waited until I thought of it, so I guess it can wait for that." He chuckled in his booming bass. "And you can bet our shadows out there would rather it did."

"That good, eh?"

"Better. How many sphere shots did it take to knock out one of those Sforan ships?"

"Six or eight. Less, if a shot hit a power room or inertia compensator."

"My new wrinkle would do it with one, hitting anywhere." The titan grinned, pleased by his friend's raised eyebrows. "The difference is like between iron cannonballs and high-explosive shells."

"How..."

"Call coming in, Captain." The Chinese telepath cut the conversation short.

Jander narrowed the pickup even further to hide Denny's presence, and Vickie's, whose anonymous psychological insights might help him in the conversation to come. "Put it through, Li-san." Steele twisted in his chair as the quantum entanglement communications system, shamelessly cloned by the Corps from the Admiral's own *Kaltim*, ballooned the image of Nil Spart onto the forward com screen. His lean, broad-shouldered form looked resplendent in the insignia-bedecked green vest over puff-sleeved gold shirt of his dress uniform.

Steele gave the image a friendly smile, "Good morning, Admiral."

Spart faked a wince at the familiar words. "Hello, barbarian." His English was properly British, the dialect he had learned prior to their first meeting in London. He noted that Orion was in uniform, with a patch below his left shoulder matching the big shield displayed on the double-doored hatch behind him. It was his first look at the Omega Corps shield, a red scale of justice topped by the golden symbol for infinity within the black Omega horseshoe. He easily deduced the symbolism: Justice for All. "It's nice to see you without being frightened out of my senses first."

"It's your own fault. Never sit with your back to anything." Jander grinned at Spart's mock frown. Steele's primary variant power was forcefield projection; he could shield himself into invisibility at will. In their previous meetings he had suddenly appeared behind the Admiral and was rewarded with absolute shock every time. "I understand you have an interesting problem for us."

"How did you know that? Surely Lady Alpha can't read my mind at this distance."

"Well, why else would you call?"

Spart lowered his head to hide a wry grin. It was

a cute game to Orion, always catching him in some semantic trap or other. "Someday, barbarian, I am going to catch you. And you'll never hear the end of it." He chuckled. "By the way, if you wanted to keep your existence secret you've done a magnificent job of blowing it."

Steele chuckled. "You're a credit to Gaean slang, Admiral. We're no longer interested in keeping our existence a secret. That's futile. We only want our origin secret—and that's in your interests, too."

"I'm quite aware of that," Spart nodded with a grimace. By unwittingly exposing Orion and his Omega Corps to the higher technology of his exploration cruiser the Admiral had broken the First Law, that no underdeveloped planet may be altered by such exposure. That Steele and his variants had stolen the information was merely a technicality; if the fact became known, Spart's career would be ruined at best. "Still, I had to tell the Director a few things, in order to explain my information about Sfor."

"Hence your full-dress uniform, I presume. I was wondering how you were going to handle that."

"I'll bet you were, you bloody bastard." They shared another grin. "You left me holding a bagful of wildcats—and I don't mean that as a racial slur. Next time, don't do me any favors."

Jander shrugged. "As you wish." He moved as if to cut off the communication.

"Wait-wait!" Spart sat up in alarm, then caught himself. Taken again! "You..."

The words were not in English, but they were volatile in any language. Jander heard a choking sound and glanced back over his shoulder; Connors was laboring mightily to suppress his laughter. He widened the video pickup to include the engineer, but still hiding the equally amused Vickie.

The knowledge that they had an audience elicited a few more remarks from the Admiral. "Orion, if you do that again I'll find a ship and come test those screens of yours!"

"Sorry, Nil." He did not look it. "Shall we go on?"

Spart took a deep breath, then burst into a laugh. "All right, Orion. A straight man is still a man. If you get your kicks from making a fool of me, who am I to deny it? I have an idea how serious your life is."

Steele sobered his grin a bit and met the other man's eyes with warmth. "No more than yours, Nil. I'll try to be nicer if you try to be less literal. You're too easy."

"Try keeping secrets from your own lifemate sometime if you want to know why I'm such a grouch. Hietzi's the sweetest woman you'd ever hope to meet, but we aren't allowed to talk like you and Alpha can." He caught a glimpse of the giant figure behind Orion turning away and sensed he had hit a nerve.

Vickie caught it, too, and conveyed it to her husband with a sharp thought. Jander rushed to divert the conversation. "I wish I could help, but I'm a bit pressed for time right now. What is it you wanted to talk about?"

Spart understood and followed the flow. "The Director wants to see how good you are, so he's thought of a problem we can watch you handle. Interested?"

"I have no interest whatsoever in proving myself. You can tell your politicians I'm good. If they don't believe it, tough."

"The Director is not a politician. He's chosen by evaluation rather than election, for administrative excellence and integrity. And he retakes the veracitor test twice a year. He is entirely trustworthy and completely trusted. Can you say the same for Gaea's leaders?"

"Quite the opposite. Don't get touchy, I apologize." Jander waved it away. "Okay, I'll listen. But I have something going on my own, and I may not get to your problem for some time, if ever."

"Fair enough. I told him as much myself and he understands. But if you do take it and succeed with it, you'll have his backing as well a mine. By the way, if I may ask, who's the big fellow?"

"Call him Kodiak. He's the *Angel*'s chief engineer, and third in command." Denny nodded and rumbled a formal greeting, conscious that he was in fatigue coveralls not in keeping with the company.

Spart gave Jander a humoring look. "Come on, Orion. Why can't you tell me your real names? I'm not about to blackmail your mother."

"No, but somebody else might. I do have family back there, and I have to protect them. I trust you, as much as I trust anyone not of the Corps, but I can name seventeen different drugs on the Confederation market that can make a man babble like a brook. Are you immune to them?"

"Most. But if I am needled, I could say you're from the planet Gaea."

"And they'd hold Gaea hostage, right? No way, not with Binary and his three hundred super-powered protectors staying home nights. One person, or a dozen, could be snatched, but the Omega Corps does not consist solely of one ship and one man." He again waved a hand in dismissal. "So how much did you tell the Director?"

Spart hit the high points of his conversation with Lim. "So, I'm director of operations concerning you, and will be your liaison with the Confederation and your source of information about the planetary powers outside of it. As for your authority and acceptance within the Confederation, we've begun leaking your existence to the public. We rather had to—far too many people know about the Sforan incident for us to pretend we aren't aware of you.

"By the way," he added with a half smile, "we named the project Operation Messiah."

"Oh, shit," Connors muttered, and hid his face behind a huge hand.

In contrast, Steele sank back, jaw and body sagging. Of all the things he considered calling himself, Messiah was not even on the list. "Oh, no!"

Spart grinned. "Got you, at last. That's the name,

like it or not. But what's a name? You can go on being your overbearing, supercilious self, thumbing your nose at honest working people and flashing about performing miracles to your heart's delight."

Steele recovered with a growl. "Spart, I'll come gunning for you if you don't watch out! What's the big idea?"

The Admiral shrugged, still smiling. "It seemed to fit. But really, the name is beside the point. What's important is that you'll get your information without having to work for it."

Steele clouded with anger. "Now I see your strategy. Nice try, Nil, but that kind of flattery won't work. If you think I'm going to dance on your strings you're mistaken. Now say your say and get lost." Behind him, Connors was the very picture of anguish. He knew very, very well that one of Orion's most forceful tenets was, "We are not gods. We will not act like gods." Any Corpsman would lose more than figurative skin by bending that rule even in the slightest.

Spart sobered. "Orion, I'm sorry. That wasn't my intention, really. I'm your straight man, remember? I'll work with you with or without sanction. I trust you and I believe in what you're doing. The name was my idea, but I meant it as a reference akin to your mythological code names, not as a sop."

"Change it. Some of our people still adhere to that particular belief system, and I don't want myself linked to the implications."

"As you wish, Milord." Spart bowed his head to the angry image in front of him. He had no intention of changing the name—that was out of his hands—but determined that Steele would never know. "But I meant what I just said. I'm not your subordinate any more than you are mine, but I'll aid you in any way I can."

Steele met the Sabarian's candid gaze and held it, judging him thoroughly. Spart met him halfway, not trying to conceal anything. Steele could see that, and responded accordingly.

"All right, I guess I believe you, at least as far as the sop is concerned. But I'll be damned careful from now on. So, what does your Most Exalted High Non-Politician want me to do to prove myself?"

Spart was relieved at that indication of Steele's returning good humor. He leaned back in his chair and settled down to business. "In recent months there has been an increase in hijackings throughout Confederation space. How many, we don't know; perhaps as many as a hundred. Most of the overdue ships have disappeared without a trace, but some battered hulks and debris have been found. All crews dead or missing, all holds bare.

"As far as we can tell, none of the merchandise has returned to the free market, although it may be going out of the Confederation—we simply don't know. All I can tell you is that if it isn't stopped, commerce could grind to a halt. The Fleet can't escort every ship. But we can't trap the hijackers, either—

they hit wherever we aren't. I wouldn't be surprised if they had an inside track on shipping schedules."

He looked up from his scanner and saw the wry smile on Steele's lips. "What's the matter?"

"Tell me," Jander said. "If someone planted a bomb under your neighbor's bed, wouldn't you notice?"

Spart grimaced. "Don't tell me, that's what you're working on."

"You've got it. And it's worse than you picture. Our research points to outright piracy, not simple hijackings. It's so big, we got wind of it as we crossed your territory to visit you on Dephlet. The *Angel*'s communications equipment is better than yours, and we can pick up calls from much greater distances. Not just your big commercial merchants are disappearing, but private yachts, liners, everything that can escape a planet's gravity isn't escaping these pirates. They're vanishing almost without a trace, though we've spotted a few distress calls. But we've also picked up a few pieces of communication between pirate units, enough to give us a lead or two. We expect a confrontation very soon, and I guarantee we'll track those murdering savages to the edge of the galaxy if we have to."

Spart repressed a shiver. The tone in Orion's voice made him very glad he was a friend. "How will you go about it? As I just said, we haven't been able to find a single hijacker when we want one. To use one of your own expressions, how does one find a needle in a haystack?"

"Use a magnet."

Spart's eyebrows shot upward. "Bait?"

"Bait. Right now, we're loafing along the Gramb-Larkant trade route, looking like the biggest, fattest, dumbest freight vessel you ever saw. And we've picked up an audience." He waved to Tsin, who caught the motion in his monitor window and superimposed the view of their six shadows onto the output being sent to Spart.

The Admiral squinted to see the almost invisible points. "Six of them. The standard Confederation squadron has five."

"I know. We saw a similar squadron a few days ago when they passed us heading toward Gramb. I didn't recognize the significance of the number then, but it may be their standard. They've been attached to us for an hour and a half, more than likely waiting to be sure no Confederation warships are lurking about. I expect them to attack soon."

"And what will you do?"

"That remains to be seen. I intend to make no offensive move—six standard cruisers can't even warm my screens. I want to see what their reaction to that will be."

"Surprise, no doubt," Spart mused. He was keenly interested in that information; six ships could blast his lamented *Kaltim* to atoms. "Will you need any help?"

"For these guys? Not if we dropped our screens and opened every hatch."

"Hm. Good point," He grinned, discomfited. It was a stupid question. "I'll just forward you our data and keep out of your way, then."

"I want you to do better than that. Keep it under your hat, or share it only with the Director. If you do have a leak providing these pirates with information our efforts could be compromised. Even the six per squadron thing could tip them off."

"Agreed. I'll leave you to your hunting, Lord Orion. Good luck, my friend."

"Thanks—and give Hietzi my compliments when you can." Steele motioned, and Tsin cut the connection. He felt that to be a little rude, but Sabarians were not known for extended salutations or goodbyes and he followed their standards.

He turned to Connors. "What do you think?"

Denny looked at him, eyebrow raised. "About what?"

"About our shadows. You've made a better study of Confederation and whatnot engineering than I have, and these guys are almost mirror images of them. Can they hurt us?"

Denny waved a hefty thumb at the screen. "We'll know in a minute. Here they come."

Steele took one glance and ordered Angela to sound general quarters.

CHAPTER 4

Vickie double-tapped a button on her chair, and the First Officer's console rose from its concealment in the deck and came alive before her. "What made them decide to attack?"

Connors answered, "They probably detected that call from Spart. It was scrambled, unlike the tidbits we used to hook them, but they could have traced its origin at least."

Steele turned back to the communications station. "Opinion, Jinwu?"

"Quite possible, sir," Tsin Li-san responded. "A quantum entanglement burst leaves a tachyon radiation residue at both ends that can be detected, as both of you know. And they are at an angle that puts them in conjunction with the *Angel* and Dephlet."

"And not by accident, I'll bet." The six raiders circled to surround the ship as the *Angel*'s ready stations reported. Jander called for the ship wide intercom as the last department checked in. "Attention, all. As you know, the plan is for us to be a target. That means we'll show no signs of life whatsoever unless I so order. Our present speed is four gravities per second, so we're sitting ducks. But remember, we compare to a duck like a brick wall compares to a marshmallow, so don't be nervous. Just relax and watch the fireworks."

He sat back and looked to Nwoye Lam, the helmsman, who gave him a bored look and nodded. Four gravities was stultifying to him. Steele winked at him and looked to his engineer. "Can you answer my question, Denny?"

Denny strode forward to the sensors console. Yukio keyed her chair into the deck and became spectral to make room for him; in essence, the two occupied the same space. Denny went to one knee to reach the console set to accommodate its four-foot-five operator. Her rich cargo of black hair waved a ghostly ponytail between his shoulder blades. "As far as I can tell, they're no more lethal than the Confederation's cruisers, maybe even weaker since they're proportionately smaller. No sweat. But it makes me nervous that they've left so many derelicts behind them. Their weapons might be something special."

"Not if they always work in teams of six," Vickie observed. "If I remember correctly, a merchantman's screens are only a quarter as strong as a warship's."

"About that. Roughly quadruple what it takes to protect them from natural radiation," the titan agreed.

"So, we wait," Steele directed. "Scatter, be ready to bounce the ship, just in case." Lam perked up at that, and his long fingers flew over his console to set the command that would teleport the entire ship to a point outside the englobing squadron.

"Ow, hello!" Li-san jerked in his seat and reached for a slide key on his console. "Tachyon interference. They're trying to block broadcast." He reduced the volume by eighty percent.

"Can you punch through it?" Jander asked. "Not that I want you to—it's just that it's our first experience with it."

"It's a blanket, so our stronger conduction could jab a needle through it. It doesn't affect our quantum array at all. They'd have to knock that out by force, but unlike Confed ships ours isn't concentrated in one spot. They can't target it."

"Good to know. I guess we're about to get shot at." Jander put his hands behind his head and became the very picture of idle relaxation.

Denny was resuming his seat when one of the six raiders opened fire with a three-shot burst from both guns of a midships battery. The six shots struck the *Angel*'s energy screen at the south pole of the sphere, spread along its curve and were dissipated with ease. The visible spectrum passed through unimpeded and was absorbed by the accumulators.

Jander dropped his charade, becoming the strong commander he truly was. "Portunes, report." As he spoke, the other five ships joined the bombardment.

"No damage, Captain," Geraldo Belocci responded from analytics. "Their guns are a bit weaker than Confederation weapons, as Kodiak predicted. Our screens are deflecting the force with no trouble." Kurino, back in her chair, nodded confirmation.

"Fine. Let's see what they'll do."

If the raiders had faces on their hulls their surprise could not have been more evident. They ceased fire after eighteen shots each, then retroed out of range— for them—and circled again, looking and behaving like a wolf pack around a stainless-steel moose.

"They've broken radio silence, sir," the Chinese telepath called back from his console. "They have a dedicated wavelength their interference doesn't block."

"Funnel it through the translator and broadcast to the Bridge." Angela's extraordinarily efficient quantum plasma-based processors could interpret virtually every signal she heard with a minimum baseline, regardless of the language or even code. The communications they intercepted during their hunt for the pirates gave her that baseline.

The speakers around the Bridge came alive, Angela giving each ship its own voice relative to its position outside.

"What is this monster?"

"Beats me. They must be asleep in that thing."

"They can afford to sleep. Those screens!"

"I'm going in for another look."

One of the ships peeled out of the circling formation and slid within six thousand kilometers, point-blank range, and jabbed again with its nucleonic bolts of power. Steele saw Kalanev shake his head and glance sideways at Kurino, who shrugged. Belocci idly waved a hand.

"This is ridiculous. Can't he see we're attacking?"

"As far as he's concerned, we're not. What do we do now?"

For a moment the dialogue ceased, then another voice came on, one with a firm ring of command. *"We must have that ship. The power there is too strong to pass up. We'll call in the Fourth Fleet and crack him somehow."*

The six ships turned away and retreated to their watch posts on the edge of sensor range. The interference faded with distance but still remained, little more than a nuisance. Lively traffic passed through the ether consisting of tachyon bursts rather than entanglement, indicating that the receiver was not a precise target. Tsin took bearings and shot his results to the navigation console. Computopathic Alexiy Pashkov had a brief conversation with Angela through his navigation console, then turned to Steele. "There is no star within their range in that direction, sir. Probably relayed to another ship, then another. Impossible to trace."

Jander frowned. "This will be harder than expected, then. We'll have to wait for the fleet."

Vickie released an unladylike snort. "I suppose you'll let them attack, too. This could get monotonous."

Jander tapped a few keys to change the red alert to amber. "No, we'll mop up the place with the fleet, then follow the remnants home. Should be gunnery practice. Speaking of which," he turned to Denny, "this might be a good time to look at your new popgun. Do you have a prototype?"

"Didn't need one. It's so simple it couldn't help but work."

"Hmph. This I've got to see. Scatter, you have the con. We'll be in Engineering."

"Aye, sir, I have the con." Lam beckoned his backup from her station against the bulkhead and left the helm for the center chair.

Steele looked to Kalanev, sitting alert but quiescent at his armaments station, and waved two fingers toward the hatch. The Ukrainian nodded, and the four officers left the Bridge.

ENGINEERING WAS ON THE VERY first level of the *Angel*, just above the wok-shaped water reservoir nestled into the south polar curve of the ship's hull. The hull, twenty meters thick, englobed the ship and contained the gravity drive engine cones, thermal and solar accumulators, primary weapons, and screen generators within its thick armor of Nokilonian nanosteel, the toughest nonconductive alloy in the known galaxy.

The *Angel* was shaped like a gigantic geodesic jewel, one hundred fifty meters in greatest diameter. The hull consisted of twenty sections built of convex panels that collectively bulged them close to a spherical shape. Each corner of each section housed a drive projector, with its conical tail pointed at the center of the ship. The open mouth of each cone, three meters across, was screened with a red-gold fractal hologram to hide the technology within.

Between those corner installations and set in from the edge of each section was either a pulse or beam weapon port. The rest of each section was dotted with silver-black stellar accumulators, interspersed with the multiplex arrays called tablicy disks that combined communications transceivers, sublight and ultralight sensors, quantum flux and warp sphere generators, and the compound defensive shields that so stoutly protected the ship and her crew. Three of the elongated tropical, or Cancer, sections also boasted the wide portals for auxiliary craft and cargo loading, and three subtropical Capricorn sections housed the telescoping tripod landing stabilizers.

In every dimension the *Angel* was thrice as big and immeasurably more powerful than any other ship in known space. Steele had at his command the power to destroy planetary systems—and Denny did not think it was enough.

His operations office, the hub of engineering, was dead center on the first deck surrounded by one- and two-story warehouses and workshops. Denny directed his audience of three to his cluttered desk shoved against one polyglass bulkhead with five monitors squeezed onto its surface. The reinforced chair creaked as his seven hundred pounds of dense muscle settled in. He tapped a key and the console came to life.

"Here are the plans. As you can see, it's a small addition to our pulse projectors." He called up a dynamic image of the massive pulse cannon on the center monitor. "As you know—you designed it, after all—this mechanical anus is the basic shaper of the force sphere. It expands from zero to not quite two meters, then contracts back to zero. That takes six hundredths of a second or thereabouts. Meanwhile, this forcefield impellor behind it is generating energy to punch it outward like a load of gunpowder. At the end of the firing process, about a quarter second, you have a hollow sphere of molecular cohesion just short of two meters in diameter coming out the twelve-meter magnetically rifled barrel like a fastball from hell. Check?"

Jander nodded. "Check."

"Now, suppose we put right here..." his fingers flew with surprising delicacy as he spun the graphic's perspective to another view, "...a small gun-type fission reactor, designed so that when the sphincter is at its greatest expansion the reactor slams the core masses together and a blast of simple nuclear energy is ejected through here, pushed into the sphere by forcefields generated here. When the sphincter closes and your process is completed you have a bucket of energy, like a balloon full of water—only absolutely rigid and safe to us, of course—that continues through the impellor process, kablooie, out the barrel and on its way. When the sphere loses cohesion, either by crashing into too much matter or simply reaching its limit of endurance, the energy is released as pure thermonuclear destruction. Makes a thousand-pound bomb look like a flash-bang grenade." He leaned back with a smug grin to allow the others a better look. "Neat, hah?"

Steele nodded slowly, intrigued. "Simple is right. And very nice. But I have to believe the pressure of all that raw energy would shorten the life of the sphere."

"I'm no physicist—that's your department—but my staff and I think it's about half. But that's still a range of three hundred thousand kilometers, four times the range of the Confed guns. Plenty to play with. Now, there is a delay when it comes to loading the payload. Right now, we can fire at a rate of four per second. The safeguards for the nuke infusion will make it two per second, but remember we'll need a lot fewer of them to turn somebody into peanut butter."

Pavel chipped in, "But we would still be losing half our range—and we would not always want to shoot to kill."

"No problem." Denny brought up a schematic of a gunnery console on another monitor and high-lighted a prominent icon. "The reactor has two sub-critical masses of U-235 crashing in from either side to combine for injection. Each individual pulse gun station will have the option to open or close the loading magazines. And I can program your master console to shut off any or all of them, at command discretion.

If you want cannonballs, close them. If you want hell-fire, just open the gate." Pavel's gray eyes gleamed as he slowly nodded. Denny went on, "The same can be said about the color of the spheres. As you know, we designed the molecular cohesion spheres to be transparent, but we added an occlusion element that makes them glow red like tracers if we want it. Now, I admit I don't have it yet, but give me a little more time and I can make them opaque instead, to hide the fireball so nobody can see it coming."

Jander clapped him on the shoulder. "Beautiful. I love it. How soon can you put them in?"

Denny grinned. "I have three in already, one on each pole and one on section eleven. Thought you might like to see them in action."

Vickie broke in, "Why nuclear? Why not nucleonic, like the Confederation guns and drive? I'd think that would be a lot more powerful—and cleaner."

"Yeah, but it's more complicated, too. With this, we won't have to redesign the whole gun. We can whip up some fast breeder reactors in no time, and we have enough U-235 on board to fuel them. As for cleaner, this is a bubblegum pop compared to a whole ship blowing up. Anyway, the difference would be between hell squared and hell cubed. Can you imagine a nuclear reaction let loose in your bedroom?"

"Easily." She looked at her husband. Jander cleared his throat and looked away.

"Ahem, yes." Denny turned a little pink. "Anyway, if you agree, I'll get my folks together and get on with this."

"Denny, you're a genius," Jander said. The titan grinned and ducked his head. "I don't need a demo. I love it already. Get them in as soon as you can. We don't know how big this fleet will be."

"You bet. We already have the reactor design loaded into the foundry code. If we put all hands on deck, we should have them all built and installed before that fleet gets here—that is, no more than two days."

"So, go." Jander swept an arm to shoo him out of the office. Denny bounced to his feet and strode for the door, bellowing to his staff to gather round. Pavel settled in at the console to study his new arsenal more thoroughly.

Jander took his wife's arm and led her toward the grav tube around the corner from Denny's central office. "I want to talk to you, lady."

She chuckled. "Embarrassed?"

"A little, but that's not what's bothering me. Let's go home." The two floated up the tube to the fourteenth level and walked hand in hand to their quarters. He remained mute until they entered their living room, then steered her to the reclining love-seat. Finally, seated himself, he broke his silence.

"One of my abilities is that I can read any variant mind without interference, just as a regular telepath can read normal minds." He knew that this was old hat to her, but he needed time to collect his thoughts. She sensed that and did not break in. "While Denny was going over his plans, I was in his mind getting the information first-hand. I was still there when you changed the subject." He paused, irresolute.

Vickie filled in the space. "And you saw Chelsea."

"Yes. And not only that, but a hell of a lot of pain. I sensed the same thing when Spart brought up his relationship with his wife, and our rapport as well."

He sighed. "Denny loves her desperately, so much so that the lack of her in his life interferes with his concentration—and that drives him to work himself half to death. And a look into Chelsea's mind would show the same depth of feeling. She has the patience of the Dover Cliffs, but with Denny, as dynamic as he is, it could be disastrous. He feels inadequate, and it could ruin him."

He sighed again. "The thought of her brings him alive in the morning and gives him peace at the end of the day. But in between he's filled with frustration, seeing her all the time, wanting and needing her, yet fearing to touch her lest she break. I can't afford to lose his productivity, honey, but for the life of me I can't figure out a way to make it work. How can a seven-foot, seven hundred-pound titan romance a five-foot, ninety-pound ghost?"

She pulled her legs up and leaned her shoulder against his. "I know they pine for each other, but do you really think it's that serious?"

"I know it is. What's worse, nowadays he's avoiding her, which brings pain to both of them. It's getting out of hand." He twisted to search her eyes. "You're the psychologist; what do you think?"

She considered the problem for some time. When she spoke, her normally symphonic voice had a clinical tone. "Frankly, I can't see why he hesitates. Denny is no gentle giant, I know. He glories in his strength, like a child with a favorite toy, or a primo don at a command performance. We both remember that time he nonchalantly tossed a mob torpedo out an eleven-story window in New York; and during our interrogation of the Sforan, Habo Esfha, he took a bite out of the poor cat's finger. But he can be, and usually is, painstakingly careful in the use of his strength. Never once has he broken even the most delicate instrument."

"But he's never been passionately in love with a delicate instrument, hon. One slight twitch of his arm and little Chelsea could have a broken back. And he could roll over in his sleep and crush her. I might go along with your opinion that he can control his strength, but his weight, never. And besides, how can you convince him that he'd be gentle with her?"

"You can't. Chelsea will have to do that. We have to throw them together somehow." It occurred to neither of them to mind their own business. They were the Captain and the Chief of Staff of a starship, and anything whatever that concerned the welfare of their crew was definitely their business. "The best we can do right now is wait for an opportunity to do so. But as you say, we can't wait long. I wish I could approach him, but he'd just turn on the charm and talk around it."

She reflexively reached to rub his chest, but stopped herself and remained professional. "The time might come for a fatherly talk. Can you do that?"

"Denny's older than I am, honey. Besides, he's my best friend. A fatherly talk with him might net me a slug in the jaw—and you'd be scraping me off the bulkhead for weeks, shield or no shield." He chewed his lip.

"You'd be surprised what you can do when you have to, dear. You've never let any of us down yet." She uncurled and stood up to pace. "But I see your point. I know Denny was bullied as a child—he was too smart, ten sizes too tall and toothpick thin back then, and kids can be merciless. The scars of geekdom are still there, including more than his share of unsuccessful crushes."

He nodded. "And I wouldn't know how to get around it, even with your coaching. The fact that I have an eidetic memory doesn't mean I know it all."

"We have to be patient. Maybe we'll have something coming up where we could team them. But it has to be logical—I don't want to lose a husband at my age."

"Thanks. I don't want you to." He smiled and got to his feet, interrupting her pacing by enfolding her in an embrace made comfortable from long practice. "You're a nuclear blast yourself, sweets. You've taken a load off my shoulders."

"The hell I have." She curled her arms around his neck and gave him a quick and open kiss. "You're still the Captain, sir, and I don't want the job. I'm perfectly happy to be your mate." The music was back in her voice.

"That job you can keep." He pulled her closer into a full embrace.

CHAPTER 5

Jander reposed in his command chair with Vickie and Denny flanking him and Cinnamon, his tortoise-shell cat, flopped purring in his lap soliciting strokes from his idle hand. Cindy had the run of the ship, with carte blanche to be anywhere safety was not an issue.

The primary crew at their stations and their backups at the wall consoles were watching the massive fleet form on the outer fringes of the *Angel*'s warp sphere. They could see at least two hundred ships —which answered one question: the hijacking operation was on a planetary scale. Steele had suspected that; the fact that none of the stolen merchandise seemed to have turned up on the Confederation black market was a pretty good indicator.

He cleared his throat. "Angela."

"*ACTIVE*," the mechentity answered, after the half-second delay programmed in to soften her otherwise instant response.

"Given as index, the known power of Confederation weaponry compared to the corresponding power of the present fleet's weaponry; given the known resistance of the *Angel*'s shielding; question: How many hits from the present fleet would be necessary to disrupt our shields? Answer."

"ANSWER: GIVEN THE KNOWN POWER OF CONFEDERATION WEAPONRY AS INDEX ONE, THE WEAPONRY POWER OF ONE PRESENT FLEET UNIT IS POINT NINE FOUR. THE ANGEL'S SCREENS MAY RESIST EIGHTY-TWO POINT NINE SEVEN EIGHT PLUS SIMULTANEOUS HITS TO THE THRESHOLD OF DISRUPTION."

"How many ships comprise the present fleet? Answer and correlate."

"ANSWER: TWO HUNDRED TWELVE UNITS COMPRISE THE PRESENT FLEET. CORRELATION: PRESUMING CUSTOMARY SALVO OF THREE OF TWELVE GUNS PER UNIT, AND USING THE ANGEL'S SCREEN RESISTANCE AS INDEX ONE, THE PRESENT FLEET REPRESENTS AN OVERLOAD OF FIVE POINT NINE SEVEN EIGHT."

"Thank you."

"WHATEVER."

Jander blinked in surprise, then swung his chair to the analytics console on the bulkhead to his left. "Was that your idea, Geraldo?"

The Italian computopath's dark eyes bulged with indignation. "I would never consider such a thing, Milord!"

Jander half-closed one eye as he opened his mind to the mental impulses around him. Instantly he discovered a guilty conscience behind him. "Denver..."

The titan jerked alive. "Harrrumph. Mr. Belocci, a computer is a precision instrument, not to be trifled with. You will please reprogram accordingly."

The accused looked utterly scandalized. "Captain..."

"It's all right, Aldo. We know where the body is buried." He glanced over his shoulder at the discomfited titan and changed the subject. "Did you get your new popguns installed, engineer?"

"Um, yessir. We can now not only destroy worlds, we can wipe them out of existence." He shifted. "A conversation with, uh, Angela indicates that with the nuclear containment our range is cut by almost half, as we thought."

"We'll see pretty soon. It looks like they've stopped juking around and are about set to mug us. Angela, full ship broadcast." The sound of a boatswain's whistle echoed through the ship. Cindy perked up at the high-pitched tweet, then hopped down from his lap and tucked herself into the cushioned cube installed for her under the command console.

"Attention, Corpsmen. We're about to go into battle with a force almost six times our relative strength. But we have gadgets they've never dreamed of, and the best crew in the galaxy to operate them. I know you're ready. So keep your ears on and your eyes open—things will be happening fast. Angela, keep this broadcast open. I'll be issuing instructions."

Now the complete commander, Steele had the look of his namesake in his eyes as he surveyed his

Bridge. "Corpsman Seshat, have you calculated the jump coordinates?"

"Yes, sir, they're at the helm." Navigator Alexiy Pashkov was just as crisp.

"Corpsman Scatter, be prepared to initiate the jumps in sequence on my command. In between, you will maximize the fields of fire for the gunners."

Nwoye Lam nodded shortly and poised his hands and telekinetic mind over his helm console. "Ready, sir." His job would take enormous precision; he had eighty-four engines to play with as well as the quantum entanglement flux energies merged with the ship's inner warp sphere that could teleport the entire ship.

"I have a signal incoming, sir," Tsin Li-san rapped. "No visual." Not only did he have his communications board to manage, but Corpsman Jinwu was also the telepathic link between navigator, helmsman, and Corpsman Kitsune, Kurino Yukio, at her sensors station.

"Put it through." Steele himself took a firm grip on Vickie's mind, relying on her psychological insights to aid him through the sparring now to come.

The message came through in Sabarian. *"To the commander of the gem-ship, attention. We have you englobed and are ready for battle. Prepare to receive a boarding party or be destroyed."*

Steele bared his teeth, and sensed Vickie's grim satisfaction as well. Despite his superiority in numbers, the speaker had his doubts. Along with the brutal threat, his respect-fraught description of the *Angel* made that clear enough.

"Jinwu, connect." The communications officer made it a two-way. "To the commander of the fleet, attention. I am obligated by intergalactic treaty to advise you to stand down your weapons, cut your defensive shields and surrender your forces at once. You and your crews will be accorded the treatment due prisoners of war. Any demonstration of power will be answered in kind, and your forces will be annihilated. You have two minutes to comply."

He waved his thumb across his throat. Tsin saw the gesture on his rearview window and cut the connection. "That should stir them up."

"There's no way they're gonna put up with that," Denny rumbled.

"Of course not. I just wanted to make then insecure enough to attack full force, no reserves to worry about. They'll charge in and give us a legitimate right to bat them all over the place. They've murdered their last merchantman."

He sat back and rested his hands on the chair arms. "Commander Cobra, prepare your gunners. Remind them that my orders to cease and commence fire will supersede all circumstances." Since the broadcast channel was open, Pavel Kalanev's order was superfluous. He simply nodded and tapped his earpiece microphone twice.

"Here they come," Denny rumbled, and sprinted out the hatch toward Engineering. Angela, coded to be aware of the stationing of all personnel under battle protocol and knowing the Bridge was clear of all but the proper crew, sealed the double pocket hatch behind him.

Steele reached for his board and pinpointed one of the enemy ships, bringing its magnified image to his console monitor. It looked exactly like a Confederation cruiser, if a bit smaller. In the broad tail of the sixty-five-meter ovoid were the main drive engines, their long nucleonic nozzles pointing sternward. A third of the way forward, at the egg's broadest diameter, was a ring of smaller engines, alternately pointed stern-ward, outward and forward, which provided drive, retro and braking thrust. A smaller ring of gimballed maneuvering retros, pointed outward, was set a quarter of the way aft of the rounded prow.

In the waist of the ship, at one hundred twenty degrees intervals, were three pairs of nucleonic cannons surrounded by the stellar accumulators and screen generators. Basically modified engines, the artillery vented their energies in near-solid pulses a meter wide instead of the engines' steady thrust. Three more such weapons protruded from the stern segment between the main drive and main retros, and another trio menaced the universe just ahead of the forward retro ring—on each cruiser, twelve guns in all.

The *Angel* had eighty-four.

The fleet formation contracted, the ships leaving their posts on the edge of the *Angel*'s outer warp sphere and moving closer and ever closer, retroing sideways into an encircling net which would surround their quarry at fifty thousand kilometers—the best effective range for their weapons without endangering their own forces on the other side of the englobement. The *Angel* continued to float along the trade route like a gigantic dirigible, seemingly without a care in the universe.

Steele's quiescence did not impede his own preparations. He spread his perception to every member of the Bridge crew to monitor their stations as thoroughly as they did. He felt a tingle of pride as their thoughts flooded into him, each prepared in his or her own way for the battle to come.

Tsin's concentration was solidly on the telepathic link he provided for Kurino, Pashkov and Lam, his outside-the-box sense of humor suppressed but lurking just beneath the surface. Kurino's flashing eyes and fixed-reference clairvoyance followed every enemy ship on the monitors and extrapolated their patterns of momentum with the trained instincts of the former world-class gymnast she was. Pashkov's hands were in constant motion as he sketched the vectors that Lam, his hair-trigger reflexes at the ready, would need to most efficiently direct the ship within what the enemy thought was a trap.

Kalanev, the seasoned warrior in a youthful body, took his feed of Kurino's patterns to direct his gunners to sequence their targeting most efficiently. Belocci at analytics was locked onto the *Angel*'s multiplex defensive screening to detect any overload and strengthen any points of weakness. And covering them all was the soaring soul of Lady Alpha, wrapping them up like a warm comforter, her subtle touch keeping them focused, alert and confident without revealing the slightest hint of her own fears.

Steele absorbed his crew's calm strength and drew a deep breath of his own. "Show them our fangs, Cobra." Kalanev touched a master key, and eighty-four spiral hatches three meters in diameter flashed open. Nanosteel tubes reinforced with shimmering energy fields deployed outward in silent menace. The gunners at their consoles near the outer hull surrounding the Bridge deck released their safeties and readied their targeting systems.

"Prepare to jump." Lam, speedball under his left hand to control yaw and pitch, joystick in his right to control direction, and acceleration and retro pedals beneath his right and left feet, rested a telekinetic "finger" lightly on a preprogrammed key.

With no further warning, eighteen of the encircling ships blasted out probing shots, which splashed on the *Angel*'s energy shield in a blinding blaze of impotent nucleonic fury.

"Now!"

Lam hit the jump key. Each of the three hundred variants aboard felt the familiar tug at the base of the skull that heralded a change of scenery. In that instant the *Angel* was teleported *outside* the fleet, making their englobement as ineffective as a rotten fishnet.

"Commence fire!"

The *Angel*'s internal gravity quivered as at least half the ship's guns came to life. Driven by a steady flood of stellar-powered thrust, the beam cannons gimballed on target and blasted out meter-wide cylinders of pure energy. The force beams crashed through the enemy defensive screens with little effort and sheared into the nanosteel hulls; then the gunners twitched their mighty bludgeons back and forth in minute arcs at that distance, hacking their victims into glittering shards.

Tremendous fireballs of nucleonic hell expanded from each target as the force beams ruptured engine rooms and gun batteries, releasing the stored energies to feed greedily if briefly on the escaping air. In the blink of an eye the ships ceased to exist, or spun away in crumpled fragments as their inertia compensators failed. The beams blinked off and the projectors swiveled to seek the next targets caught by Kurino's sensors, leaving behind nothing except expanding clouds of debris.

But the pulse cannons! At half-second intervals, two-meter incandescent spheres of force incarnate spat from the mouths of the guns and flashed toward the enemy ships at better than half the speed of light. As with the beams, the shields and hulls of the enemy were as inefficacious as vacuum against the sheer kinetic force of the mighty cannonballs. But once the spheres encountered solid matter, they lost their cohesion.

Instantly Denny Connors' brainchild was unleashed within the unprotected ships, and the power of six kilotons of TNT ran rampant through bulkheads and atmosphere alike. The result was indescribable, inconceivable. With the beams, the targeted ships ceased to exist. With the spheres, the victims may never have existed at all.

Jander watched hard-eyed as ship after ship dissolved into shards and globules of molten metal or crumpled like so many tin cans. Lam played his part with consummate skill; an instant after the jump he flashed fingers, feet and mind over his console, spiraling the *Angel* toward the concentrated formation of ships at twice their speed. With only sporadic return fire the survivors increased their drives and fell back in panic, desperately powering away from their far more maneuverable nemesis and closing with those behind them that were foolishly trying to get into the action.

When the range was down to thirty thousand kilometers, Jander spoke again.

"Attention, all. I will give a countdown. On the two count you will cease fire; on zero, we will jump. Then you will pick your targets. Ready. Four. Three. Cease fire. One. Jump! Fire as your guns bear!"

As the first set of victims fell back, their counterparts on the other side of the englobement dashed in. The *Angel*'s one hundred thousand-kilometer jump put the big ship *behind* the fleet—giving the gunners on the other side of the ship their own choice of targets.

Scatter literally flew over his console, hovering centimeters over his chair as his left foot flipped the gravitic drive from one end of the ship to the other and his right foot poured on the power. At a speed that would have torn any other ship in half she braked her outward momentum and, with hard shoves on the stick in Nwoye's right hand, retraced her path through the vacuum to bear down on the shocked pirates.

The gunners had another skeet shoot, howling cheers and curses from their stations as they exploded raider after raider. Almost half the fleet was already gone, and it seemed the others would fare no better. By the score, they were blasted into incandescent atoms. The shattered remnants gave back as their fellows had before them, turning their previously perfect global formation into a shambles of twisting, spinning, scrambling rabbits.

"Prepare to jump. Four. Three. Cease fire. One. Jump! *FIRE!*"

With whoops of delight, the gunners recognized their position. They were right back where they started, in the center of the englobement! The enemy fleet, retreating from the *Angel*'s previous positions, now found themselves driving right at her. Now every gun had a target. Every target had a short life. The combat became execution.

"North and south polar gunners, safety your nukes. Leave us some debris." Directly above and below the *Angel* the ships no longer exploded. They were simply riddled through and through by the spheres themselves, minus the brimstone that was still devastating the other ships.

"Cease fire." Taut-jawed, he intruded on Kurino's mind to check the score.

Of the two hundred twelve units of the mighty fleet, less than thirty were left to run away. And run they did, in utter panic, scattering to every point of the galactic compass.

Steele sat back in dour satisfaction as Denny, from his engineering station far below, bellowed at the top of his robust lungs, *"Who's your daddy now?!?"*

Jander hastily cut the shipwide broadcast, but too late for the clarion roar of victory to be cut off. From Engineering below and the Gunnery stations on the Bridge deck, from the Hangar deck, from Environmentals and the isolated Damage Control stations, even from Sick Bay and Hydroponics, the triumphant cry was echoed and reechoed by three hundred jubilant warriors.

Jander allowed himself a tight-lipped grin and looked at the timer on his console. The entire battle had taken less than twelve minutes.

"Angela, stand down to amber alert." An alto tone repeated the Morse code for the letter "A" three times throughout the ship.

"Cobra, I want a list of aces. Can you do it?"

"Absolutely, Captain!" Kalanev proudly turned to his board.

"What now?" Vickie, the least bloodthirsty of people, was nonetheless content with the carnage they had wrought. Her thoughts, as were the thoughts of every Corpsman on the ship, were on gutted merchants and massacred crews. "Are we going to let them get away?"

"Not hardly. We'll pick one of them and follow him home. Give us a look around, Kurino-san."

Jander turned as his engineer cleared the opening hatch and planted his huge hands on the curved back of the right-side secondary chair. Connors bent forward and smiled grimly at the main monitor on which Yukio was displaying the devastation. "We sure made a mess, didn't we? I want a raise."

"How about a field trip instead?" Jander returned. "I want to drop you and a team off to look at those hulks, Denny, or what's left of them. We'll be back to pick you up as soon as we get a line on the pirates' base."

"Sounds good to me." He straightened to full height, glad for something other than the thousands of casualties to think about. "Who should I take?"

"Load up a Sprite with salvage gear, and take a clairvoyant—better yet, a ghost. They're used to zero G maneuvering. Take Winschell—she's a med tech and can look at the bodies, too. And you'll need a computopath, and an eidetic to store whatever you pick up, and a telepath to use as a link. Mançon, Wize, Crawley. I'll give you Banshee 106 as top cover. Whitney and Soames are still pretty green and need some time in the saddle. Anyone else?"

Denny almost flinched at the sound of Chelsea's name, but he did not question the order. "That oughta do it. When do I start?"

"As soon as you can. I want to get on someone's tail pretty quick."

"Yessir." Connors strode to the Bridge's backup engineering command station and settled into conversation with Angela to make his arrangements. Steele hoped he was too busy to recall that he had three ghosts in the Engineering department who were better qualified for the mission than Chelsea. But, by choice or by chance, Denny elected to stay with his lineup.

CHAPTER 6

Denny dropped in on Engineering to hand off departmental command to Hal Summers, his Canadian second, then rode an elevator up to the hangar deck on level 20. He stepped out and ran his eyes over the twelve bottle-shaped, ten-meter Banshee fighter ships, six of which were still crewed after being on fruitless standby the entire time the *Angel* was on combat alert.

Their canopies were hinged up and he could see the disgruntled looks of the two-person crews through their vacuum suit helmets as they went through their check-down procedures. They were the best of the Banshee teams, all of them with battle experience in aircraft before joining the Corps, and were clearly disappointed not to have the chance to fight their new rides.

A steady stream of Kannada curses came from one cockpit as its Indian pilot made his opinion very clear. A ground mechanic knelt on the stubby wing of each of the ten-meter interceptors to help pilot and gunner disentangle themselves from the plumbing that kept them very personally attached to the deep, windowless cockpits.

A full ground crew was swarming over another Banshee to prepare it for flight, gauging the tempered aura of the glowing retro cones prominent on the nose and wingtips and forming the main engines in the stern. The cones, hiding beneath their red-gold fractal hologram disguises that made the ship's profile appear seamless, gave the little ship the thrust and maneuverability of a terrified cockroach, and the twin twenty-centimeter pulse guns in the gimballed nose delivered a devastating punch. That ship would be his top cover, crewed by a team that needed flight experience and got the draw for what was expected to be a milk run.

Denny looked through the broad double hatches separating the combat hangar from the one housing the six shuttlecraft and two Banshee-T trainers, and saw the tail end of a Sprite being similarly prepared. That would be his ride.

A third external hatch opened to a separate loading dock, with room enough to allow two shuttles to land and unload onto the telebooth platform intended to move the cargo to storage. Its interior hatches connecting it to the hangars were currently closed.

Denny strode to the ready room that took up most of the central bulkhead between the two hangars, where the other members of his team was gathering. The hangar itself was a double level with seven meters of headroom, but the ready room was divided into two stories with the upper serving as a billet for the duty watch and the lower as the locker room.

The Banshee crew were already suited up on standby, seated on couches with their helmets hinged back to rest on the backpack that contained the suits' rebreather, recycler, environmental and internal power components. Freddie Soames, an Australian teleporter with longish dark blond hair and a full ginger beard, who once had designed computer war games, was the gunner/navigator reading something on a tablet as he waited. The pilot was the telekinetic Zach Whitney, an erstwhile criminologist who briefly flew a Harrier for the U.S. Marines.

Zach's brunette wife, Ann, sat hand in hand with him on the couch trying to look calm. Denny noticed that her makeup had left a brush of light powder on her husband's dark cheek. He gave them a smile and a thumb's up as he made his way into the men's locker room.

Bill Wize and Simon "Slim" Crawley were already suited to the waist, both still grimacing from the application of the EVA suit's plumbing. Slim was muttering something about chicken sexin' in his twanging East Texas drawl, which had Bill trying not to laugh because it would hurt. Denny grinned, then grimaced as a pair of techs held up his own suit and beckoned him forward.

Ten uncomfortable minutes later—a flight crew could do it in less than three—they emerged to find the blonde Chelsea Winschell strolling out of the women's locker room with Elga Mançon, the women having taken the plumbing much more equably than the men. The irrepressible Chelsea grinned up at Denny with a wink, while thin-faced, brunette Elga, an ascetic and consummately nerdy computopath, nodded and settled into a chair with as much dignity as the bulky suit would allow.

Seeing her, Denny had a sudden brainwave. "Elga, could you please gather up all our wristpads and get Angela to upload what we have on the pirate language? We don't know what kind of data we're going to find, so let's go out as prepared as we can be."

"A good thought," Mançon acknowledged with a nod and a smile, happy for something technical to do. She unbuckled her own instrument as she rose to collect the others.

"Okay," Denny started, knowing Elga could both listen and work at the same time and not miss a thing, "everybody link with Slim and get the plan in your heads. Here's what's expected of us..."

Twenty minutes later the big hatches at the base of two Cancer hull sections slid open and two small shapes emerged. From one side of the mother ship came the Banshee, with Whitney piloting and Soames slotted in behind him with the weapons and navigation systems.

Denny piloted out from the other hangar at the

controls of the longer and much broader Sprite, a loaf-shaped and unarmed shuttle sixteen meters long. Designed as an all-purpose exploratory platform and cargo carrier, the wingless Sprite sported six command consoles to cover all the tasks a first-landing expedition might require. Chelsea, all business now, sat beside Denny at the copilot/navigation console.

The others were seated at the sensors, analytics and engineering-environmentals stations behind them, leaving the communications console unmanned. The rest of the ten-meter interior capsule was empty except for their salvage gear, with the six passenger seats flattened into the deck to leave cargo space for whatever they collected from the debris field.

Jander watched them go, a bit embarrassed by his pairing maneuvers. With a quirk of his lips he dismissed the feeling and called to Yukio, "I'm assuming enough of this wreckage still have warp spheres intact. Can you double-check for me?" Every ship's quantum tachyon mass-time compensator sphere not only created a bubble of normal space that negated superlight distortions, but also protected anything within its two million-kilometer infusion zone from crumpling like a paper cup.

"Yes, Milord. No fewer than six of the wrecks are intact enough to maintain the former fleet's velocity and keep our own ships with them. Our friends are in no danger from inertia flux as long as the power lasts—a minimum of ninety hours for three of the wrecks. I detect no sign of life, though. Apparently, these people were so confident that they didn't bother to wear environmental suits into combat."

"Well, so were we. Can you find us a fugitive, Nwoye?"

"Kitsune gave me a line on several, sir. Which one do you want?" Lam highlighted seven of the smaller viewscreens surrounding the main monitor. Their borders, glowing in colors from bright red to deep violet, indicated their direction and course relative to the ship. It was Angela's job, under the direction of Belocci, Pashkov, and Kurino, to keep track of where they were relative to the galaxy, but from a tactical standpoint the universe revolved around the *Angel*.

"Let's take that one on a heading out of Confederation space, screen eighteen." Jander pointed to one of the viewscreens that showed the drive flare of a cruiser beyond the fleet's warp sphere but still visible on tachyon sensors. Lam nodded and got busy with hands and feet, and the *Angel* sped in the direction of the fleeing ship. "Li-san, shoot our vector to Kodiak and Peregrine so they know where we're headed. Pavel, let's have the baffle."

Steele's two greatest variant talents were force projection and wave analysis. By combining the two—and his sizeable intellect—he and his engineers had designed mechanisms to duplicate many of the shields he could generate mentally.

The ship's offensive weapons were based on those talents, as were the enhanced collision and deflection shields. Parallel to them was the inner warp sphere that reduced their normal two million-kilometer infusion zone to thirty thousand, just wide enough for Angela to dodge anything solid enough to threaten them.

Extending to the same horizon was another shield infused with the energies necessary to refract all lengths of light and sensor waves, including super-light speed quantum particles. The Ukrainian tickled a few keys on his armaments console, and the *Angel* became invisible and undetectable.

Denny saw them disappear, and felt more alone than ever in his very active life. No, that was not quite accurate; he had Chelsea beside him.

"Well, you great lummox, are we going to sit here all day?" Temperamentally, the jaunty pubmaid-turned-medical technician was clearly complimentary to her towering secret love.

"Just feeling a little homesick." He shook his head to settle his closed helmet and blinked at an icon in his heads-up display to trigger his short-range com. "Sprite 202 to Banshee 106."

"*Peregrine here.*" Whitney's Marine-strong baritone answered immediately.

"We'll start with the carcass just above my horizontal plane and forward. I need you to stand off somewhere about here and keep us covered."

"*Roger, Kodiak, we'll keep you warm.*" The Banshee, under the impetus of the retro cones covering its short, thick wings and turreted bow quarter, slipped like a fish and took station above them, nose idly rotating in a broad circle. Connors wafted his stout shuttle toward the derelict, weaving through the drifting debris blitzing along at the same relative speed as his Sprite.

"THERE SHE IS, ORION-SAMA." Yukio at her sensors station pointed with her hand palm up to the forward screen. Lam was good to his word, as usual; his magic fingers had directed the *Angel* to the edge of the fleeing raider's warp sphere. The Nigerian spun his speedball and typed briskly, setting his steed into the warship's wake at precisely its speed, then relaxed back in his seat to let Angela take over.

The *Angel*, back down to blue alert, settled in for a long ride.

DENNY STABILIZED THE SPRITE near a wreck with much of its mass intact and gave control to the computer to maintain their distance. The five occupants dropped their solid nanosteel faceplates into place over the plexiglass visors of their helmets and switched on the sensors that would thereafter be their sole view of the outside.

No ship or EVA suit could ever allow its occupant to see the universe beyond the horizon of a warp sphere; experiments by many species of space travelers had proven that the intense distortions and chaotic mirages of superlight speed was more than enough to drive any sighted entity to the point of insanity. Any being that relied on vision had to depend solely on tachyon sensors to survive the experience.

Since nanosteel was non-conductive and non-magnetic, each suit was equipped with circuitry that formed gravity fields from the boot soles, gloves and seats to keep them in place. Once all of them were protected and sealed, Bill at the engineering console pumped the atmosphere into holding tanks, switched off the Sprite's internal gravity and popped the broad loading hatch.

Denny was the only one of the party unencumbered by his EVA suit. Not that he was not wearing one, of course; simply put, the strength that could bench-press a minivan found the man-made atmospheric pressure of the suit almost non-existent. The others would have trouble moving without the built-in servos.

Still, it was Chelsea who carried the tether from the Sprite to the wreck. Even though she was unable to turn spectral in the vacuum of space, her experience as a free-flying ghost made her a natural for maneuvering through the floating junk using her compressed-nitrogen thrusters and finding an anchorage for the strong cable that would serve as their mooring line.

They entered the derelict through a huge rent near where the stern used to be. The internal gravity was gone, but the inertia compensators had held long enough so that the acceleration of the demolished drive engines had time to dissipate and allow the wreckage to revert to drifting without forward thrust.

Elga took her time orienting herself, blandly ignoring the horribly distorted yellow-skinned bodies floating about, then opened her mind to that of the ship. "I sense nothing," the dark-haired Swiss reported. "We'll have to set up a portable power source to get the computers thinking again."

"I'll get it," Denny said. He hooked onto the connecting cable, released the gravitic plates in his boots and pushed himself out the tear toward the Sprite.

Chelsea and Simon "Slim" Crawley, the telepathic Texan, were already at work, she "seeing" the ship's structure and he relaying the information to the eidetic Bill Wize. There the information would wait, in perfect detail, until they were back in the *Angel*. Then the Calgary native would sit down with a cybernetic feeder helmet and relay his stored knowledge into the barely more efficient memory of Angela.

They worked for several hours, until Wize's mind was crammed with esoteric science and he had to take a break. His brain buzzed with mechanical illustrations, three-dimensional cross-sections and wiring charts supplied by Chelsea, and processing shunts, pathways and data gleaned from the binary-based computers by Elga. Also within his copious memory were the grumbled musings of his chief. Denny had hooked into Slim's telepathic link and made spot assessments and diagnoses of the ship's infrastructure. One thing was missing, which they all noticed.

"We'll have to grab us another hunk 'a ship for the nav stuff," Slim drawled. "This'n here musta been too far down in the T.O. to have it stored."

"Right," Denny agreed. "We'll take a few minutes off in the Sprite, then find ourselves another wreck." The five floated toward their impromptu door.

"You know," Connors mused, "If I didn't know better, I'd swear this was a Confed—"

"Banshee to Kodiak, come in."

"Here, Peregrine. Gettin' bored?"

"We were, but not anymore. We got company. Two five four mark oh four niner from your position."

Denny shot a look at his companions, then leaped for the outer hull of the derelict and snagged a handhold. He scanned his sensors with squinted eyes until he spotted the moving specks.

Four of the raiders had returned.

CHAPTER 7

Denny leaned back into the derelict and waved his crew toward the tethered Sprite. "How is your Banshee shielded?" He knew the answer, but the commander in him wanted Whitney to think about it.

"Tachyon sensors and defense. We don't have room for baffle screening. They can pick us up on visuals. I just hope they don't look at 'em too closely."

"My Sprite's fixed the same way. Small craft baffles are my next project, believe me." Bill was first up the line, bearing a towline attached to a net full of wreckage samples; the engineer would power up the shuttle. Next went Slim with a huge load of their equipment in tow, then Elga with more samples. Chelsea powered across on her own dragging the generator behind her.

Denny detached the tether and held on as Slim winched it in along with the towlines. "Peregrine, Kodiak. We'll try to sneak out on them and find a place to hide. Stay put until we're ready to go."

"Roger that."

Within the tight cockpit of the Banshee, Whitney stared dry-mouthed at his sensors. Behind him,

Freddie Soames flipped the switches to bring his twin pulse projectors to life. He shared a grim look with the image of his pilot displayed in a corner of his console screen. Neither of them was combat experienced. No amount of simulator training gave them much confidence against four cruisers.

Denny was aware of that queasy feeling, also. "I'll bet they're here to get rid of this junk," he said as they strapped in.

The hatch cycled shut as Slim and Elga tied down their cargo and the ship's computer poured heated air into the cabin. Denny raised his solid faceplate as the interior lighted up. "They're just as anxious to keep their base secret as we are to find it. I'll also wager they have their sensors on full tap right now." He waited with shortened breath while the little ship came to life under his hands.

Wize was at the engineering station, triple-checking their minimal defensive shields. "After the beating we gave them, I'd have thought they'd still be running."

"All of us did. Maybe they're more afraid of their bosses than us." All his lights were green, and Bill joined him up front and strapped himself into the co-pilot's seat without protest from Chelsea. The ghost was a good pilot, but she was no match for the half-Scottish, half-Lakota engineer and she knew it. She chose to float free and spectral behind the two front seats.

"Here we go." Denny shared an impulsive look

with Chelsea, then rammed his weight down on the drive pedal.

The Sprite shot away from the derelict at the velocity of almost sixty meters per second squared. On his console monitor he watched Whitney flip his much faster and far more agile Banshee into a curve and speed away at a tangent, flanking the shuttle while putting as much distance between the two targets as possible.

"Slim. Get on the horn and put out a mayday. Try to tight-beam it in the direction Orion said he was going."

Crawley grunted an acknowledgement, unstrapped and skimmed toward the shuttle's sixth chair in front of the long-range communicator, motioning for Elga to take over the engineering console. He unfastened and stripped off his gloves so he could handle the keyboard barehanded. Suddenly he yelped and pointed at the forward monitor. Two of the raiders were peeling out of formation and speeding in their direction.

Denny cursed and opened his short-range channel. "Jack, old buddy old pal old friend, do you see what I see?"

"Coming around now, Senior Commander. We'll intercept."

"Watch yourself. You're a match for any one of them, but there are four out there."

"Yeah, I noticed. But we have one big advantage over them. We're Corpsmen!" The Banshee looped

around and corkscrewed in to protect its defenseless charge.

Connors broke contact. "Good luck, *men*," he rumbled.

Zach Whitney felt the beginnings of a maddening itch on his shaven scalp and scraped at it with his telekinesis. "Got a bead, Freddie?"

"Aye." His gunner's voice was barely a croak. The enemy was so close he disengaged his targeting computer and relied on his crosshairs. He deselected the tracer-like visible wavelengths from his projectors and stared unblinking at his targeting monitor.

The pilot spared a brief glance at the photo of Ann taped to his console, then returned to his heads-up. He eased the stick in his right hand in a circular motion and aligned the Banshee's nose with the nearest cruiser. "Let 'em have it!"

The Australian tweaked the speedball that directed the gimballed gun turret and leaned on his joystick trigger. Twenty-centimeter spheres of energy erupted from the fighter's twin cannons in rapid one-two succession, eight per second.

The first two shots puffed deep and deeper flashes in the cruiser's defensive screen, then a double string of holes blossomed in the stern quarter of the enemy ship as the spheres bored in, punching their way through the weakened screens and into nanosteel. A tiny geyser of light spurted from the retro ring, then the ship was an inferno, the chain-reaction from the ruptured engines consuming the oxygen-rich atmosphere up and down its length.

Abruptly it exploded in a blinding flash of hellish brimstone, quickly snuffed by the vacuum of space. A rapidly expanding hail of debris soared outward.

"Splash one!" Whitney roared in triumph, then tingled with alarm as a thought struck him like a fist. He jerked at the controls, flipping the Banshee over on its side and whipping away from their course. No more than a second later a series of twin nucleonic bolts flashed through their previous position.

Spinning back on their previous course, the Corpsmen saw two of the other raiders retroing toward them as the other one continued after the shuttle. As Whitney spiraled his craft at dizzying speed, Soames snapped off quick bursts as his guns bore onto each of the cruisers in turn. One of them yawed away as its control room was riddled, but the other, though hit, juked around its stunned partner and altered its course away from the Banshee to go after the Sprite it was obviously protecting.

The fighter spent a few precious seconds drilling lethal holes in the cripple before it could reorganize, then looped around again to race for the others. Too late!

The first ship, the one closest to Denny's craft, twisted to show its broadside and unleashed a salvo in the Sprite's general direction, flooding the vacuum around the unarmed vessel with raw energy. One of the bolts made spattering contact with the shuttle's energy screen, a glancing blow intended to disable rather than destroy. The hit sent the shuttle spinning end for end, the aura of its shielding flickering like a dying flame.

"They've lost their defense!" Soames shouted, shoulders hunched over his console. "Get me back on track!"

Whitney uttered a guttural curse as their wounded foe spiral into their path. Its guns flashed, and only his reflexes kept the Banshee from annihilation.

Soames howled again as he watched the first ship fire once more at the Sprite, knocking the shuttle into an even wilder spin. *"Dammit, mate, get me back on track!"*

"Oorah!" Whitney dropped his own sensor shield, flipped his fighter hard over and stomped his drive pedal to the floor. Instantly the game little fighter was fully detectable to the raiders as it drove straight at the Sprite's pursuer. Guns pounding, ignoring the deepening peril from their own flank, the Corpsmen bulleted in to protect their helpless friends.

"CAPTAIN! I'M GETTING A SPURT over our emergency channel."

Jander stiffened. "Unscramble and give it to me, Tsin." Vickie tensed behind him and dropped to one knee beside his chair.

"Mayday! Sprite 202 to Angel, *mayday! Four of the raiders returned to the scene and spotted us.*

Attempted to run, but took two big hits and lost upper retros, internal air and gravity and defensive shields, along with the computer and most of our accumulators. We still have our warp sphere and inertia compensator. We're still running, mostly on battery power, but it won't last long at this speed."

There was a pause.

"Banshee 106 gave themselves up to give us a chance, but they took three of the bastards with them and bought us some valuable space. The last one, damaged, is following us, but we have a good head start on them. Pecos was uncovered when the first hit came and suffered a fatal decompression. Dominique has a compound fracture in her arm. The rest of us are all right, but we'll have to set down somewhere— you can't intercept in time."

Denny gave a string of numbers representing their line of flight. *"We've located a G1 yellow star ahead of us. Look for a Gaea-like planet if there is one, you'll have to hunt for us if there isn't. Gotta cut this short—conserve power. Wish us luck. Kodiak out."*

Vickie, mouth open in shock, looked up at Steele, then shrank away from him. He was livid, his strong face twisted into a mask of bitter fury. He jerked to his feet, stepped around the command console and advanced with deliberate, stiff steps to the armaments station. Kalanev, hardened killer that he was, recognized the look on his face and hastily vacated his chair.

Jander fumbled with the keyboard, taking gun

after gun from its operator's control, until a full third of the *Angel*'s armed might was concentrated in one key. Slowly, with bitter deliberation, he raised his arm, cocking his fist to his ear. Then, with a guttural snarl of towering rage, he smashed his fist into the board. The entire Bridge crew jumped with the blow, while the ship lost a noticeable percentage of her momentum to the violent shove of thirty guns. The raider on the screen before them vanished in a blossom of violent energy.

"Pashkov." His voice was deep, deadly. "Get us back there." He gripped his broken hand, glaring at the empty viewscreen with a terrible stare. "And I don't want to see an atom intact in our wake, Lam..."

He spun on his heel and strode toward the starboard hatch, ignoring the stunned crewmen who stared after him. "I'll be in sickbay—having my head examined!"

CHAPTER 8

They replaced Slim's gloves, closed his blocking faceplate and strapped his vacuum-ravaged body into the communications chair. Mourning would have to wait.

Chelsea, who was trained as an emergency medical technician after joining the Corps, did her best to set Elga's shattered left arm inside the pressure suit with the help of her clairvoyance, and wrapped it in an elastic bandage as tight as she could without cutting off the airflow within. The impact from the first near miss had hurled the computopath against the bulkhead, jammed her arm in the narrow space between consoles and splintered both forearm bones plus several in the wrist, and destroyed the medical auto injector next to the skin beneath her wristpad as well. She was in intense pain, but with the loss of most of their atmosphere Chelsea had no way to administer an anesthetic.

Denny was sweating over his controls, his face a picture of concentration. A patchwork repair job had restored part of their shielding, but not enough to handle the larger chunks of cosmic debris in "empty" space. Bill's attention was glued to the forward observation screen, warning the pilot of obstacles ahead. At their velocity, multiplied every second by more than three gravities of thrust, a multitude of small bodies of matter flashed toward them at terrifying speed, any one of which could destroy them by collision. Their small warp sphere was still intact, which helped protect them by normalizing anything within ten thousand kilometers to their own relative speed, but that was designed to be effective only at sublight speeds and was a fragile margin at best. The Sprite was never intended for interstellar flight.

While the men toiled on the razor's edge the ghost flitted about the cabin, unencumbered by the loss of internal gravity that forced the others to labor under more than triple their normal weight. Thanks to Bill's frantic efforts to reseal the sprung cargo doors there was just enough residual air in the cabin to afford Chelsea the molecules through which to maneuver. She was jettisoning all their cargo and any unnecessary odds and ends by the simple expedient of turning them incorporeal and pushing them through the hull. The resulting tiny increases in speed gave them a comet's trail of wreckage samples, seats, tools, salvage equipment and other debris in their wake.

Connors, with his tremendous strength, found the added gravity no great problem. "Chelsea, check the battery levels. We don't have enough accumulators left to keep them at capacity. I think we'll have to set down pretty quick."

Chelsea floated to the engineering station and

her hollow voice rattled off a string of numbers. The eidetic Wize made some rapid mental calculations. "We'll make that star we want, but we won't be able to do much maneuvering." He shot a glance at another monitor. "No sign of pursuit, but their sensors are stronger than ours are now. They might have us in sight."

Denny answered with a grunt. "We'll have to take that chance. I'm sure Zach and Freddie hurt them before they went out, or we'd be junk by now. We gotta use what they gave us." He studied his flickering monitor. "With our upper retros and some of our drivers gone it'll be pretty rough, but do you think we could bounce off that star to slow us down?"

"You mean, slingshot around it?" Bill consulted his mental navigation file. "It might work, at that. But I think it'd take more than one orbit if we want our pals behind us to have a hard time catching up. If we start to decelerate too soon, we'll get nailed. Let's hope there's a Jupiter sized satellite."

"Well, if we weren't lucky…" Denny did not bother to finish the thought.

"THERE." TERRY KIRKLAND, THE SHIP'S Chief Surgeon, unclamped Jander's hand and stepped back from the diagnostic chair. "Good as new. But from now on if you want to explode, at least wait until you have a decent target."

Steele just glowered at the wall, opening and closing his restored fist.

Terry sighed. "All right, Jander. Talk to me."

He met the transmutator's eyes with a silent scowl. She stared him down until he spoke. "Three good people dead, and four more may be, including my best friend, because of my stupidity. There was no real reason for me to leave them so naked." His eyes darted around the small diagnostic room in frustration.

She flickered an eyebrow. "Oh? How else could you get to a navigation computer?"

"Hell, we could get a line on them by following, just as we were doing. Instead, I used any old excuse to throw Denny and Chelsea together, and probably doomed them both."

That was no news to the doctor. Hers was the responsibility for the physical and mental health of the crew, and she was very good at her job. "And you did the right thing. Denny was going to pieces."

"Yeah, play that again. Going to pieces, right." He tossed himself from the chair and started pacing in the narrow space. "I should have known the pirates would come back. They wouldn't leave that debris around for anyone to pick over. They're too smart for that. So I make the mistake, by underestimating them. You can't make mistakes in this business—one slip could kill thousands."

He flexed his hand again. Other than a slight stiffness, Terry's mental surgery was perfect. "And all I can think to do about it is smash my hand."

"We're going after them, aren't we? We'll get them back."

"That's a big maybe. After I've killed three and jeopardized the lives of four others."

"Bullshit!" she rapped, causing his head to snap toward her. "Look, I understand how you want to blame yourself. Hell, I've lost patients who haunt me to this day. But you are *not* to blame for putting them in danger—that's what commanders do. They are members of the Omega Corps, and we're fighting a war. They knew the risks when they joined us. You may have sent them to do a job more hazardous than you thought, but you sure as hell didn't pull the trigger on them. As everybody's so fond of saying, no plan survives the actual event."

"Tell that to Ann Whitney." His voice was bitter with remorse.

"I don't have to. She, too, is a member of the Omega Corps. I'm not saying Zach and Freddie became heroes by dying. If they didn't already have that mindset they never would have had their variant genes activated. All that did was give them better tools. Theirs was no futile sacrifice; it was the discharge of their duties. They were charged with the protection of the Sprite and that is exactly what they did. And Slim made himself vulnerable doing his sworn duty as a teammate. It may sound funny to hear a transmutator talking about destiny, but it is always the dedicated who die in battle, and we are all, 'all in'."

"In other words, we may all be doomed." He threw his head back and slammed his eyes shut.

"Surely," she shrugged. The thought did not seem to bother her in the least. "And if you knew without a doubt that that was the case, would it change your way of life? Not a chance. In your own words, our battle is hopeless, doomed to failure. Zach and Freddie, and Slim, and the four who may die in the next few hours, knew the odds when they pledged themselves in your service. I dare you to tell them you're giving up. They're yours, body and soul, and I know you return that love in full, but if you try to keep them from risk you'll find yourself without a job—and I don't mean it as an ego stroke when I tell you that more would die without your steady hand to guide them. And you can bet your life you'd lose Vickie. She doesn't want to just live by your side, but fight by it, and if necessary, die by it. And we all feel the same way."

He opened his tortured eyes and stared at her. She met his gaze with all the sincerity in her dedicated heart. "I mean it. Look into my mind if you like. I'm a doctor, and my solemn oath is to fight death. But I can deal it, too, and face it without the slightest hesitation, because I'm a charter member of the Omega Corps, and fighting this fight is my chosen destiny."

Jander dropped his eyes and sank back into the chair. "All right, Terry, I'm convinced." He did not sound it. "But I don't have to be in love with the idea."

Her lips twitched at the feeble attempt at humor. "No one's asking you to. All we ask is that you do your best, and let us do the same. And together, we'll bring those despicable bastards to just and total destruction."

He sighed. "Right now, all I can do is scramble after Denny, running for cover in a little ship with no screens, no guns, no power and no gravity... hold on..."

He slipped from the chair and stood erect. "Angela! Tell Engineer Summers I'm on my way down." He turned, his confidence rising. "I'm going to make sure that when Denny gets back, he can have a life!" He strode out the hatch.

Terry watched him go, sighing with relief. "When Denny gets back" was just what she wanted to hear.

CHAPTER 9

"This isn't going to be easy without a telepath," Denny rumbled. The Sprite had flipped end for end long since and was back-driving at three gravities per second per second. They were now below light speed and had a clear if long-range view of the target system.

The big engineer was doing most of the maneuvering, with the eidetic struggling against the g-force to make delicate adjustments at the copilot's board. The shuttle's computer was so damaged by the physical battering it had suffered that it was little help.

"I think our line's about right, now." Bill squinted at the ever-decreasing readouts at the edges of the monitor showing the star rushing toward them at frightful velocity. "This will swing us three times around the sun and out towards the third planet—two is a trojan of three, but much smaller than its partner—which will in turn throw us at big six."

He let the triple gravity pull his head back to the cushioning of his chair and hauled in a heavy breath. "With any luck, the result will be having that pretty little fourth planet right above us. By that time we'll be slow enough to land—I hope."

"Remind me not to play billiards with you, pal. Everybody ready?"

Chelsea floated in the center of the cabin, escaping the crushing gravity by remaining spectral. She winked in response, her infectious smile the most solid thing about her.

The Swiss computopath was beyond caring, her face ashen and drawn with pain from her shattered arm made even more torturous by the acceleration. Denny's lips tightened in sympathy; he wished Elga would just pass out. But she, too, was a Corpsman, and she stubbornly held onto consciousness.

"Hang on, gang, it's gonna get rough." Connors steeled himself for the torment to come. They passed the star's equivalent of the Kuiper Belt and continued to lose velocity as they traveled inward. They rushed toward the primary on a path that would allow its gravity to capture them and slow the shuttle enough to stay in the system.

As they continued to lose speed Wize switched off the warp sphere and diverted as much power to the radiation screening as the damaged shield generators would allow. The star became a disk and then a blazing sun, forcing them to cut the brightness of the scanners.

Insidiously the pressure of gravity increased as the vessel came more and more under the star's sway. Closer, and the pull became even fiercer, pressing them backward, straining them against the straps that held them secure. With the Sprite's tail pointed just below the star's horizon and pushing as hard as her battered motivators could drive, the faint atmosphere within the cabin echoed with the creaks and groans as she was stressed well past her design limits. Elga at long last fainted, and a few moments later the gallant eidetic too succumbed.

Higher and higher rose the gravity, eight, ten, twelve times normal, until Denny was struggling under the torture of over four tons of his own flesh. With gritted teeth he hung on, keeping the craft steady, guiding it in its violent battle against pressures it was never designed to handle, knowing full well that if the energy shield failed not even Chelsea would live long enough to know it.

The wraith hovered at his shoulder, her ghostly voice whispering meaningless and unheard words of encouragement to her chosen man as he fought the greatest battle of his life.

Sweating, straining, eyes glaring from deep in their sockets and hot breath rasping in his crushed lungs, he drove his battered strength to its limit and far beyond. On and on he fought, until the hours became only another villain in his struggle for their lives.

The straining ship whizzed around the star three and a quarter times, glowing within its energy shield as violent ejections of corona far hotter than the star's surface flickered around it like fingers after a fly. Somehow Denny stayed on top of the fluctuations, masterfully adjusting the joystick and speedball to counteract the constant battering.

As gradually as it had insidiously intensified, the crushing force began to release them. By the midpoint of their third orbit the Sprite had slowed enough to begin pulling away, widening the distance between star and ship until the straining drive allowed them to escape the fierce pull.

Through burning and misted eyes, Denny watched as the chronometer crept toward the cutoff time. On the mark, he fired an eight second burst of gravity impulse from a stern keel retro, flipping the craft away from the star, then loosed another burst to straighten her out.

The Sprite slowed even further as her drive engines battled to escape the star's gravity, until equilibrium was reached and they started pulling away. At long last they built up enough speed to break free, allowing Denny to cut the drive engines. Weightless, under no impetus other than its greatly reduced velocity, the tiny craft bulleted away from the star's mass and toward the third planet.

The sudden cessation of pressure came close to doing what the pressure itself could not. Fighting the urge to vomit, Connors fought the waves of dizzying blackness from his mind and focused dazed and burning eyes on the monitors. It did not look right to him.

He turned his head to check on Wize, and yelped in pain. Every muscle of his body was on fire, trembling with the strain of the past few hours. Chelsea moaned in sympathy and materialized, floating in the zero gravity as she had in spectral form. Her own fatigue from hours of maintaining her conversion, always a conscious choice and constant burden, was borne with British stoicism. She slid her arms around his bull neck and tried to massage his shoulders through the spacesuit. "Denny..." Her tone spoke tender volumes.

He reached up with an effort and touched her gloved hand. "We're not out of the woods yet, hon. We went off the track somewhere." His abused vocal chords squeaked in protest. "Try waking Bill—I can hardly move." The titan had been straining against the pressure rather than relaxing into the contoured and gel-padded seat. His punishment had been terrible.

Chelsea pushed away from his chair and floated to the copilot's station. She grabbed the eidetic's shoulders and squeezed with her suit's servos, trying to bring life back into the knotted muscles. Bill stirred and groaned, then opened bloodshot eyes to the monitors. Muddled as he was, his remarkable brain nonetheless set to work. "We're off..."

"I know. Think, buddy, we don't have much time." Denny rotated his aching shoulders to try to loosen them.

With painful effort Bill pushed his organic computer into full operation. "Uh... two point two seconds on the southwest forward retro, then one point six on the south rear." He closed his eyes and let his head drop back, exhausted.

Denny floated his aching hands to the board. "Hang on, Chelsea." He keyed in times and combinations, then pressed the execute.

Nothing happened.

"Oh shit, we're going to miss. Most of our retros are offline." He fumbled with his straps. "I'll go aft and try to find the trouble there. You start thinking about how we can get out of this."

"Unh... okay." The eidetic shook his head, trying to dispel his grogginess. "But I can't do much until I know what we have to work with."

"Go forward, then, and see if you can find what's wrong in the nose. I'll send Chelsea when I'm done with her."

"Hurry. We have sixteen minutes to the third planet, and the only other one within reach is seven—ten hours, maximum." He stiffly unstrapped and floated himself out of his chair.

Chelsea was hovering over Elga. "How's she doing?" Denny asked.

The girl probed with her second sight. "We have to get her out of that suit soon. There's too much stress on her heart, what with the pressure and the pain." She looked up at him, her eyes misted. "She's dying, Denny."

Lips set and wordless, Connors pushed himself aft.

DENNY TOOK SEVERAL SWALLOWS from the feeder tube that pulled nutritional fluid from his environmental pack and adjusted his suit conditioner a shade cooler. "Okay, Bill, we have three southern forward retros, four southern and two port rear retros, five of the eight drive motivators, and thirty-four minutes. What can we do with them?"

Bill studied the nav board, haggard eyes gauging the position of planet seven. "Well, since we missed the curl around the third planet, we'll have to go straight from seven to four. We don't have enough directional options left to brake around anything else."

He pulled his lips back between his teeth as his remarkable mind danced with equations. "Set up a six point four second nudge with the four retros on our southwest corner. That'll swing us around so we can use the big ones." The connection between the pilot and navigation consoles was severed, and without Elga to repair it the two Corpsmen would have to coordinate their efforts by voice alone.

"Gotcha." Denny tapped a few keys, then poised his thumb over the button atop the control stick. "Ready."

"Okay. On my mark. Three. Two. One. Go." Denny pressed the button, and the ship lurched as the retro cones under the portside aft of the shuttle started to swing the tail around. "Let me know when to hit the drive."

Bill tightened his straps and yawned, never taking his eyes off the screen. The retros cut off at the programmed time, and the eidetic watched his digital timer count down. "Steady. Two. One. Now."

Denny stomped on the drive pedal, pressing them into their seats. A moan escaped from the unconscious Elga. Chelsea, in spectral form, drifted back to keep an eye on her though there was little she could do.

"Two. One. Cut!" Denny jerked his foot back, and Bill leaned forward to analyze the results.

"We're still swinging away," Chelsea observed with studied calm.

"No problem," the Lakota assured her. "When we're not under drive it doesn't matter which way we're pointing. That first pop was to line up the drivers so we could push ourselves in the right direction. We'll swing tight around seven, which is a methane giant, then re-cross our own path, almost —four hundred twelve degrees around the horn, and seventeen degrees below our line of flight as it is now. That will aim us right at the atmosphere of friendly four. We'll come in hot, but controllable." He shot Denny a wry smile. "For you, anyway."

Denny pulled out the power cord of his suit and plugged it into his console. Since the accumulators had managed to top off the ship's batteries while they drifted, he could replenish his backpack batteries from the reserve. "Bill, if you get us out of this…"

"Don't say it, Chief. I know how close we were to

Roche's Limit when we went around that star. I owe you, too," He, too, plugged himself in.

Chelsea harrumphed. "You make me feel like a bloody freeloader."

"Well, okay, let's see." Bill swung his helmet around to give her a grin. "Who are you kidding? Without your clairvoyance to show us the trouble with the retros we'd still be heading for east nowheres, as ol' Slim would say. We're one hell of a team, the three of us."

"I think so, too, mes amis."

The three twisted to look toward the voice. Elga favored them all with a weak smile.

CHAPTER 10

Planet four, positionally third from the sun since two and three shared an orbit, was even more appealing up close than it looked from deep space. It approximated Venus in distance from its yellow-green sun and its diameter was somewhat larger, but the cooler luminary gave it the same mean temperature as Gaea.

The damaged sensors, cantankerous as they were, still promised a healthy nitrogen-oxygen atmosphere and a strong, protective magnetic field. A study of its seven small moons by the eidetic led to his conclusion that its gravity, too, was near Gaea normal, thus promising a denser mass with rich deposits of heavy metals. They could detect no evidence of industry, architecture or broadcast, limiting the possibility that they were about to break the Confederation's First Law. Its natural blues, browns and greens made the observers a bit homesick.

Under Bill's chess master guidance Denny jockeyed the Sprite until its tail was pointing at an oblique angle toward the planet's atmosphere. The daylight side had two large triangular continents in hourglass formation, separated at the tips by a narrow strait.

As the southern continent was densely forested, they chose the northernmost of the two as their landing zone. Touchdown would be along the border between a vast plain of khaki grassland and the verdant forest stretching to the north of it. The area was now in bright daylight but would be approaching dusk by the time they got there, giving them the cover of darkness.

The titan was not going to rely on the jury-rigged retros until they were near the surface; the sputtering motivators had more than once upset their delicate maneuvers. Their shielding, overstressed by the solar flyby, could not be trusted, either, so they would go down like the almost powerless Apollo capsules of Gaea's past, butt first and bouncing in a fiery arc and hoping the tough nanosteel hull could take it.

They bound Elga securely with several cargo straps, paying special attention to her compound broken arm. The Swiss woman was drenched with fever and gasping from the pain caused by the wrenching maneuvers of the craft, but her eyes were still open and glittering with determination.

"Get ready," Connors warned them. "We're about to start our first penetration. We're way too fast still, so we'll be doing one full orbit to slow us down enough, I hope. If this isn't timed right our entry will be more terminal than I'd like to think about." He was sweating, too, but not from fever. He felt the beginnings of a quiver in his overtaxed leg, the one poised over the drive pedal. He automatically sucked on his nutrition tube, then remembered it had run dry hours before. His energy would start to wane before much longer. "Chelsea, I want you to bail out when we reach decent atmosphere and follow us down. We won't be in any position to see the lay of the land."

As before, Chelsea was relying on her spectrality to keep her safe. A ghost's only limitation was the scarcity of molecules available for her psychic form to flow through. The air in the shuttle was not thick enough to be breathable, but it did allow her to maneuver. But if she left the Sprite too high in the troposphere where the air was too thin, she would be stalled in orbit.

"I can see just a well from here. I'd rather stay with you."

Bill discreetly turned his gaze from the look on Denny's face. "Thanks for the vote of confidence, gal, but I want you gone with the wind. And cheer up. We'll be the first Gaeans to land on another planet. We're making history." He frowned at the monitors. "I just hope we don't become history at the same time."

"Don't talk like that, you'll frighten me. Besides, Orion's been on two planets, Sfor and Dephlet." said

"Orion doesn't count. Everything's easy for that big dope—including finding us, I hope. Bill, do you see what I see?"

"I'm afraid so. Our wounded playmate has caught up with us." They watched the glare of nucleonic fury grow behind them as the pursuing raider backdrove into the system. "I don't think they can see us against the planet, though, not through their drive effluvium, anyway. They're backing in to cut their arrival time, but thanks to our ponging around we've still got the upper hand. We'll make it down."

"Yeah, but this thing will be as obvious as a moose in a parking lot," Denny replied. "Their sensors will pick us up in no time. We'll have to destruct the shuttle and start running as soon as we... hit." A slight tremor buffeted the ship as they arched downward at eighty thousand kilometers per hour. "We've touched air. Brace yourselves."

The trembling grew stronger as they penetrated the troposphere. On a sharp word from Bill, Denny pressed his poundage down on the pedal. Elga groaned and blacked out, her aquiline features pulled out of profile by the tremendous force of the propulsion. Bill, pallid lips bloodied by his clenched teeth, somehow held onto consciousness. With supreme effort, he grunted the cutoff signal. Denny lifted his foot and was thrown hard into his straps like the others. The friction forced them back upward, but at a considerably reduced speed. Chelsea whipped forward and was almost thrown out the nose before the denser matter in the chassis allowed her to retard her transparent form.

"That's one," the eidetic gasped. "Two more to go before we're slow enough for entry."

"Save your breath, pal, just tell me when." The

titan shook his head and glared at his readouts. This had long since become a personal battle with him.

"Now!"

Again the pressure, greater than before, took its fury out on bodies already half crushed from such punishment. The Sprite bit deeper into the atmosphere and skipped out again, glowing with the friction despite its partial shields, fighting its pilot like a living thing.

Denny held on with all his strength, growling deep in his throat, his left hand flickering over the speedball to keep them steady as his joystick channeled carefully gauged surges of power into first one cone of the gravitic drive, then another. Gradually the ship slowed, its angle of descent leveling a bit against the resistance of the thickening atmosphere, then as its pilot regained a semblance of control it dropped again into the turbulent air.

This time it stayed and fought, nanosteel hull blazing cherry red as it fell like a stone. It took long, rough minutes to slow the shuttle enough for the nanosteel to cool and allow the sensor ports to pick up the planet's surface. The sun behind them glittered off the cold ocean below as the shore of the northern continent grew to fill the horizon.

"Bail out, Chelsea," the giant growled through gritted teeth.

"I want to stay, Denny." She hovered at his shoulder, her gloved hands seeming to rest on his neck. "Please let me stay."

"That's an order, damn it. Bail out!" He knew what their chances were, and he did not want her in the middle of it.

She started to protest, then bit her lip and floated toward the hull. She took a last look at her four fellow Corpsmen—the blanket-covered body of Slim; the unconscious and feverish Elga; Bill, ashen-faced and bleeding; and the snarling, straining, valiant man she loved. Eyed filled with tears, she slipped through the hull of the Sprite.

They had just passed the coast. She hovered for long moments, watching the scorched and battered shuttle plummet toward the surface at an ever-increasing angle, leaving her behind as her own momentum diminished. Then she materialized and allowed herself to freefall several thousand meters, until the air was thick enough to breath.

Her eyes still glued to the Sprite, she again turned phantom and flashed out of her pressure suit, which continued to fall to its ruin in the thick forest below. Unencumbered by anything but her snug green jumpsuit, she could achieve a far better speed through the molecules of the atmosphere. She lofted herself after the shuttle that was rapidly widening the distance as it fell.

The loaf-shaped Sprite was never designed to glide to a landing. Descending slower and slower under the increasing influence of its drive, the crippled ship pitched over backward until it was almost vertical. At six thousand meters Denny redoubled the power, and when the nose dropped he triggered the weakened forward retros and increased the drive even more.

Under his gifted touch the ship continued downward tail first at a thirty-degree angle, quivering violently as it plummeted toward the plain below. Lower, slower, the retros somehow retained their glowing power, leveling out the flight path to ten degrees and holding steady. Sobbing with relief, the watching ghost raced toward the landing zone.

Then, a scant one hundred meters from the tall grass, the glow of the retros died. Denny cut the drive too late by a split second, and the shuttle nosed over in a dive. Chelsea screamed as she watched the Sprite smashed cruelly into the turf, the tough nanosteel prow crushing like tinfoil and flipping the little ship back into the sky. For several seconds the battered hulk whirled silently through the air.

Denny flashed the drive in a desperate attempt to straighten the craft, but the stern hit with a piercing crash and rebounded, driving the nose even deeper into the ground.

Again, the madly battling engineer had no time to react. Under the sporadic influence of the sputtering tail engines the Sprite flipped end for end, pinwheeling violently over and over for hundreds of meters at horrific velocity. Countless brutal flips and spins crushed and shattered the wreck, sending screeching shards of nanosteel and great clumps and islands of grass and dirt flying wildly in every direction from the helplessly disintegrating mass. Far too gradually, the awful momentum was reduced from crunching bounces to shrieking slides in a torn trail of rutted turf and twisted metal, until at long last its force was spent and the crumpled shuttle careened squelching to a halt.

Chelsea dove for the steaming wreckage and flashed through the ruined hull. She scarcely glanced at Elga, lifeless body distorted by her straps, or Bill, dark eyes wide and staring at nothing, his head tilted at an impossible angle. She materialized beside the unconscious Denny and shoved away the long-dead Slim, whose body had come loose in the madness. Only when she tried to call out to the titan did she realize that she was still screaming.

She made a swift scan of his body with her clairvoyance. Somehow, his internal organs were not ruptured; his iron bones were intact. She crouched over him and shouted in his ear.

"Denny! Please wake up! *Denny!*" She glanced over the flickering control board and her eyes widened at what she saw. The supercapacitor safeguards were offline, and the surviving accumulators were pouring solar energy into the batteries like a firehose into a teacup. She studied the few remaining readouts and banged key after key to no effect.

"Denny! The power's backing up, and I can't turn it off. It's going to explode!" She tore off his helmet and slapped him again and again, putting all her negligible weight behind every stinging blow. "Denny!"

"Unngh..." His heavy head swayed on his shoulders.

"Denny, you've got to run!" Desperately she pressed her mind into action. Becoming transparent, she whipped to the stern and touched one of the scores of heavy batteries, then wafted the now-intangible cell through the hull and dropped it on the torn and smoking ground. She went back for another. "Denny, the power's backing up! I can slow it down, but I can't stop it! Get out, Denny!" She made another round trip and whipped back to slap him again. "Run, Denny!"

"Ngh..." The titan opened bloodshot eyes and tried to focus on the console.

"Run!" Another battery left the bank.

He fumbled groggily with his straps. Chelsea took the time to flit over and help him. "Get out, darling!"

That last word did what no amount of slapping ever could. Connors jerked loose from the collapsed seat and swayed to his feet.

"Run!" He stumbled to the cargo hatch and pushed against it. It stuck, squashed out of articulation by the crash. Chelsea slipped over and touched the hinges; the hatch fell out, taking the giant with it.

"Run!" Denny stumbled to his feet and staggered for the woods.

"Run!" Swaying, he increased his pace, tripped over the uneven ground and fell heavily.

"Run!" On all fours, he managed to move again.

"Run, Denny!" He blundered into the woods, even

in his battered condition faster than any other man alive.

"Run!" Cracking into trees, tripping over roots and bushes, spinning in full circles and staring blindly in all directions, he staggered forward.

"Run!" He stumbled over a huge log he could not see and crashed to the ground behind it. The fall undoubtedly saved his life.

The Sprite burst into flames, then exploded like a heat-concussion bomb as the death of the computer triggered the self-destruct charges. Denny was again flattened by the force of the blast, while white-hot shrapnel peppered the log behind him and sizzled through the air above. For the second time in a matter of moments, his mind was flooded by blackness.

CHAPTER 11

"Welcome back."

Denny groaned and pried his eyes open. The English blonde sat like a pixie on the log above him, grinning soberly, her white teeth and pallid skin barely distinguishable in the faded light.

He forced his senses to open up to his surroundings, groping for the jumbled memories of what brought him there. The winking stars pierced the canopy of breeze-sighing trees, the shadows lightened from three directions by moonglow. The ground beneath him gave off a loamy smell, offset by a more distant stench of scorched vegetation. His ringing ears detected chirps, peeps, chortles, grunts and gronks from the local wildlife that seemed to have become accustomed to their presence.

He raised a heavy hand to wipe the gunk off his eyelids. "Uh... how long was I out?"

Her smile wavered at the tortured sound of his voice, but she forced herself to keep her tone light. "Well, you may have noticed it's rather dark out here. We came down just in front of the sunset line, so I guess it's been two, three hours. You looked like you needed a spot of rest."

He let his arm drop. "I could use some more, too."

"I'm sorry to disappoint you, but we really need to flit. I've seen a flare overhead more than once. Comes the morning, they'll see the burnout if the grassfires haven't been enough."

Denny sat up, and indicated the cost of the motion with a deep groan of pain. Every muscle in his body was tormented with stinging agony.

"Ooooh," she sighed in sympathy. "Careful! I nipped you out of your suit and tried to massage some of the lumps, but it was like molding steel without a hammer. No bones broken, but you're blue from head to foot." She grinned. "Lovely, really."

He raised his hand to his shoulder and yelped again. "I'll bet I am," he grunted. "Any sign of radiation sickness?"

"None, I'm pleased to say, but there may be some residual effects that could pop up later. It appears our energy shielding held up long enough to protect us from most of the solar radiation. Not so much can be said about our collision shields, obviously."

"Obviously. The internal gravity went offline with our first bounce." He twisted his arms in front of him to try to loosen his knotted back. "Everything after that is a jumble. How'd I get out of the Sprite?"

She came down from her perch and went to both knees facing him. "You were out of it, weren't you? You got out on your own hook, though you were apparently unconscious at the time. You don't think

I carried you, do you—though I was screaming at you loud enough to move rocks."

"I'm sure it helped." He held his breath a moment before the next question. His own condition told him the answer, but he had to hear it. "Where are... the others?"

She sobered. "They didn't survive the crash. And the ship exploded as soon as you got out. I tried to stop the battery overload, but mucked it. Since I was spectral the blast didn't touch me."

He grunted, "Why didn't you pull the plug?"

"I tried. The controls were dead, so I was yanking out the batteries. I slowed it down but couldn't stop it."

"All you had to do was disconnect the three main cables to the accumulators."

The filtered light from three of the seven moons showed the tightening of her jaw. "Well, if I were an engineer, I wouldn't need you, would I? I'm a medic, not a bloody button pusher."

He sighed and reached out to touch her knee. "I'm sorry, honey. I'm still a little dazed."

She gave him a wan smile and shook her head. "I know. I shouldn't have snapped at you."

"You saved my life, and I'm sure not complaining." Denny struggled to his knees and moved over to his pressure suit, fumbling through its exterior pouches and shoving whatever he found into the pockets of his cargo slacks. "Damned little to eat here. We'll have to hunt for food. My lucky plierench, one multitool jackknife, a little precision tool kit, small roll of plastic sample bags, not even a match. Sweet."

He unbuckled the wristpad from the arm of the suit and adjusted it to fit his bare arm, then started using the knife to scrap cut anything that might give a clue to the suit's origin. "While I'm breaking this down, why don't you get some altitude and take a look around? See if you can find us a place to hole up until the *Angel* gets here."

"Good idea. Just be sure to keep your eyes open until I get back." With a grin and a wave, Chelsea soared upward through the trees.

Denny used the multitool to detach the environmental pack from the back of the suit and tied strips cut from the suit's legs to fashion it into a backpack. His supply of nutritional fluid was drained, but the recycling unit would assure them of clean water, at least. His helmet had gone up with the shuttle, so most of the suit's technology was already unusable. He yanked some of the electronics from the its interior, shoved the telltale chips and scraps into a recess of the pack and tossed aside the ruined suit.

Denny scanned it all in the dim light to ensure he had done everything necessary to protect their anonymity, then he groaned to his feet. He was very conscious of the fact that Chelsea would have had to disengage the suit's very intimate plumbing in order to remove it. But then again, she was a med tech.

He shrugged it off as the ghost spiraled back down to rejoin him. "So, where are we?"

"We're in the tongue of the forest on the edge of the savannah you were trying to hit—um, land on." She pointed through the trees toward the crash site, then swung her arm in the opposite direction. Some creature in the tree she gestured toward gave a chittering squeak and scrabbled to the other side of the trunk. "Off in that direction, about four hundred kilometers, the mountains rise. They look rather rough—we can lose ourselves there if we don't find a hidey-hole sooner. Between here and there it's dense forest, a few small lakes and lots of rivers and streams. We learned from the Sprite's sensors that the polar ocean is beyond the mountains, another two or three hundred kilometers. I've detected a lot of animals, no birds, billions of bugs, but no sign of intelligent life—present company possibly excepted."

"Possibly. That's a lot to pick up in a ten-minute scout. Thanks."

She treated him to a little curtsey. "At your service, sir."

He pressed a button on the multiplex instrument now on his left wrist and said, "Bangle, display compass." The wristband complied and he touched another button to illuminate it. The planet's magnetic pole was a few degrees west of where she pointed.

"Did you notice any opposition? I mean, carnivores?"

"I heard something that makes a lion sound like a frightened hare. I'm happy to say I haven't seen the bugger." She watched the titan twist his hard body into contortions, trying to loosen his tortured sinews. "Can you walk?"

"I can run if I have to. We need distance—I'm sure that pirate has called for backup, maybe even another fleet." He fished a snack bar out of a shirt pocket and broke it in two, handing her the smaller piece. "Chew on this for now. We'll hunt in the morning."

"I shouldn't have let my own suit drop. Stupid of me. We'll never find it now, and my wristband went with it." She bit into the bar and lost her teeth in its gummy hardness, guiltily aware that his accelerated metabolism would need six or eight times the calories hers did just to survive. "Keeping it would have slowed me down, and you were almost out of sight by the time I dashed after you."

Denny used his free hand to help his sore jaw. "You can't foresee everything," he told her. "I'll bet Jander's kicking himself all over space for losing us—and I wouldn't want to be in that pirate ship when he gets here."

He swallowed the rest of the bar. "Let's get moving, if you're okay with it."

Denny pushed his arms through the backpack straps with a soft grunt. He made a note to himself to find a way to camouflage it. Its shiny aluminum plating, deliberately polished to be visible, made a fine target. He himself was clothed in the blue-gray shirt and cargo slacks common to the Corps, but a little mud would disguise that.

Chelsea was reasonably safe in a jumpsuit of deep

emerald green. The snug Kevlar and neoprene ankle boots designed to fit inside the pressure suits would protect their feet for as long as the trek required.

"I'm up for it." Chelsea licked her fingers clean and rose from her perch on the log.

Denny oriented himself with his compass, then peered through the gloom in the direction they would have to take. The tongue of forest was as tangled as he had ever seen in Montana or his native Colorado. Young trees and bushes filled the gaps between the more established growth, and vines and brambles dug their roots through years of seasonal detritus and climbed high into the broadleaf trees in search of the light. Enough of it was wilted and torn from the explosion that he could pick out a path in the moonlight, but he expected that their trek would become more arduous the farther they penetrated.

With a glance and a nod to his tiny partner, he set out toward the deeper forest.

They did not get far under the triple moonlight before Chelsea stumbled over a root and fell hard into the underbrush. Denny reached for her in alarm, then stopped himself, irresolute.

"Well, help me, you big ox," she whined crossly.

Hesitantly, he held out his arm. She caught hold of it and pulled herself up. "I won't break on contact, you know. Don't you think..."

She saw the stricken look on his face and stopped in mid-sentence. She moved to rub her shoulders against his ribs. "I'm sorry, Denny. I'm tired, too."

"Have you had any rest?" He gingerly rested a hand on her shoulder.

"No, I haven't, really. I was watching over you while you recovered." She sighed and snuggled into him, her fingers curling the cloth of his shirt.

"We have to stop, then, and let you get some sleep." He squinted around for a suitable spot.

"We can't do that. We have to keep moving." She looked up at him. "Do you feel well enough to carry me?"

"Car—uh, what if I trip or something?" He was still looking around, as if searching for an avenue of escape.

"No, you wouldn't Denny. I know you wouldn't hurt me." She reached to the limit of her arm and pulled his chin down to look into his eyes. "If I didn't trust you, I wouldn't suggest it. Now, don't you be afraid of me. I promise I won't bite."

He smiled uncertainly. "Well..." He stooped and slid his arm under her knees, lifting her easily.

She curled an arm around his neck and rested her head against his massive shoulder. "Am I too heavy?"

He chuckled, a trifle uneasily, but with a warmth that thrilled her. "I could throw you to the mountains."

"Thank you, no." She patted his chest, then pointed toward the north. "Onward, gallant steed."

He set himself in motion, picking his way with exaggerated care through the light of the moons. Chelsea sighed and dropped off to sleep, leaving Denny with a gentle, pacific smile on his face.

DENVER CONNORS WAS ALMOST TWO inches over seven feet, and appeared to weigh in at a solid three hundred twenty pounds. His actual weight was over seven hundred; his strength was as great as any five Olympic class weightlifters. His variant gift was only partially latent; the brain-tearing impulses of the alien activator that had triggered the spectral genetic coding of Chelsea's physiology had done little to Denny. His cellular structure had always been different; the cells were smaller, more compact. Activation made it possible for him to add cells through bodybuilding, to bring his scrawny frame up to normal-appearing bulk, and to help his nervous system coordinate the extra tissue. Like most variants, he looked perfectly normal.

Meshzner was a shade over five feet tall and looked every ounce of his seven hundred fifty pounds. His thick legs were short and his arms disproportionately long to balance his huge torso. He had inherited his strength by being born on a high-gravity planet; his squat, gray-skinned body was at least as strong as Denny's. The two had never met—as yet. In fact, neither knew of the other's existence—as yet.

Meshzner stood hulking on the Bridge of the *Rannz*, his deep-set eyes glaring from under the short black fur covering his head and backbone from brow to cervix, glowering at the planet depicted on the monitors. He was one of the thousands of Liev denizens in service to the battle fleet of Ertain. His brother was another; his brother had been on one of the three ships destroyed by that insignificant little fighter craft, completing the annihilation of the *Rannz*'s five squadron mates. He had pledged that the fugitives would die by his own massive strength, crushed under his own tremendous weight.

"I know what you're thinking, Meshzner, but the Head wants those killers alive for questioning." The Ertainian Captain felt no remorse over the thousands of defenseless merchant crews, passengers male, female, multisex and juvenile, and all the other innocents they had slaughtered in the past; that was business in the course of manifest destiny. The ruthless destruction of the Ertainian Fourth Fleet was murder. Still, if he allowed his bodyguard to have his way, his own head would roll. "After they spill their guts, you can have them, I promise."

"They'll spill their guts." His voice was immense in what was, to him, the thin atmosphere of the ship. It matched his expression perfectly.

Captain Z'zschou sighed to gather his temper. The brute was not very bright—anyone whose ancestors voluntarily settled a triple-gravity planet could not have inherited much sense—but he had his uses within the cutthroat politics of the Ertainian military. "I cannot emphasize enough that they must be taken alive, and undamaged. Through great good luck, we were not implicated as responsible for the loss of the fleet. But we are being watched by the High Command, including the Head. If we acquit ourselves well in the search, we have an excellent chance of coming through unscathed." He was irritated that such a long-winded explanation was necessary; as were all Ertainians in positions of authority he was accustomed to being obeyed without question, on pain of death. But one of the many things he could not afford was a rampaging Lievan, which is what he would have if he tried to dictate to Meshzner. The combat-scarred oaf was dead-set on vendetta.

"You will be in charge of this ship's contingent of searchers, but yours is not the decision as to whether they live or die. That decision belongs to the Head, and he has decreed that they live for a time."

"I understand, master," the monster grumbled. "But I don't like it."

The Captain clapped his six-fingered hand on the bodyguard's shoulder. "I know, Meshzner, but we must all follow orders, mustn't we?"

Meshzner shrugged away from him. "Don't talk to me like I'm a child!"

The Captain started at that unexpected burst of free will. The gray-skinned behemoth's greatest value to him was his pliancy; if he lost that, he may as well lose his life.

"At ease, my man. I'm sure you'll do your best, and that you'll bring the killers back. But if you kill them, the Head will execute you—and me. You are sworn to protect me, and in this case that means not hurting the killers. You understand that, don't you?"

"Yes, master." He said nothing more.

"Good. Good." Z'zschou eyed him warily and edged away, then strode out of the control room. A short and cautious search found him the two Ertainians he wanted, two crewmen whose familial gens owed him favors. He ushered the pair into his day cabin and bade them sit so he could talk to them from above.

"You will accompany Meshzner at all times on the planet's surface," he told them. "You will make certain that he does not harm the fugitives. If he tries to do so, you will kill him. Understood?"

The two crewmen muttered their assent and glanced at each other. Not the easiest of assignments!

"Dismissed." The Captain watched them go, then returned to the Bridge feeling more secure. If Meshzner did get out of line, he could protest to his superiors that he tried to prevent such a thing from happening. By such precautions more than one captain's life had been spared.

THE *ANGEL* AT LAST RETARDED HER velocity and was now hurtling back toward the scene of the recent battle at her maximum, with Tsin Li-san taking the duty shift in the command chair. He had reconfigured part of the captain's command console to keep an eye on his communications station, where his backup was busy intercepting, interpreting and recording the tachyon broadcasts flashing through the trade route. It was clear that the pirates had sent other squadrons to the battle sphere to clear the debris, which now included two unfortunate merchants who blundered onto the scene while the sanitizing was in progress. Tsin kept silent, knowing that his dog shift crew were as grimly set on mission as he was and would overlook nothing.

In the bedroom of the captain's suite, Vickie stood at her full-length mirror indulging herself in one of womanhood's more soothing tasks, that of brushing her ash-blonde hair into a gossamer cloud of moonbeams. Her eyes drifted often to glance at the refection of her man, lying on his back on the gel-bed she could see in the mirror.

Finally she put down the brush and sat next to his sprawl on the bed. "What's the matter, honey?"

He stared at the overhead, fingers locked behind his head. "You know what's the matter."

She tried a smile. "Yeah, I know. Terry told me you were having a case of the blithering dolts. Of course, I had to break her arm to get it out of her—something about ethics—but she said you were blaming yourself for our loss. Hell, I counseled Ann Whitney after losing Jack, and not even she feels that way." She rolled onto her side and tenderly caressed his muscular chest. "You've been like a zombie lately. You don't eat, you don't sleep, and last night you didn't even twitch for me. You can't help anybody by freezing over, you know."

"Well, how am I supposed to feel? I'm pissed at the pirates and I'm pissed at myself, both for good reason." He closed his eyes and sighed sharply through clenched teeth. "I know it doesn't help them, but it sure as hell helps me."

"That's news. You're running yourself into the ground. You've done everything you can, including the engineering job that will ensure Denny and Chelsea can make a go of it when they get back. What more do you want?"

His eyes flew open, glaring at nothing. "I want blood, Vic. We have a chance of wiping those murdering, thieving bastards out of business. They're not only going to bite the dust, they're going to eat their whole goddamned planet!"

He ground his teeth and continued in a low voice, "It's not just revenge for losing our friends or justice for their victims. It's destiny. We *have* to do this. We have to do it because of all the people in the galaxy, we can. And if we don't do it, someone else would have to try. Someone not nearly as strong. Someone who could get killed trying to do the job we are better equipped to do. I want to not just avenge Denny and the others, dead or alive, but all those innocent victims who never had a chance to fight for themselves."

"As do we all, darling. And we'll get them, you'll see to that. But until then, stop being avenger and try being husband." She nuzzled his neck. "I'm human, too, you know. Here, roll over and let me give you a massage."

Grudgingly, he did so, and she straddled him and set to work with fingers and mind. Firmly at first, then more gently, she kneaded his neck and back. Soon he began to relax as Vickie used all her skill to loosen his tensed muscles, until the hardness left him and he fell asleep.

When she was certain he was out, she lifted herself off him and settled again at his side, running her fingers across his shoulder. "Just get them within reach, darling."

CHAPTER 12

After ten minutes of striking sparks with the file blade of his multitool and a flint he found in a stream, Denny managed to get a good fire going. He and Chelsea watched the meat hungrily, the girl staring inside the skewered body to check its progress. The titan managed to snag a greyhound-sized creature with a head like a hornless deer or a primitive horse (or a skinny camel or a short-necked giraffe, or maybe a combination of the four), a three-toed herbivore that balanced on six stick-like legs.

Now the fragrance of roasting venison mingled with the organic scents carried by the leaf-sighing breeze. A thickness in the air hinted at fouler weather to come.

Connors raised his head and looked around them for the umpteenth time, unconsciously taking on the natural reactions of the hunted. Nothing overtly threatening had come along, but in the growing light of dawn, he was feeling more than a bit vulnerable.

Within a few hundred meters of the plain the treetops soared higher into the night sky, and the combination of voracious grazers and deep shade had opened the forest floor for easier travel. But it also limited their cover. His senses were on full alert, and when the little hexapod deer/horse rustled a bush he was passing he shifted the sleeping Chelsea to free a hand and snapped the animal's neck.

"You sure we can eat Bambi, here?" Denny asked.

"I'm no microvoyant, but it seems all right to me. It smells good, I can tell you that." She gave it a deep sniff. "And its food supply seems to be quite ordinary leaves and grass. It's got three stomachs and its heart's in the right place, anyhap."

She ducked down for a different view. "Still, we'd be remiss if we didn't cook it thoroughly. It's pretty unlikely that any native parasites can harm our alien physiology, but a proper roasting should kill them regardless." She jabbed the center haunch with a long needle-like thorn she had pulled from a bush they had otherwise avoided, and watched the clear juice flow. "I think it's ready."

The titan reached and lifted the spit, stripping off a hunk of the meat with his bare hand and handing the stick to Chelsea. She dropped it with a squeal of pain.

He snatched it out of the loam and waved it in the cooler air. "Sorry, honey. I've got skin like a walrus, can't feel the heat." He held it out to her with one hand and offered her his knife. With the blade in one hand and her thorn in the other, she sliced off a chunk and sniffed at it. Assured that she was all right, Denny returned the spit to its cradle above the fire and bit into his own chunk. "Mm. Pretty good."

Chelsea dematerialized her piece and watched the dirt drop away. "You could wait for me, chum. It's bad enough you have to look like a troglodyte without acting like one, too."

The titan watched her cleanse the meat with interest. "I was wondering how you managed to keep so clean. You just phantomate and step out of the dirt, huh?"

She nodded over a mouthful of the juicy meat. "If I could affect living matter I'd love to do the same for you. Though I suppose I could flash off the thickest of the crust." She took another bite. "Not bad cooking, for an engineer. Anyhap, my body is the only animate matter I can convert—something about not being able to affect nervous energy other than my own. Most variants can, with personal contact, sort of connect energy—'aura', you might call it, or 'life force'—and therefore share powers. Mine doesn't work that way."

"Mph. How does it work?" He wolfed down the big chunk of meat and reached for the spit for another. The aching pit that was his stomach would need a lot more.

"Jander tells me I turn into some kind of pseudo-energy, some psychic wave form even he doesn't understand—which relieves me, in a way. I was afraid he knew it all. In any case, I can pass through anything, even other forms of energy. Which reminds me—how is it that, if you have twice as many brain cells, you're not twice as smart?"

Denny waved his handful of roast. "That, Jander was able to explain. You'd think I'd either be dense between the ears—don't say it—or super-intelligent —don't say that, either."

She giggled.

"Fact is, I do generate two or three times as much synaptic energy, but it has to bounce off two or three times as many cells to get from one place to the other. The two effects cancel each other out."

He took another mouthful, then started strongly and fumbled the meat. "What the hell was that?"

Chelsea shrugged with a half smile. "Anything it wants to be, I'd imagine."

The sound resonated again, a terrifying, tremendously deep roar of bestial challenge. The monster had to be hundreds of meters away, yet the volume was chilling.

"That's the rabbit I told you about, the one who made his presence known while you were unconscious. Odds are he smells the meat."

"If that's the Easter bunny, I'm my own grandmother." He picked up his venison and brushed it off with his fingers, glancing askance in the direction of the sound. The voices of other creatures that had been hushed by the roar gradually resumed their volume. "We'd better get moving as soon as full light comes."

Chelsea clucked through her teeth. "Afraid of a little kittycat."

"You can say that, shady lady. All you have to do

is let him go right through you. If I tried that you'd be scraping me off the walls of his belly. That sucker's *big!*"

"So, stick close to the trees. I can distract him while you scramble." She licked her fingers, then dematerialized and dropped away the remains. "Though it might be best to avoid him altogether."

"Uh-*huh*." Still staring over his shoulder, he pulled a plastic sample bag from the roll stored in his backpack and scraped the rest of the meat into it off the spit, then extended a huge boot and stamped out the fire. "Suppose you go up and take a look around. I might have gotten turned around in the dark."

Chelsea treated him to an elaborate curtsey and soared aloft.

Denny got up and stretched his back, fighting the fatigue that threatened to overwhelm him. Carrying the woman through the night had not tired him in the least—in fact, he enjoyed the duty immensely—but he was still suffering from the effects of the brutal day before. He was bruised to the bone, so deeply that even his rapid metabolism would take days to heal.

He attached the bag of venison to his belt and pocketed the tools, including Chelsea's thorn, and reached down for the backpack. The stiffness attacked again as he pulled it on. He spread his arms wide, twisting his torso from side to side. He felt a slight increase of weight on his right forearm and turned his head to see his elfin companion perched there.

"I have some good news and some bad news," she

said.

He flexed his bicep and caught her as she dropped. He had almost completely conquered his fear of hurting her. "Shoot."

"The good news is that we're still heading for the hills." She pointed in the right direction. "The bad news is that our pursuers are circling about eighty kilometers up, over the crater where the Sprite used to be. No doubt they can see the scar. And we're only about twenty kilometers from the edge of the plain. You made splendid time last night, but we could use some more."

"I heard that." He finished stamping out the fire and kicked the ashes into the loamy turf, hiding their traces as best he could. "Let's go, then." He started through the towering trees in the direction she indicated.

She tapped him on the breastbone. "I can walk by myself, don't you know."

"Oh, yeah." Reddening slightly, he put her down.

MESHZNER STOOD UNMOVING IN THE center the *Rannz*'s Bridge for hours, occasionally scratching his deep chest through his maroon coveralls, ignoring the irritated crewmen who were forced to dodge around his massive bulk. He was oblivious to the fact that he stood right in the middle of the hologram that projected the ship's position in space. He watched the forward monitor almost unblinking as the sunrise line crept across the face of the planet, searching for the slightest sign of his quarry. Suddenly he pointed, and his bull bellow stunned every man in the ship. "There!"

The Captain, sitting at his console at the top of the inward-facing circle of Bridge stations—a weak, uncomfortable replica of the configuration found in Confederation ships—and peered around his body-guard whose vast breadth obscured his view of the monitor. In a few seconds he found it, a long, broken line of ripped terrain and scattered debris terminating in a shallow crater that glowed under the infrared. "The ship exploded, Meshzner. The killers probably died in it."

"I'm going down and make sure." His tone allowed no denial.

The Captain considered reprimanding him for that, then decided to let it pass. The opportunity to get the grumpy giant off the ship was too tempting to pass up. "Very well, Meshzner. You and Schaus and Gazenhout will take a shuttle down and check it out. I need every other man to repair our battle damage, so you'll be on your own. If you find no sign that the killers survived, you will return. If you find traces of them, you have my leave to pursue."

He paused, then went on as casually as he could. "Schaus and Gazenhout will be armed, but there is no reason for you to be. Your strength will be enough to subdue them. I require you to keep in touch. If there is sign, I am ordered to contact the Second Fleet for more search parties."

The giant turned his square body around to set his baleful eyes on the smaller man. "I want them, Master. You don't need other searchers."

Z'zschou rubbed the dusky brow fur that flowed up and over his skull above his small ears and down his backbone, a genetic trait shared by both races, and shook his head. "I do not make such decisions. The Head himself has left those orders. They are to be found at all costs. Who finds them is unimportant to the Great Plan, as long as they survive for questioning. Remember that, Meshzner. If they die, for whatever reason, I will have your head."

The ogre glowered at him, then dropped his eyes. "As you say, Master." He set his massive frame in motion sternward, toward the cramped hangar bay and its tight-fitting auxiliary craft.

Under the thundering lash of Meshzner's bull bellow preparations were made in record time. The *Rannz*'s crewmen resented the dumb mercenary's direction, but they were not foolish enough to protest. The Captain's bodyguard had carte blanche in all things, no matter that he was a vicious, brainless, supercilious, arrogant son of a misbegotten stink-lizard. Or perhaps because of that.

Meshzner stood—it was impossible for him to sit without a specially-designed banana stool—behind Schaus and Gazenhout as they brought the rocket-jet down toward the surface. Their velocity forced them to angle downward to diminish their speed, which brought them to a hover two thousand meters above the smaller, lushly forested southeastern continent.

Gazenhout felt the full weight of Meshzner's impatience as he ran tests on the atmosphere, radiation and gravity to be sure they could survive on the surface. He found it to be rather richer in oxygen than their home world, which would make them feel more invigorated, but overall it would be a very welcome change from the recycled air they had been breathing for months. He stepped around the hovering Meshzner and spoke to Schaus. "We're good to land."

The pilot nodded and turned to his console. The hovering craft pointed its laser-armed nose to the horizontal and accelerated to take them north and west, cruising at mach two over the jungle and across the long, narrow strait to the northern continent where the shuttle went down.

In contrast to the southern landmass they found themselves flying over a harsh desert that gradually merged into a verdant prairie, and on toward the forested northern mountains. It was some time after local noon when they arrived at the southern edge of the finger of woodland where the cratered crash site still steamed.

Seconds after they scorched to a landing near the edge of the forest, Meshzner was out and bounding through the blackened stubs of moist grass toward the crater without so much as a glance at the surrounding landscape. The two Ertainians collected their backpacks and laser rifles and dismounted, cautiously running their wide-irised eyes through a full scan of their environment before following Meshzner to the crater's edge.

There was nothing left, absolutely nothing. Not only had the Sprite's volatile battery assemblies exploded, but its strategically placed self-destruct charges designed to obliterate its advanced mechanisms had gone off at a predetermined five minutes after the computer ceased to function. Barely a shard of metal was left to identify. Schaus unhitched the portable communicator from its loop on his hip and raised it to his thin lips.

Meshzner slammed the instrument out of his hand. "We're not done yet!" he roared.

Schaus backed away, nursing his numbed forearm. Gazenhout edged his hand toward his shouldered laser, then slumped in resignation. He would have liked nothing better than to burn the monster down, but he wanted to be at least two hundred spans away when he tried it, and behind him, and hidden, and ready to run anyway.

Schaus mollified himself by turning a wary eye to the magnetic south, where the low rolling hills flattened into a vast prairie of green and blue grasses broken only by small clumps of trees and bushes all the way to the horizon. Occasional thick clouds provided a moving patchwork of shadow. A long, thin line of trees to the southwest marked the river he spotted as they descended. He saw movement at the limit of his vision to the southeast, a substantial herd of large beasts moving away from what to them was a frightening, fire-breathing predator. Schaus had flown over them as they descended and saw them start to stampede in all directions at the ear-splitting noise of his engines. Those beasts were no threat to them unless the stampede came their way.

He turned away and looked north, where the others were already moving toward the tongue of forest angling out from the distant mountains. The clouds were thicker there, but few showed rain. Schaus retrieved his communicator and hooked it back in its place, still flexing his six two-knuckled fingers as he followed them.

With sweeping gestures from his knuckle-dragging arms Meshzner directed the smaller men to his right and left. "They would've headed for those woods. Spread out and look for tracks." They obeyed, keeping a wary eye on him as they started their search.

The nearer trees were peppered with shrapnel, and the intelligent pair of the search party wondered about radiation. They both concluded that it was unlikely: one; the foliage appeared to be withered only by heat; and two, the consensus was that the killers did not use nucleonic propulsion.

To find out what they did use was the purpose of taking the fugitives alive. It was assumed that the scavenger party the gem-ship left behind at the sphere of battle would include engineers.

They moved into the canopy of trees and waited for their eyes to adjust to the relative darkness, then wove their way deeper, checking every shadow. Schaus and Gazenhout kept their eyes moving everywhere, noting the teeming insects and occasional reptiles inhabiting the strange plants that themselves could prove to be threats. They well knew that the planet was untouched by advanced development and could harbor myriad unknown dangers.

Meshzner, far more animated in the light gravity than the Ertainians, bounded back and forth on his barrel-sized legs stupidly ignoring everything but what might further his single-minded quest. Everything near his blundering progress either fled or froze at his noisy approach. Quite a few native creatures were crushed unnoticed under his broad, flat feet.

Suddenly he bellowed an ear-splitting roar and leaped at least four feet in the air, gesticulating wildly. The crewmen rushed over to see what he discovered.

"They're alive! I'm gonna get 'em!" The ludicrous troll hopped up and down in his agitation, leaving deeper and deeper impressions in the loamy surface and thoughtlessly obliterating the very clues he spotted. "Two of 'em! Look! One was big, and carrying somethin'. His feet sink way in. The other one's a little guy. An' here's a suit!"

He cleared a shrapnel-laced log in one prodigious

broad jump and thudded back to ground next to Denny's discarded pressure suit. He picked up the mutilated garment and held it by the shoulders. He reached up and up, and still the knees dragged. "A big one! I'm gonna tear 'im apart!"

An evil gleam was birthed and grew in his piggish eyes. "Call it in, Schaus. We're goin' after 'em!" He dropped the suit and, bent as double as one of his race ever could, started nosing out the trail.

The Ertainian unhooked his communicator and pressed the button on its side. "Party one to *Rannz*."

"This is the Captain. Go ahead."

"We have evidence of two survivors, Excellency, including the remains of a discarded spacesuit. The wearer is at least half again as tall as we are, and the prints of the other one are small. The huh—Meshzner has started to trail." He bit his lip and awaited the results of his blunder.

"Make sure you find them before the hunker does, or at least be ready to shoot. That particular gentleman has outlived his usefulness."

"We'll be careful, Excellency. You'll have at least four of us alive."

"See that it is so." Captain Z'zschou cut the connection and settled back, frowning. He regretted that order, not only because he was losing a body-guard, but if the story got out they might lose a lot of Ertain's Lievan mercenaries. The behemoths were useful, and trustworthy to a point, but their sense of clan loyalty was overwhelming.

He shook himself. "Communications, send a signal to the Admiral, Second Fleet. Two of the fugitives are alive, and we may have to search a good portion of the forest to find them. Put it just that way and wait for instructions. The admirals like to make their own decisions."

"Right away, sir." As the officer bent over his console, the Captain reflected on his last remark. He was getting too familiar with his crew; they might soon start to think of him as soft. Without his bodyguard beside him, he would have to be extra careful.

UNDER VICKIE'S URGING, JANDER was now off the Bridge and getting his first good dinner in several days in a corner of the crew's lounge. Instructed to present comfort food, the chef served tender herb roasted chicken with dirty mashed red potatoes and Parmesan broccoli, a meal sufficient to soothe the angriest of omnivores. The crew members sharing the lounge kept their distance as he enjoyed his dinner alone with smooth jazz playing softly from state-of-the-art speakers nearby.

Richard Ford, Steele's self-appointed adjutant, teleported in to find his boss savoring a stemmed glass of white burgundy and waited silently until Jander accepted him with a nod. "Tsin intercepted this exchange between the pirates, sir." He extended a tablet, speedball first.

Jander scanned through the data, reluctantly allowing the afterglow of the meal to dissipate. "Call Vickie and Pavel to a conference in the briefing room in ten minutes. I want you there, too, with Rosenberg, Kiaga and Sharon Gibson. Hop."

"Yessir." Ford disappeared. Seconds later Angela repeated Jander's summons.

Stocky, hirsute Walter Rosenberg, who also happened to be a werewolf, was the first to join the African American in the conference room. "What's happening?"

"We'll find out in a minute." Ford shook his head. "I can't get over Orion's gift for instant decisions. He reads a message and names some names, and you just know he already has a detailed plan. Here he is."

Jander strode in and took his seat at the head of the table as another teleporter winked in, spread around some glasses and pitchers, and vanished. Vickie strolled in from her office down the corridor, read Richard's mind and sat at the opposite end from Jander, her features unrevealing but her expressive eyes narrowed.

Ford and the Bavarian found seats of their own and waited for the others to arrive. Kalanev, off duty as Steele had been, strode in wearing sweat-stained warmups, and Gibson, a smallish brunette, came in her light blue lab coat. Last to appear was Cielo Kiaga, five feet, eight inches of Sudanese femininity, clad in a rumpled sari and blinking sleep out of her amber eyes. She had been catnapping in the park.

"Thank you," Jander began. "Our information is by no means complete, but we have enough to build a plan on. Tsin intercepted communications from the last, damaged, ship of the bunch that jumped Denny and the others. Denny managed to land on a Gaea-like planet 'way outside Confederation territory, the coordinates of which we have been able to triangulate from the signals. It's a G1 star dim enough to escape notice in the past. The Sprite exploded soon after touching down, but the indications are that at least Denny and Chelsea got out alive."

Sighs and whispers greeted that news, and Jander used the time to fill his own lungs.

"Now the bad news. The pirates have decided to put a balls-out effort into finding them. If they succeed, they'll do their best to bleed them dry, believe me. Oh, Chelsea can escape them, but I doubt that she will as long as Denny and any other survivors are in danger. In any case, they'll need our help to pull them out of it.

"The planet is a bit smaller than Gaea in diameter, if we interpret their distance measures correctly, with gravity a bit high for its size and a solid magnetic field protecting what's a good atmosphere, at least by pirate standards. No known intelligent life to get in our way, but that means we'll need tracking skills to hunt them up. I will lead the relief force, with Pavel in the second spot. Walter and Cielo will act as trackers, Richard as scout. Sharon will scout in another manner: her zootelepathy will guide us by finding animals that have run into the strange new critters. Vickie will provide our top cover in command of the *Angel*. Oh, we can expect at least another two hundred or so ships—the usual strength of a pirate fleet—over the planet."

"I thought we destroyed the fleet," Sharon put in. Her voice was smooth and calm.

"They wouldn't have sent their entire force to capture one ship," Jander pointed out. "Actually, the fact that they could spare two hundred for the job worries me. It means they have ships to burn. The *Angel* will stay under cover unless absolutely necessary, but it sure will be a comfort to have her close. Other questions?"

"Do we go down to stay?" Rosenberg asked.

"We'll go down by telebooth and remain until we find them. We can't take the chance of an auxiliary ship or any extra quantum teleportation energies being spotted. We don't know enough about their technology to risk it. Communication will be by telepathy, between Pavel on the surface and a strong team here. I figure it would take six or seven to get the necessary range."

"How will we be armed?" Pavel, ever the warrior, wanted to know.

"Pulse pistols should be sufficient, with plenty of extra batteries. I don't want us to be hauling around a lot of heavy weaponry, especially since the metamorphs won't be able to carry packs. We'll be moving as light as possible, living off rations and whatever we can catch. Sharon, I know you're vegetarian. We'll be sure to pack plenty to keep you going."

The zootelepath smiled and nodded her thanks.

"Our arrival at the planet will coincide with dusk tomorrow at the Sprite's landing site, say, thirty hours from now. We'll be hitting the ground soon after that. So get as much rest as you can—you won't get a whole lot down there. Anything else?"

Walter hesitated, glancing at the expert biologist Sharon, then said, "I've interacted with a lot of exotic creatures in my past life in the pet trade, and I can tell you that some of the cutest animals you'll ever see can kill you. A slow loris, for instance, looks like a stuffed toy, but its bite can be lethal. And we're likely to see creatures that make a platypus look as common as your cat. So even though we have no idea what kind of wildlife we'll encounter, we need to assume that anything we meet is dangerous until proven otherwise."

"A very good point," Sharon agreed, to Walter's relief. "The same goes for plant life, by the way. I'll pack a variety of antitoxins, but I can't guarantee or even guess if they'll be effective. I'll also pack some equipment to analyze anything we run up against, but again, the taxonomy may be so different from what we know that it'll be useless. So, Walter's right—the best prevention is avoidance."

"So my idea of our hunting for provisions is off the board?" Jander said.

"I won't know until we get samples. I can test for

protein and sugar chirality, which will tell me if you'd get nutrition out of the local wildlife. If the amino acids aren't left-handed, for instance, you can fill up on it but it won't sustain you. We can pack supplements just in case."

"Is that something we can test for from afar? Or do you need specimens?"

"Hmmm... Let me get with Chloe and Kitsune and see if there are any markers we can scan for from orbit. If there's a way, we'll find it."

"Sounds good. Keep me posted, and if you need more pack room let me know and we'll distribute it around. Any other thoughts?"

No one spoke.

"All right, then, dismissed."

The Corpsmen filed out, save for Vickie, who stayed rooted to her chair, arms crossed in body language as obvious as a scream. She had been frowning darkly throughout the meeting. Even without probing, Jander knew what was on her mind, and he set himself for the inevitable argument.

"You're keeping me out of the action again," she said, too sweetly. "Why aren't I going with you this time?"

"Because you're my best officer, and I need you to stay on top of us. With you in the command chair, I'm not the least bit worried."

"Yeah? How do you think I feel, seeing you dive into danger like that? Why is Pavel going, and not me? He can fight the ship. And I'm not only telepathic, and the stronger, but also telekinetic and telehypnotic."

"Pavel can hit ninety-nine bullseyes out of a hundred, and the other would be on the line," he reminded her. "And for sheer killer instinct you can't beat a trained assassin. You are my First Officer, and not just because you're a good sounding board. You're the most capable officer I've got, and I'm leaving you in command because you'll give me the best possible top cover."

"Bullshit!" she fumed. "You're just trying to protect me. Who in hell told you I couldn't take care of myself? I'm not going to just sit up here and let —"

He slapped the palm of his hand on the table. "Enough!" She stopped and inhaled sharply, eyes flashing. His voice was harsh. "Who am I?"

"You are my *husband!*" She sprang to her feet, fists balled at her hips. "You were my husband before we built this ship, and you will be my husband, my man, to the last breath I have to defend you with! My place is at your side where a woman is *supposed* to be!"

The emotions that played over his face were everything she longed to see, but they were quickly replaced by determination as the lifemate stepped aside and the commander returned. He kept his voice soft.

"That honors me far beyond my worth. But we both have greater responsibilities now. We're not just husband and wife, but the heads of a family that depends on us for guidance and protection."

"But—"

"No... buts!" he gritted. "If I were trying to keep you safe, I'd keep you with me, as any man would be compelled to do. But I need you here, in our home, to guide our family as they defend it against odds beyond anything we have ever faced."

He leaned forward, both palms on the table. "I'm going down there because some of our family is in a danger that I put them in. I should have known the pirates would want to cover their tracks—hell, they've been doing it all along. My strategy to draw them out was based on it. Yes, they fell into my trap, but I never thought to extrapolate their response to the setback. Anyone with any military experience at all wouldn't have made that mistake. I'm culpable for that. It was my amateur decisions that put our people in jeopardy, and you of all people know it's eating me alive!

"So it's up to me to go get them, and I'm taking a team that I hope will keep me from being so stupid while we're looking. I'm leaving you here to safeguard the rest, and to be ready when I need you. And I will need you, Vickie. I'll need you right here, with the full strength of our home and family, to pull us out when I get our kids back. That is my decision, and all your love for me won't change it."

Vickie opened and closed her mouth several times, then turned away in frustration. She bowed her head and fought with herself, and finally found her voice.

"I should have predicted this," she sighed. "I'm your wife, and it's my duty to be by your side, and to hate it if I can't be. But you're also the captain of this ship, the head of the family, yes, and your word is law. I am your first officer, and I am sworn to obey and support you."

She turned to face him. "You're right, the brutal fact is that your decisions led to this, but nobody else thought it through either. We never thought to question or advise you, because we're just as amateur as you are. None of us is Annapolis or Sandhurst. So we left it all on you and never thought you might be wrong. It's a guilt I have trouble accepting." She shrugged, a winsome half-smile returned to her lips. "Orders, sir?"

He wanted to go to her, but resisted. "Can you accept why I'm needing you here?"

She nodded ruefully. "You've picked a great team to go with you, and the best possible officer to command in your absence." She smiled, her buoyant spirits returning. "I guess I have to agree with you on that."

Jander sighed in relief. "Okay, then. Now, the way I see it, we have thirty hours to stock up on togetherness before the lid blows off."

He rose and came around the table, met her halfway and pulled her close. "Come on, I left a bottle of great chardonnay on the table."

Arms around each other, they left the room.

CHAPTER 13

Two moons were beginning to win their competition with the setting sun as Denny and Chelsea entered the clearing. They traveled at least fifty kilometers that first day, paced by the untiring stride and triple-strength soles of Denny's feet. Chelsea alternately walked, drifted or perched on his shoulder to keep up.

Throughout their hike they spotted myriad forms of animal life, some with four legs and some with six, from naked and blubbery piglike beasts with a head like a duckbilled hippo to clawed and armored things with compound eyes that looked like animated rocks.

The several varieties of ungulates, some solitary and some in small herds, froze and stared at the sight of them, then sprang away in ground-eating leaps. The smaller weasel-like or rodentine creatures either dove for burrows or scrambled higher into the trees. Lizards of all sizes, many of them carnivorous and a few likely poisonous, relied on staying still in their camouflage colors.

Insectivores of many species feasted on the abundant insects that had four to twelve legs each. Some of the bugs were the size of Chelsea's hand and fearless in their search for anything edible. Far too many had wings and came at them in swarms. Denny was constantly slapping them away while Chelsea opted to turn spectral and let them drop off. Few of them lingered in any case; it seemed they had no taste for Gaean flesh or blood.

"This looks like a good place to rest." Denny paused at the edge of a forest clearing and looked up into the partly cloudy sky, which carried more vapor trails than he would have liked. "We'll duck under that big tree, there." He indicated a huge pseudo-maple that dominated the grassy glade with its broad umbrella.

The pair moved beneath the sheltering foliage. A hawk-sized blue lizard with four greenish wings hissed at them from an upper branch and launched itself into the air to find a space less crowded.

Chelsea sighed and settled onto an exposed root next to the trunk. "Bloody well time for it, I dare say." She paused as the forest reverberated to that awful roar. "That blighter's getting close. We'll have to watch ourselves tonight."

He thumped to the ground beside her and shrugged off his pack, wincing a bit from his still-knotted muscles. "How're you doing?"

"I can hold up as long as you can, with your bruises and all. Better, if you keep letting me hitch-hike." She grinned her pixie grin and ruefully fingered her neck-length pixie bob. "I must look a sight."

He shook his head in sympathy. "Sorry about that

sap tree. At least you didn't get those leaves full in the face." He handed her a sample bag half filled with water from an artesian spring they passed. They elected to trust its purity without running it through the recycler, since they had no idea how long they would be marooned and the appliance was never meant to last forever.

Denny untied another bag dangling from the vine around his pack and pulled out a shoulder of the tasty little creature they chose to call a "dorse". That, too, gave them no gastrointestinal problems and thus appeared safe.

"Dinner." He used his pocket tool to cut off a healthy chunk of meat cooked earlier and extended it toward her.

"Cold?" She took the greasy offering and eyed it with distaste.

"Gotta be. We don't have much shelter here. A fire could be spotted too easily, especially if they're using infrared. It's bad enough to risk it at midday under a canopy." He tore off a mouthful of his own meal. "Not too bad—a bit gamey, maybe. Of course, I don't suppose you get much venison in London."

"Of course not." She copied his efforts with her own piece, waving the meat as she jocularly continued, "Fish and chips, biscuits with your tea, that's about..."

She stopped, her eyes widening. "Uuuuh, Denny..."

He followed her stare and froze. Out of the underbrush of their back trail stepped the most gigantic predator he could have ever imagined. At least two meters at the shoulder, with a bear's thick legs and deep chest, the big springy haunches of a cat, and a mouth overflowing with eight-inch teeth. There had to be at least a ton of supple muscle under the tawny, gray-striped hide.

"Smilodon," Denny breathed.

The beast did bear a resemblance to the saber-toothed tiger of ancient Gaea. The great, curving canines were relatively shorter, but they were in pairs rather than single daggers. The body was much larger and more ursine in bulk, and the tail was long rather than bobbed, but those deviations detracted nothing from the horror of the thing.

Denny's nerveless fingers let the meat slip to the ground, and the monster caught the sound and movement and turned in their direction. The shaggy coat bristled as it coughed a warning.

"I wonder if he's hungry?" Chelsea was maddeningly calm.

Denny swallowed convulsively. "Could you, uh, could you..."

"Cover your retreat? My pleasure." The two rose with exaggerated care, never taking their eyes off the tiger. As any alpha predator would, the beast perceived a challenge in that stare and returned it with tenfold malevolence.

Chelsea stepped forward, countering the behemoth's advance while Denny edged around the huge tree at their backs. Smiley sidled forward, gave her a chilling once-over and opted for the better meal. With an ear-splitting roar intended to freeze his prey, he charged.

It had the opposite effect on Denny. He stepped back from the tree, gathered himself and with a prodigious twelve-foot leap attained the lowest branches. Growling through his teeth, he hauled himself higher with bone-cracking force.

Chelsea uttering her best shriek and raced forward into the beast's path. The tiger swept a disdainful paw, gnashed his huge teeth through her head and neck, and kept on going. He almost reached the tree before his dim mind recognized that he had run right through her. He stopped dead in his tracks and looked behind him.

Chelsea grinned, curtseyed and twiddled her fingers at him. "Booga-booga."

Smiley blinked, looked away, looked back again, then shook his head and coughed. Since such a thing as transparent prey was impossible, it obviously did not exist. He turned and leaped, sinking his great claws into the tree eight feet up.

"Shit, it can climb!" Denny squawked, his deep bass reaching new heights. He scrambled upward.

Chelsea showed concern for the first time. Shouting, she flashed after the snarling beast, flitting around his head, shrieking in her best ghostly manner. Smiley ignored her. Once he formed an opinion, he stuck to it.

"Jump, Denny!"

Huge as it was, the tree was shuddering with the seven hundred pounds of Denny high above the rapidly gaining ton of tiger.

Connors struggled onto a creaking limb and leaped for the ground, chopping at the cat with his hard hand in passing. Knocked off balance by the power of the blow, the tiger screamed in rage, aimed a few licks at his stinging shoulder, and retreated backward down the tree. Connors, groggy from his ten-meter fall through the branches, got slowly to his feet—too slowly.

"Move!" Chelsea screamed as the cat reached solid ground with a decidedly un-catlike thud. Denny sidled away, fearing to turn his back.

In desperation Chelsea flitted around in front of the beast, materialized at ground level, jumped as high as she could, and aimed a right cross at the tiger's nose. Smack, her tiny fist made wet contact with all her negligible weight and leverage behind it.

"Rrrrngh?" Smiley flinched to a halt and turned his attention to the little morsel he had discarded as unreal. Tentatively, he blundered his massive paw through the phantom's head and shoulders.

Nothing? He tried another swipe, then gave it up. He started forward again.

Chelsea leaped into his path and swung with her open palm. Smack.

The tiger erupted. With a guttural snarl he leaped full onto the phantom, teeth gnashing and claws ripping through the empty air. He expected something, anything, to break his plunge, but found himself on his chin and haunches with nothing under him. He twisted catlike and looked over his shoulder, to see Chelsea sticking out of the middle of his back. She stuck her thumbs in her ears, poked out her tongue, and created a masterful Bronx cheer.

That did it. Roaring in rage, the tiger spun, all four paws and his tail cutting the air, curved double canines champing on flickering, tenuous pseudo-flesh. He contorted into all the shapes that only a cat could manage, using every trick in his primitive mind to catch this incredible meal.

Chelsea goaded him on, using every gambit in *her* book to bedevil him. She shrieked and cackled as piercingly as she could, flitted over and through and around him, and employed every opportunity to gain substance and pop him in the nose or smack his ear.

Denny had circled around them and regained the tree, but he did not climb. He could not. It was all he could do to remain standing, leaning on the trunk and howling with mirth, peering through tear-blurred eyes as he watched her go through her spectral paces with the wildly enraged behemoth.

He should have climbed.

Eventually the extra sound effects filtered into Smiley's infuriated consciousness. He paused in his fruitless tail chasing and ignored two raps in the snout to look around. His blazing eyes met Denny's.

The titan's Herculean mirth turned into equally

enthusiastic alarm as the cat crouched, gathered all the power in his mighty muscles, and launched himself into a full sprint. Denny scrambled behind the tree.

Chelsea uttered a few choice barmaid's remarks, turned on her power and sped after the predator. As she flew right up behind the beast, she materialized, lashed out with her size five boot and planted it squarely in the tiger's most tender spot—not, incidentally, his nose.

Smiley shrieked in an entirely different key and whirled. Chelsea bared her own teeth and presented him with another raspberry.

Roaring hideously, the cat charged, blundered right through her and stopped, tail whipping with fury.

Chelsea did not allow the opportunity to slip away. Again her toe flashed, with the same rewarding effect.

This time Smiley bounded at least six feet straight up, spun in mid-air and landed on his haunches. The ghost shrieked and hopped forward, arms flailing. The cat answered her with a coughing roar and gave ground.

Again Chelsea leaped; again the tiger retreated. Back across the clearing they frog-marched, the ghost allowing the distance to increase between them.

At last the tiger was backed up against the forest wall and Chelsea was bouncing up and down in place, content to see the monster disappear. With one last defiant bellow, Smiley turned tail and vanished into the trees.

Denny leaned with his shoulders against the tree, sick with laughter. Chelsea drifted over to him, grinning from ear to ear, turned solid and hopped up to catch her arms around his neck. "You bloody fool, you almost wrecked it."

"I'm sorry, honey, it was just so..." He relapsed into weak laughter.

She giggled and swung from his neck, planted her feet on his hip bones, chinned herself and gave him a moist and healthy open-mouthed kiss. "It was great good fun."

She paused with wide eyes at the new expression on his face. "What's the matter?"

He could not speak. He just stared at her, shocked wonder in every line of his face.

"Why, of course I love you, you bloody fool." She kissed him again, lingering, then leaned back and searched his eyes.

Slowly, tentatively, he closed his arms around her lithe form, gingerly taking her weight and pressing her against his chest. Incredulously, he heard her say it again.

"I love you, Denny."

Groaning softly, he met her lips.

CHAPTER 14

Through long hours of reminiscing and not much sleep they pressed on during the night, putting as much distance between themselves and the plain as they could. The terrain was changing to rolling hills as they pushed north, with the dense woodlands interspersed with stretches of younger growth that told of past forest fires. The frequent rain often included thunder and lightning that foreshadowed both the strikes to start the flames and the showers to quench them.

As the crisp dawn broke, Denny hunted for breakfast, hurling rocks at one startled creature after another without success. Even Chelsea's shepherding could not slow his targets enough for him to strike a lethal blow, and he was reluctant to pitch at anything that might escape with a crippling injury and a lingering death.

With no more substantial weapons close at hand, it appeared they would go hungry that day.

"You know, you might think me a spinnaker short of full sail, but there's something I haven't ever tried that might work to get us some victuals," the ghost murmured in her hollow voice. "I can't affect anything with a nervous system, but I can shove a stick into something with the best of them. The question is, would there be anything left to eat?"

Denny considered the idea as he swatted away a huge flying insect. "I swear, that one had a tail number. You mean, have your stick and the dorse occupy the same space?"

She nodded.

"Hm. You're talking molecular fusion. In my book, that would cause the biggest explosion since Krakatoa." He thought about it. "But maybe not. If you use something tiny, like, and shove it deep, it might work. We can try it."

Chelsea floated parallel to the ground, her nose a foot from the loam, and found a flat pebble little more than half a centimeter wide. "How's this?"

"Okay. Happy hunting."

She grinned and flitted to treetop level.

Floating above, around and through the trees, she scouted the shrub-carpeted forest with her fixed-reference clairvoyance. Several times she dipped, checked out a shadow, then soared aloft again.

At last she found one of the solitary-roaming dorses resting beneath a bush. The creature bleated at the sight of her and scrambled away, but Chelsea kept up with it easily. She reached her hand into its torso, said, "Sorry," and let go of the pebble. It immediately rematerialized.

Two hundred meters away, Denny did not hear the blast. It was so tremendous that he was instantly deafened, and the concussion staggered him a dozen meters into a clump of shrubbery. The trees around him quivered and bowed and a hailstorm of wood and soil rained down, unfelt over the thumping pain in his skull.

Favoring a brand new set of bruises, he staggered to his feet. Chelsea found him leaning against a tree shaking his ringing head and flung herself into his arms, tears streaming. He gestured his health and pointed to his ears, and waited as she probed with her second sight.

After what seemed a long time, she sagged against him, sobbing with relief. She said something that he felt rather than heard.

"What?" he shouted, feeling the vibration dimly in his skull.

She stepped back and gesticulated, getting across the idea that his deafness was temporary.

"Okay." He sat down at the base of the tree and checked himself over.

Chelsea, her cheeks streaked with relief, busied herself pulling shrapnel from his tough hide: splinters, hard-driven gravel, even a slice or two of animal bone. Denny paused to rest his head against the tree as the ringing in his ears increased, and gradually it diminished to a sizzle until he could hear again.

He swallowed away the worst of the tightness. "I'll do the hunting from now on."

"By all means, be my guest," she moaned, and pressed her head into his shoulder. "I was afraid I'd killed you."

"You made a good try," he said lightly. "The concussion was tremendous. If my skull weren't so thick it'd be splattered all over the forest." He grinned to comfort her and lowered his head to touch hers. "I take it we won't have breakfast after all."

"Not unless you want it already digested, no. There's nothing left but a crater. Dorse, bush, dirt, everything, *pouf*, gone. Luckily enough, atmospheric waves don't affect me in spectral form. I can hear, but it's on the order of clairaudience rather than vibration. In any case, anything else that can hear is doubtless long gone."

"No doubt. Except the bad guys, maybe."

She gasped. "You're right, we'd better flit. Come on."

They got up and started on their way.

"Well, we learned one thing," Denny observed. "If we're cornered, we've got one hell of a weapon."

SCHAUS AND GAZENHOUT CHEWED tiredly on their rations, both keeping an eye their monstrous guide. After almost a full day of marching Meshzner at last consented to a rest stop. He leaned with his massive back to a tree, studying the prints on the ground in front of him. He had not eaten or slept since the pursuit began.

"That hunker's going to run us into the ground,"

Schaus muttered, careful not to let the Lievan hear the slur.

Gazenhout grunted and squeezed his aching feet through his low boots. Shipboard life did not make for strong calluses. "Why is he in such a rush? We'll catch them eventually."

"The Captain says they're landing parties from other ships in the forest. Meshzner wants to find them first—and you know what he'll do."

"And what we'll have to try to do. I tell you, friend, we don't have much chance against him." Gazenhout grimaced and stretched his arms. "I'm slowing down fast."

"So am I, Gaz. I wonder what manner of creature this alien is—the big one. Have you seen his stride?"

"Makes two of mine, with prints as deep as the hunker's. I'm beginning to doubt he's carrying anything but his own weight. There's been no sign of anything being set down."

"You mean someone half again taller than we are, with a Lievan's weight?" He shook his head. "Meshzner's welcome to him. If we do catch up, I want a front-row seat." He considered. "Correction—I want to be on the other side of the galaxy."

Gazenhout chuckled and nodded. "The other one, now, is light enough to be female. The Confederation always takes their women with them—a convenience I wish the Head would agree to. She's a tiny one, too." He smirked. "Quick and easy."

Schaus snorted. "Right, son. You take care of her

boyfriend, and I'll let you go second."

"Thanks. I'd do the same with your mother."

Muttering and chuckling to each other, they stretched out on the fragrant loam as the new day began. They were nearly asleep when the ground twitched beneath them and a distant *crump* reached their ears. Both sat up in a hurry. "Explosion!"

The Lievan bounced erect. "In front of us!" He hopped up and down, not the least bit fatigued by the pace he was setting. "We're runnin' 'em down! Come on!" He bent to the ground as well as his thick body could manage and bounded down the trail.

Schaus and Gazenhout looked at each other, then sighed in unison. "We have to keep the bastard in sight," Schaus put it into words. He struggled to his feet, then gave his partner a hand up. Shouldering their packs and rifles, they plodded after their secondary target.

"*CAPTAIN ON THE BRIDGE*," Angela announced.

"Anything new, Alexiy?" Jander strode through the double hatch to find the navigator in the center seat. The primary bridge crew were accustomed to taking turns in the command chair even as the *Angel* sped toward the gathering storm.

"A few things, Captain," Pashkov said as he rose and stepped aside for his commander. "One, I believe we have to accept fact that Kodiak and Nebula are only survivors. We have five comrades to honor."

Jander felt the burning eyes of every member of the Bridge team. "We will, gospodin. Trust me, we will. What else?"

Pashkov nodded shortly in acknowledgement, and went on, "We intercepted reports of some kind of explosion in middle of forest—meaning halfway between steppe and mountains, if our geography projections are accurate. No one on other side can account for it. I can't see how it could be Denny, though. What do you make of it?"

Jander scanned the array of monitors on the forward bulkhead as he thought about it. "No pirate casualties?"

"No. sir. Explosion was reported by closest pursuers, two pirates and one Lievan, whatever that is. They've put search parties in area but haven't found anything yet. Only thing they could come up with is that Denny himself caused it, and we know he's not armed."

Jander grunted. "Not with a bomb, at any rate. But on the other hand, that guy could make a flashlight out of a dirty boot... hmmm." He pondered for a moment. "Yukio, have you ever tried to release one item of solid matter inside another?"

"Oh, no, Orion-sama. I imagine it would cause a... big boom." She looked at him through a dawning light.

He winked at her, acknowledging the fun side of her playing to her childlike appearance. He knew the truth of her mature and indomitable intelligence. "That's what I think, too. A gas, like air, has enough fluidity to get out of the way, else you'd blow up every time you rematerialize your clothing. But anything with molecular complexity would be disrupted. Maybe Chelsea was experimenting. Alexiy, I'd say our friends are definitely armed, with a living, breathing blonde bombshell. That makes me feel a little better."

He frowned. "I hope she was careful with Denny. 'S funny, our strongest man is also just about our most vulnerable."

"To blonde bombshells, at least," Vickie smiled as she glided through the hatch. She apparently picked up the conversation telepathically as she approached the Bridge. So delicate was her control that she could fleetingly tickle a variant mind entirely unnoticed.

Jander grinned back at her. "Anything else, guys?"

Li-san was at his com station. "A ton of fleet movements, sir. They're bringing in everything but your grandfather's Chevy. Abnormal precautions, judging from the amount of com traffic. Their leader seems to take us none too lightly. He's called the Head, by the way."

"The Head?" Jander and Vickie looked at each other. "The Head of what? The fleet? The pirates? The planet?"

"Sanitation?" some wag from the periphery put in. Tittering traveled throughout the Bridge.

"Hold it in, guys." Jander turned his back on the strangled laughter and assumed his command chair.

Vickie sat on the electronics-covered chair arm next to him, trusting Angela to ignore any butt commands. "Something nags at me, about the team you'll be taking. Walter and Cielo don't seem to get along too well. You might have a little trouble."

"They're Corpsmen," he said. "It's in their training that the team comes first. Sure, they're strong personalities, they wouldn't be Corpsmen if they weren't. But they'll cooperate, if I have to bang their furry heads together." He shrugged. "Besides, that's mostly tradition. They don't really dislike each other, they're just supposed to."

He leaned toward her, elbow on her thigh and chin in his hand. "Squabbling critters I can handle. I'm more worried about how Richard looks at Cielo, and vice versa. Their minds might not be strictly on the job."

She chuckled. "Come, now. Whatever Denny and Chelsea can do—or not do, as the case may be—those two can equal. And if you ask me, it's a little late to start worrying about your cupidity."

He winced. "I'll be glad to get there, if only to get away from the puns. Okay, you made your point."

Yukio's soft voice interrupted. "I have more bogeys."

Jander scanned the bank of viewscreens. "Where away?"

"Section seventeen." She switched the view to the

front monitor without being asked. Steele stared at the sizeable glob of faint nucleonic flares.

"Dozens of them," he mused. "This is turning into quite a party."

CHAPTER 15

Under the Head's personal, if distant, direction, the Ertainian Second and Eighth Fleets sealed a meteor-tight blockade around Planet Four. More than four hundred warships crowded into the system, filling the vacuum almost screen to screen and probing, probing to ensure that no strangers entered.

Unfortunately for them, they were looking for something either visible or detectable. The *Angel* was neither. The collision shield, the energy deflector and the baffle screen were all reduced to their minimum footprint of six thousand meters, making her nigh impossible to even bump into.

In solid telepathic contact with his comrades, Nwoye Lam guided his charge between the combined fleet of fast cruisers and the larger battleships, armed transports and supply ships surrounding the planet. Within the protection of the *Angel*'s innermost shielding, he dropped into the shadow of one of the smaller moons, taking up a powered station so as not to disturb the misshapen rock's orbit with the ship's mass.

Steele watched in silence as Angela spotted and

Yukio marked the swarms of armed shuttles that had landed and were still landing on the planet. Scores at the edge of the plain, dozens in forest clearings, even more a third of the way up the mountain range. The continent was crawling with pirates.

"If Denver gets through that, I will hand-feed him breakfast," Pavel muttered. Like Steele, he was already dressed in a generic pattern of nanosteel-reinforced forest camo, a best guess outfit selected to blend them into the environment they assumed they would be traversing. The Ukrainian's eyes gleamed with the call to righteous battle. To the Omega Corps as a whole, the eradication of criminal injustice was a necessary war. To Pavel Kalanev, the steel-eyed ex-assassin, it was a crusade.

"If he reaches the mountains, it'll take a battalion to dig him out," Vickie said. "They're as rugged as any one of the moons."

"They have at least a division on the ground already, Lady Alpha. But if that forest is as thick as it appears to be, I could almost pity them. In small groups, Chelsea will tear them apart—if she has the fortitude to try."

"She does, trust me. That is one tough little Brit. And I doubt 'pity' is in anybody's vocabulary right now." Vickie broke away as Jander turned from the screen. "When are you going down?" she said.

"Very soon, at full dark. I'd like to land in the middle somewhere, but we might miss them altogether. We'll start near the crash site and parallel their trail, maybe strike once or twice at the pirates to confuse them. How's the weather, Yukio?"

"You have a cold front moving in from the northern ocean on the other side of the mountains," she told him. "Things could get nasty if it's strong enough to survive the passage. But before that you have several days of mostly cloudy, maybe a scattered shower or six, and balmy to warm temperatures. Good for hiking." She flashed her puckish smile. "Are you certain you don't need a ghost?"

Jander smiled his appreciation. The sweet young Japanese with the compassionate soul of an artist also was a Corpsman. It warmed him to know that everyone on the ship would have volunteered just as readily. "Thanks, but I expect we'll be picking one up down there pretty soon. Let's get ready, Pavel."

Steele led Vickie and his top manhunter from the Bridge toward the telebooth down the corridor. As the double hatch closed behind them, Jander said quietly, "Did you speak with the others?"

Vickie nodded. "I met with each of them, as you asked, and explored their feelings about going into combat. I made certain that they understood that they were going to have to kill fellow intelligent beings. I was pretty blunt, and my analysis was thorough. Every one of them knows that this is total war in a just cause, and I can safely say that they won't hesitate to pull the trigger. You can count on them."

"Super. Thank you."

They paused at the open hatch of the telebooth.

Pavel stepped in and faced the back of the booth to give husband and wife their privacy. A whispered moment later, Jander joined him and punched in the code for the hangar.

They strode into the ready room to find the rest of the squad already gearing up. Richard and Sharon Gibson were also clad in forest camo, cargo pockets bulging with supplies selected from the long table under the shuttered window.

Walter, Doppelwulf, on the other hand, wore only a pair of gray trunks; when he triggered his metamorphism the shorts would be tucked into a pocket behind his matching gray chest holster. The shoulder straps of the holster were infused with nanotech that would change their shape when he phased into his wolf form. One strap housed an extra battery and the other a heavy folding knife.

The Sudanese metamorph, Cielo Kiaga, wore nothing but black bikini briefs with her holster, a fact that caused the perfectly normal American male, Richard Ford, no end of trouble. He had to call on all his vaunted variant determination to control his sensations—although the sight of the pistol strapped high between Corpsman Raankhak's athletically firm breasts may have had something to do with it. She moved around the room with unconscious feline grace, feeling his eyes on her and enjoying herself immensely.

Jander picked up his combat-furnished utility belt from the table and checked the twin weapons. About the size and shape of a Colt 1911 but with a longer barrel, they were filled with intricate microminiaturized circuits, most of which served to generate and propel five-millimeter bubbles of coherent energy at any selected speed from subsonic to mach three. Sensors in the triggers and electronic elements assured that no one but activated variants could fire or strip them. Their range was two kilometers, with little recoil and no loss of trajectory; as with the *Angel*'s primary weaponry, the spheres eroded away through friction and vanished at the end of their coherency. Accuracy, of course, was in the eye of the holder.

In the grip was a replaceable supercapacitor battery, charged with solar energy and effective for fifty shots. Everything they carried that needed power ran on those batteries, from the flashlights to the cook stove. Needless to say, a large percentage of their equipment load was batteries.

Steele did not intend to use his weapons himself; his own variant power was parent to the child. He carried them for spares, in case of electronic failure. He had the cook stove in his backpack, along with a complete change of clothes, a lightweight jacket and blanket, and plenty of nutrition bars to supplement their hunting. He also carried sets of clothing for the metamorphs.

Kalanev examined his own rig with a professional's care. The hawkeyed Ukrainian also strapped on two pistols; Cobra was actually as proficient as his reputation would suggest, which was phenomenal. His pack included a water purifier, extra mylar blankets, and a few spares for the electronic wristpads they all wore.

Sharon, Harmonia of the Corps, though the least imposing of them physically, was nonetheless a trained fighter with Sai daggers in crossed sheathes between her pack and her well-toned shoulders. Richard and Sharon carried one pistol each, since their pack loads carried heavier equipment: Sharon had medical supplies and a compact analysis kit structured to test for anything that may harm them, and Richard, the solar charger for the batteries and a disassembled hover drone with its controller.

Everyone's belt was loaded with batteries, combat knives and canteens with the exception of the metamorphs, who by necessity travelled light and were far more capable of foraging. Steele inspected his team with pride, knowing he had the very best of Gaea at his back.

"All set?" He met the eyes of each of them in turn.

One by one they nodded, each with the same look of confidence and determination.

"Good. I want to emphasize that we work as a team, so feel free to contribute any observations or advice you wish. If I've learned anything this past week it's that I don't know it all, so don't assume I do."

The nods were solemn.

"Let's go."

He opened the hatch and stepped out, and paused in surprise. Every flight crew and all the ground personnel lined the route from the ready room to the cargo chamber in two solid ranks. On telepathic command, the assembly snapped to attention, and every man and woman slapped their right fists, fingers in, to the Corps insignia over the left breast in formal salute.

Jander stared, a bit stunned by the honor, then straightened his shoulders and set himself in motion. Pavel, Richard, Sharon, Cielo, and Walter followed in single file. The six strode between the ranks in broken cadence without a word.

As they passed, each Corpsman snap turned to face the cargo hold. When Jander reached the broad open hatch, his expedition squad spread their formation, turned and straightened to attention in line abreast. Orion sharply returned the salute of the honor guard and held it until the double hatch rolled closed.

Richard broke the long silence in typical Richard fashion. "Well, we ain't doin' this for the money, are we?"

Jander joined in the soft laughter. He pretended not to notice that even Pavel's eyes were moist. With a deep sigh, he turned and stepped up onto the big cargo 'porter that was their launch pad.

The cargo teleporter worked on the same principle that Richard's variant power did: total dematerialization and instant relocation to a predetermined spot, by trading a mass for the less dense atmosphere from the destination through quantum entanglement. If the landing spot was within solid matter the subject was detoured to the nearest empty space.

Arai Osamu, a clairvoyant-clairaudient engineer, was manning the console. He blinked away the sight of the nearly nude Cielo and positioned the six on the big 'porter's square platform.

Steele checked the positioning to make sure they had three hundred sixty-degree observation for the landing. "Got the coordinates, Osamu?"

"Yes, sir, I tested with dry ice. Four hundred meters into the forest, three hundred northeast of the crater. I'll set you down like babes in a cradle." The clairvoyant looked forlorn. "Sure you don't need any help?"

"Consider yourself lucky. You can watch from here." He shrugged his broad shoulders to check the comfort of his pack.

"Well, if you need a samurai, just holler," he grinned. A master of bujitsu, he was one of the Corps' best martial arts trainers.

"Thanks, but I'd settle for some horses. Ready when you are."

Osamu took a last sensor look at the landing site to ensure it was unoccupied, checked his weight readouts to verify the energies needed, and typed rapidly on his keyboard. He watched the load bar fill to the right, and when it touched the end line he tapped the command key. The pent-up energy was released in one powerful wave, and the six adventurers were gone.

Next time, stupid, Jander told himself, turn down the lights in the 'porter room. He stared blinking into the sudden darkness, and took a slow, deep breath. For the first time in long months his feet were pressed into fragrant, loamy soil; his ears were saturated by the mysterious sounds of the forest at night. He thought the *Angel*'s park was a good substitute for the real thing, but it was still only a substitute. The real forest filled his senses with memories.

Pavel had no such thoughts. His eyes were tightly closed long before the trip, and when they arrived he was ready, in a crouch with pistols out and mind and eyes questing. The mottled illumination from the glow of four crescented moons filtering through the trees showed him no threats, and he slowly uncoiled.

Richard, too, teleported with his gun drawn, but like Jander he was temporarily blinded. He pointed his weapon skyward as Pavel had taught him.

Jander vision started to adjust. "Walter," he called softly as he glanced at the compass mode of his wristpad, "Change over and scout out Denny's trail. It should be in that direction." He pointed with two fingers of his right hand.

Walter nodded, slipped out of his shorts—he was forever embarrassed by that action—stuffed them into the small pocket behind his holster, and crouched. His body seemed to flow, and in a few seconds he morphed into a huge, mottled gray wolf, testing the air with keen nose and sensitive ears. The holster that had scraped against his human chest was now just above and between his forelegs like a guide dog harness. He took a moment to orient himself, then trotted into the underbrush.

"Cielo... where is she?"

"Hrrrr."

He had to squint to find her.

The sleek black panther sat in a shadow of her own creation, her ebony fur with its dotting of slightly darker leopard florets blending so well with the moonlit night that she was next to invisible. She raised a heavily armed paw and licked away an imaginary blemish, then curled her tail around her toes. One hundred forty pounds of beautiful, dynamite pussycat.

Steele, who loved cats, felt a wash of emotion he had trouble shaking off. "I want you to scout the pirate camp," he told her, keeping his voice low in enemy territory. "See what kind of people they are, how they're armed, and so forth. You know what to look for. Be careful!" He waved her out.

She stretched full length to loosen her feline muscles and padded toward the trees, looked back and gazed languidly at Ford, then flicked her tail and disappeared.

Richard sighed and sat down on a rotting log, his city-bred senses unmindful of the horde of insects that was surely in residence. "That lady's gonna kill me."

Jander chuckled and turned to the humanform woman. "What do you hear, Sharon?"

The zootelepath was standing in the center of the clearing, eyes closed. "Everyone's awfully upset," she reported, her voice barely above a whisper. "The pirates have been killing them at random for sport, chasing them all over the place. It's so against the cycle that even the top of the food chain can think of nothing else. Their minds are too full of that to recall a pair of harmless ones. As for the animals themselves..."

She paused, marshalling her impressions. "Some are four-limned bifurcates, somewhat similar to Gaea's but more diverse. Others have six limbs and are so alien to our phylum they're more difficult to read. It seems the two families evolved in parallel. Most correspond to the Gaean Eocene period; big, dumb four-legged brutes on the plains, smaller six-legged ungulates in the forests, or little cowards from either order in the treetops and shadows. A majority of the little ones are insectivores—you may have noticed there are a lot of bugs around—but I've detected a huge variety of hoofed or pawed herbivores and a fair number of carnivores in good natural proportion. There's no such thing as a bird as we'd define it, but there are reptiles in plenty, some warm-blooded, and a few of them can fly. All in all, pretty much like the interglacial fauna of Gaea, but far more diverse than we know from our fossil records. That's all so far."

"Very good, Harmonia. That's a hell of a lot more than I expected from a first report. Cobra?"

"A lot of people," the telepath muttered. "Too many to sort out very well. The conscious thoughts that I can focus on have a sibilant tone to them, which interferes with my probes much like white noise to the ear. In appearance, they are comprised of two distinct types. The majority are first-level intelligences somewhat similar to us in appearance, with a yellowish skin—lemon yellow, not Asian. Their planet is called Ertain, a term from an ancient language, like our Gaea. They are about a meter and a half tall on average, and wear maroon one-piece jumpsuits with centered insignia. They have short black fur from just above the eyes down the length of the spine. Otherwise they are even more thinly haired than we are. They think of their skin color so much because the other type has gray-white skin. The gray ones are great monsters of limited intelligence, called 'hunkers' in contempt... Lievans."

He opened his eyes and looked to Jander. "Denver and Chelsea are being chased by a Lievan, are they not?"

"Right. Giants, huh?"

"They think of themselves as giants, but they are no taller than the pirates—oh, and almost as wide as tall, I see it now. They are beings of tremendous strength."

He concentrated. "Mercenaries, not pirates, from a heavy-gravity planet but of the same species as the master race. The Lievans are colonists many generations removed from Ertain, it would seem. And quite dimwitted, for the most part, retained for their loyalty and ferocity. None of them have higher rank."

Jander nodded, then stiffened. Jander could read variant minds without interference, but his unconscious defensive shield prevented him from communicating with even the strongest of them, including his wife. He now caught a concentration of thought from Walter, intensely focused in the hope that Steele or Kalanev would notice it. He sent his direct probe in the metamorph's direction.

<*"I have a trail, though it's so trampled it's hard to read. These pirates stink to high heaven. It wasn't easy in this rat's nest, but I've spotted footprints that could only be Denny's."*>

"Pavel, catch Walter. Tell him to watch himself; hunters." Pavel switched mental stations and passed on the message.

<*"Understood, sir. Should I return, or follow?"*>

"Stay put. We'll move soon, and parallel your tracking until we're out of the area."

<*"Jawohl."*>

So basic had the werewolf's mental processes become that the normally unilingual telepathic impulse reverted to his native German.

"Recall Raankhak, Cobra, and we'll get going." Pavel narrowed his eyes, and a few moments later a stealthy silhouette padded into the clearing behind Richard. The cat slinked closer and flashed her tongue over his neck. Only an instant gag provided by Steele's forcefield prevented the man from crying out.

"Kiaga, attention!" Steele growled.

The African flowed, then stood naked on two legs.

"We are on a covert mission, encircled by ruthless monsters who would like nothing better than to know we are here. You almost gave our position away with your foolishness, and I won't have it. One more such lapse and I'll send you back to the ship. This is no time for practical jokes. Understood?"

"Y-yes, sir. I'm s-sorry, Milord." Feeling more naked than she ever had in her life, her muscles twitched as she stared into the darkness over his shoulder.

Orion left her at attention, using her embarrassment to press the lesson home. "Report."

"I-I didn't get far, sir." She swallowed convulsively to regain her composure, and her broad Dinka accent was heightened by her determination to redeem herself. "But I counted at least twenty armed shuttles in a half-kilometer area, each capable of carrying a squad or two of men. All men, sir, no females. Most of them are our shape and average a hundred fifty centimeters tall, but there are a few many times heavier with long arms and short legs. They are armed with shoulder guns, but they're not nucleonic or projectile rifles. A few are armed with projectile pistols, probably for officers."

"Let Cobra in." Jander was already within her

mind, but a regular telepath could only communicate with another activated variant if invited. "What do you think, Pavel? Lasers?"

"If you say so, my lord—I cannot learn it for myself. Their minds are too... well, noisy for me to pick one clean. But this weapon appears to be different from anything the Confederation has, and I know they are behind us in wave science. There are certain to be some species ahead of us in that respect."

"We'll take a few with us when we go. All right, Raankhak, as you were. Remember my warning."

The woman sighed and dropped to all fours.

Richard reached out a conciliatory hand and gave the now feline form a scratch behind the ear. "Find Walter on the trail," said Jander, "and zigzag behind him to check for anything trailing him. We'll keep our distance on the right flank."

Cielo coughed acceptance and whisked away.

Steele adjusted the hook and loop belly strap that snugged his pack to his back and met the gaze of each of his team in turn. "Let's go, people. I'm point. Pavel, watch our six." He sent his mental probe in Walter's direction and set out to follow him.

Richard caught up with Steele as he led the way through the forest. "Hey, boss?"

"Is this business, Hermes?"

"Um, in a way, sir. I'm just as much to blame as Cielo is. I haven't exactly treated her like a sister." He paused, not sure what to say.

"That's your business, not mine. You're my adjutant, my good right arm in thought and deed before I even knew I needed one, and I sincerely thank you for that. But you should know as well as anyone how I feel about mixing business with pleasure. I've been known to show a pretty keen interest in my Chief of Staff, but certainly not in the middle of a battle."

"In a word, discretion. Scratch her ear, but quietly."

"And be ready to shoot right past it," Jander nodded. "I have no objections to romance, or joking, or anything else human. But I don't want to lose any more lives because of it."

Richard looked at him, puzzled. "Any more lives?"

"I have five on my conscience, Richard, because I wanted to get Denny and Chelsea together. Maybe he was thinking about her instead of business when the pirates sneaked up on them. If I hadn't insisted on pushing, Zach and the others might still be alive."

Richard pondered that. "Who would he have been thinking about if she hadn't been there?"

Jander gave him a sideways glance, silently conceding the point.

CHAPTER 16

The fugitives ate that day, after all. They walked only a short distance before discovering the carcass of a terrier-sized insectivore, which proved to be so stringy only Denny could chew it.

Chelsea scouted around and found another victim of the concussion, a six-limned arboreal herbivore knocked out of a tree along with a blast-harvested crop of pod-like blue berries the size of grapes. Now, at the dawn of the next day, they had a plentiful supply of meat and sugar-rich fruit. If Denny's calorie-scorching vigor was any indication, the local fauna and flora seemed to be quite nourishing to humans.

Denny built a fire on the shore of a deep stream, under the cover of a broad overhanging cliff that had sheltered them from the previous night's rain. The walls of the flood-cut cave showed layers of sandstone, limestone and breccia that told of seas lifted long ago by continental drift.

The terrain was becoming more broken as they moved beyond the foothills into ridges and gullies that showed evidence of glacial activity in eons past. The tall trees and leafy shrubs were giving way to creeping vines and smaller hardwoods mixed with conifer analogs. They followed the numerous game trails paralleling the fast-running streams that teemed with fishy creatures too quick to catch.

Denny felt quite at home here, having grown up in the Rockies, but he was alarmed more than once by the weird and sometimes aggressive creatures they encountered along the way.

His response to that was curing in the fire. In addition to providing heat for warmth and cooking, the deeper coals were tempering the tips of three saplings Denny had selected and trimmed with the tiny saw and knife blade of his utility tool. Two were long, slender shafts that would serve as javelins and the other was a shorter, thicker pole to use as a close-combat spear.

His encounter with the giant cat had taught him the wisdom of being better armed. And lessons learned from bear hunting as a kid in his native Colorado told him that if you throw your weapon at a bear, the bear had the weapon whether you hurt him with it or not. So, he created two to throw and a sturdier one to hold onto for defense.

"I wonder if Jandy is here yet," Chelsea mused. She was probably the only one in the universe who could call Steele that and survive.

"Prob'ly. Though how he's gonna get us out without a pitched battle is beyond me. The bastards almost caught us yesterday." The thought made the muscles stand out hard in his jaw as he turned the shafts hardening in the coals.

"Right-o, but they're even worse woodsmen than I am. They went right past us." She tested the meat with her second sight to ensure it was well cooked. "It's done. Odd that they went east to west, not following our tracks. Casting."

Denny sliced and served up the venison on a thick leaf, to which Chelsea added a side of berry pods. "They've got to have some people capable of reading a trail. Especially my prints—they look like dried-up lakes."

A squat, flat lizard with four legs and a neck frill of red feathers pattered around the corner into the shallow cave, spotted the two big creatures staring at him from the other side of the fire and quickly reversed course, scuttling stubby tail first with bared fangs and erect feathers until it reached the safety of the wall and scrabbled out of sight.

"Well, he was cute," Chelsea mused.

"Wanted nothing to do with us, I guess." Denny glanced back the way they had come. "I'll bet Jander's using one of our resident bloodhounds. Perfect country for it."

Chelsea nodded and gazed outward into the forest. Exhaustion was starting to show in her puffy eyes. "It is lovely. I wish we could enjoy it more."

They finished their meal in the silence of fatigue. Denny pulled his three crude weapons from the coals and set to scraping each fire-dried tip with the file blade of his multi-tool as Chelsea scattered and buried the embers and gathered up their leftovers into a sample bag.

Denny was starting to tie the extra food to his pack when Chelsea perked up and hissed him to silence. Her undamaged ears had detected the crackling of heavy footsteps the giant's hearing was too impaired to pick up. She put a finger to her lips, floated to treetop level and glided down their back trail.

Seconds later she was back. "We're being followed," she whispered. "One biped, rather dim by the looks, wearing what appears to be a uniform. Bloody buff scoundrel, though."

"Alone?" He let the load of provisions drop beside his improvised backpack, his brows knotting.

"And unarmed. Maybe we can get something out of him."

They left their supplies behind in the cave and followed their back trail to the shadow of a low-branching tree beside a small clearing. Denny twitched each of his javelins in his right hand to find their balance as they waited.

Before long, even he could hear something large and careless blundering toward them. The snapping of branches and the scuffing of leaves increased in volume, driving a few forest residents to escape through the clearing. Minutes later a blocky form bounded into the clearing, swinging his long, thick arms and muttering in his native dialect. The squat monster was wearing a filthy, sweat-stained maroon jumpsuit with no belts or pockets.

Denny's lips curled in a bitter snarl. His first sight of the enemy brought to his mind an instant comparison to the friends he had lost: the droll and easy-going Crawley; the cerebral and courageous Mançon; the solidly levelheaded Wize; and Whitney and Soames, who took on a responsibility far beyond their experience and paid the ultimate price. That they could be lost to the likes of the ignorant monster before him infected Denny with a rage he had never before known. The wave of adrenalin that rippled through him washed away all his fatigue and all his mercy.

He touched his wristpad. "Bangle, translate between Sabarian and the pirate language." He rose with his arm extended, gratified that he had directed Elga to upload the sibilant language from Angela.

"Hey, fatso!"

Meshzner snapped erect, his piggish eyes darting everywhere. "Where are you, little man?"

Denny laughed harshly. "I could be up your nose and you wouldn't find me 'til lunch."

Meshzner glowered in the direction he thought was true, and his voice rose to a bellow. "You killed my brother, little man! Come out and fight me!"

"You killed five of mine, and murdered thousands of innocents all over space. It's time you paid for it!"

Leaving his new weapons behind, Denny stepped around the tree and advanced bare-handed. "And I might leave a piece of you alive, to show your stinkin' bosses the kind of warriors you're dealin' with!"

Meshzner stopped dead at the sight of the titan, who topped him by a long arm's length. Now he grinned evilly. "Big words from such a skinny guy," he growled. "You're not worth the trouble of makin' you eat 'em."

"You just stand there thinkin' that while I knock your ugly head off!" Denny boomed in return.

To his surprise, the behemoth grinned mockingly and did just that. Denny strode to within reach, bared his teeth, and swing a terrific roundhouse right. The crash of fist meeting jaw was louder than any other sound in the forest.

Meshzner spun on his heels and fell heavily, his rock-hard mass shaking the ground. His forehead bounced off the turf and he stared down at it in astonishment.

Connors lashed out with his foot, levering the rotund Lievan onto his back. "What are you?" he roared. "You're too stupid to run a shithouse. Who do you work for?"

Meshzner struggled to lift his girth upright. He succeeded just in time to step into another smashing blow. This time he stayed down, shaking his head.

Denny, normally the mildest, most compassionate of men, had at long last reached his breaking point. "Traders," he gritted, livid with long-suppressed rage. "Merchants. Liners. Women and children. Thousands of them! And my friends, who saved our lives by flying into your guns. You'll pay for all of them, bastard. Get up!" He kicked the barrel-shaped body again, his voice rising to a roar. "On your feet, murderer, and see if you can take it!"

Meshzner rolled out of reach, scrabbled to his feet and lunged. Denny sidestepped around the lashing arms and chopped him in the beefy back, crushing the flesh and bruising the edge of his hand on thick bone. Meshzner stumbled forward and fell on his face again.

"Get up, bastard!" Denny roared.

The Lievan rose slowly, moved forward carefully. Suddenly he lunged again, read Denny's sidestep and slid into it, wrapping his long arms around the titan's waist. Gripping his own wrists, he *squeezed*.

Chelsea gasped and slid from her hiding place. She knew what had happened; her Denny had read the monster's earlier attacks as the norm. Now Meshzner had regained what little mind he had and was fighting with all the ability of one who used such skills for a living.

But Connors was far from out of it. He gritted his teeth against the pain and chopped down with both hands, hard on the neck. Meshzner grunted and loosened his grip. Denny chopped again, this time slamming his cupped hands over the Lievan's tiny ears. His opponent howled and backed away, clutching at his ringing head. Seeing the opening, Connors turned sideways, raised his leg flat against his chest and side-kicked with all his strength, straight into Meshzner's midriff.

With a tremendous explosion of pent-up breath

the monster spun backward, staggered and fell, striking the ground almost at Chelsea's feet. She skittered back as Denny thundered his challenge and closed to finalize the match.

Meshzner, feeling fear for the first time in his life, used his long arms to lever himself to his feet and cast about for a weapon. In a move made swifter by the lesser gravity, he reached out snatched Chelsea off her feet. Caught by surprise, she shrieked in agony as he crushed her to his chest.

The ogre showed his broad teeth in a wild sneer of triumph. "Back off, or I'll kill her!"

With a strangled wail of pain, the struggling ghost transformed and slipped through his arms. Stunned, she lost her concentration and solidified, stumbled a few steps and collapsed, gasping and clutching her savagely compressed ribs. Meshzner stared, dumbfounded at the sight.

He never saw the blow that killed him.

With a thunderous roar of rage, Kodiak leaped forward and swung with all the power of his arm and torso. Denny Connors was able to repeatedly lift more than a metric ton in normal exercise. Now he was furious, his gigantic body overflowing with adrenaline. No jaw, no neck, no skull, however thick or hard, could have survived that blow.

Meshzner never felt it. Nor did he feel himself fly through the air and land ten feet away, neither did he feel seven hundred pounds of tyranosapient berserker crash down on his corpse.

Chelsea gasped and forgot her own pain as her eyes widened to take in the sight.

Roaring with every blow, no longer quite human, Connors was methodically breaking every bone in Meshzner's body. The sound was horrible, the snarling, thundering giant and the snapping, crunching corpse blending in a vicious cacophony out of times long gone. Again and again Denny's cleaving hands rose and fell, spewing gore for yards in every direction, accompanied always by the crunch of bone and sinew and the grunts of a god gone mad. Again and again and again, and again. And again.

Enraged as he was, the titan still caught a movement from the corner of his eye. Schaus and Gazenhout, panting from their exertions, burst into the clearing and stopped short, frozen in shock. Kodiak, soaked in blood, growled and made to rise. With one mind, the pirates turned and ran.

Connors reached down and wrenched, snarling, and threw with all his power. The missile flew at least three hundred kilometers per hour, straight and true at the running Gazenhout. Meshzner's head caught the pirate square in the neck and he pitched forward in a wildly flailing spin. He crashed face first into the ground and skidded to a contorted stop.

Schaus did not see his companion fall. He was blind with fear, stumbling over bushes in his path as he blundered toward the safety of the trees.

Connors thundered his feral challenge and stormed after him, took nine gigantic strides and pitched himself through the air. Feet first, he crashed into the fleeing Schaus and caught him between his boots and a tree. Seven hundred pounds traveling at forty miles per hour ground to a halt and rebounded, the soles stopping three bloody centimeters from the bark. The thick tree shuddered and branches showered down from the impact.

Connors fell away, and the pirate folded at an impossible angle and sank to the ground, leaving the tree drenched with gore. Sternum, ribs and backbone were pulverized.

Still snarling, Connors sprinted over to Gazenhout. Satisfied with his aim, he spun and stared around him, massive hands opening and closing, searching for any other enemies who might dare to threaten his woman.

Woman...

Chelsea stood alone, wide-eyed and trembling, looking impossibly tiny in the center of the clearing.

Swaying, Denny came to his senses in a rush. Stunned by the abrupt transformation in his psyche, he stared at the carnage he had wrought. The Lievan, a bloody sack of jelly; Schaus, his chest no longer there; Gazenhout, his skull and neck crushed by Meshzner's head...

The full horror of his deeds struck him more savagely than Meshzner ever could have. Blinded, half-conscious, smeared with the alien blood and gore that were his to own, he sobbed and sagged to his knees.

He had no idea how long he slumped there, alone, inhuman. It took him a long time to become aware of the fragrant pressure enfolding his head.

Reluctantly, he opened his eyes. Chelsea held him with his head cradled against her breasts, weeping for them both.

CHAPTER 17

It was a peaceful dawn in the deep forest. The nocturnal animals sought their dens and nests and burrows as they always did, some still hungry, many content with full bellies.

Their daytime counterparts awoke to take their place in the food chain, each in their own way following the pattern of nature established by eons of evolution. Sustenance was available to be taken; hazards were known and could be avoided. Few were yet aware that the pattern was changing, that the products of other evolutionary designs were encroaching on their domain and would forever alter it. But for now, in this place, it was life as usual.

Jaws working on his latest bite, the little six-legged deer/horse/antelope swiveled his head through all points of the compass, scanning with wide eyes and long, twitching ears for anything that might prove a threat. Satisfied he was in the clear, he arched his front spine, rose up on his four hind legs and reached his long, slender snout upward to the higher branches of the bush that was his current meal.

Thirty meters away, a dark shadow detached

itself from the ground and took a half dozen gliding strides forward, skimming barely above the loam, sleek muscles rippling beneath the floreted black fur. Swift yet patient, soundless as a falling leaf, Raankhak was on the hunt.

Her prey (she could not know that Denny and Chelsea had chosen to call it a "dorse") tore a mouthful of leaves from the bush and tongued it to his molars while dropping back to all sixes. Instinct again made him scan his surroundings.

Cielo dropped her belly to the ground and froze, blending into the gloom of dawn like a rotting log.

The dorse looked upward into the bush, intent on finding his next mouthful. Cielo crept closer. Twenty meters.

The dorse reached for a leafy branch, closed its soft mouth around it and pulled. The branch bowed, then snapped back as the leaves stripped off. Cielo used the sound of the rebounding foliage to skim closer. Twelve meters.

From the direction opposite her approach came a huffing snort from another animal. The dorse spun his head in that direction, muscles tensed, all senses focused on the unknown sound, poised to leap away if it proved to be a threat.

Cielo wriggled her hips and sprang, reaching forty kilometers per hour in a few silent steps. The dorse sensed her rush and bolted, but far too late. The panther slammed into the smaller animal like a cannonball, long front claws digging into the forequarters and hind legs pounding the flanks. The dorse went down with a bleat of pain and terror, abruptly cut off as the cat twisted and clamped her teeth into his neck below the jaw.

The creature that had provided the distraction rushed in with a guttural snarl, sounding like a freight train to Cielo's sensitive ears. She twisted again to raise the dorse's head and shoulders.

Doppelwulf skidded to a stop in a shower of turf and lunged for the exposed spine. His powerful lupine jaws snapped down just behind the dorse's skull and shook violently, breaking the neck with a crackling pop. The animal spasmed once, twice, then shivered to the stillness of the final sleep.

The wolf released his death grip and backed away, snorting and shaking the blood from his snout before he returned to his human self and squatted beside the kill. "Well, that worked."

Cielo detached herself and rolled away, morphing to languid woman as she moved. "Not as satisfying as a solo kill, but it was easier." She stretched her sleek figure full length on her side and licked her lips, savoring the taste of blood.

Walter pulled the folding knife from his harness and snapped it open. "That's the difference between us. I'm a pack animal. I like the teamwork."

He splayed the dorse onto its back, gripped one hind leg by its three-toed hoof, sliced a long incision through the hide around the hip and dug the blade into the joint. "Besides, he got a quicker death this way than suffocating."

"True." She reached out a hand to ruffle the victim's soft pelt. "He is kind of cute."

"Oh, please. I'd rather be observer than butcher." Walter had run a pet shop in Hamburg prior to joining the Corps and was now a veterinary technician, and although he understood the rules of survival he still regretted its necessities. His knife sliced through the flesh surrounding the loosened joint and pulled the leg free, then started on the other shank.

Cielo watched him work, feeling the adrenalin drain from her system. "Me, too, but I come from a different line of work." Her background as a game warden, battling poachers, hungry tribesmen and even the army to protect the Sudanese preserves, had hardened her to violent death long ago. When recruited into the Corps she was missing an eye, two fingers and a lot of skin. The magic of transmutation restored her body but had done nothing to soften her feral soul.

Walter finished his work and laid the two legs side by side. "These are for the others, when Pavel calls." He eyed a trio of squirrel-shaped creatures staring hungrily down from a branch of a willow-like tree a few meters away. "Those poufy-tailed weasels are back."

"Well, let me set the table for them." Cielo rose to her knees and opened her own knife. Showing a touch far more decisive than Walter's, she sliced a vee from the amputations to another vee at the dorse's damaged neck, taking a double detour around the genitals behind the center limbs. Four more quick slices exposed the muscle of the four remaining legs. She wiped her knife on the pelt, returned it to her harness and started pulling the skin away from the carcass with her hands. "Breakfast is served."

Walter rocked back on his bare buttocks and removed his harness to keep it clean. He took a last look around with his human vision, far more acute to a canine's, then flowed into his wolf form. Trusting his animal metabolism to handle the raw meat, he sank his teeth into the crevice his knife had dug in the dorse's rump and tore out a huge mouthful.

Cielo, not bothering to protect her holster, resumed her leopard form, planted a paw on the genitals of the carcass and gnawed into a leg.

Both flinched when Richard Ford suddenly appeared a few meters away.

The teleporter took half a step back as he met the fierce glares of the huge predators, then raised his empty hands. "Easy, guys. The boss says you caught breakfast and sent me to pick some up." He looked askance at their blood-moistened fur and added, "Though I was thinkin' we might cook it first."

Seeing he was an ally and not a competitor, Cielo resumed her breakfast. Walter pointed with his dripping muzzle at the two butchered flanks, then went back to his own meal.

"Oh... kay." Richard skirted the primeval tableau and picked up a leg in each hand by the phalanges.

"Thanks, guys. We'll be ready to move in half an hour or so. Check you later."

He vanished. The wolf and the leopard never looked up.

THE TRIO OF SQUIRREL-TAILED SCAVENGERS came down from the tree as soon as Cielo and Walter had eaten their full and moved off to clean themselves. Their tiny bodies were hip deep in the offal even before five kits scrambled down to join them in the feast. Nothing was wasted in this forest.

<*"Are you decent?"*> Pavel's call was addressed to them both. The words, of course, were from Jander, speaking through the telepath with sense of humor intact.

Cielo rumbled deep in her throat and turned human. Unlike the strait-laced Walter, she was totally unself-conscious about her nudity. <*"We're digesting. The catch was really tasty. How was your breakfast?"*>

Pavel answered in his own words. <*"Lord Orion microwaved your gift by molecular acceleration. It was delicious."*>

Since they were no longer on board the ship, Pavel the Precise referred to Steele by his Corps title rather than as "Captain".

<*"Harmonia is rather subdued, however. Our dietary choices are difficult for her to stomach, as it were. Your victim may have been one whose mind she*>

touched.">

<*"Better she wasn't with us, then,"*> Walter, still in wolf form, put in. <*"We had ours tartare."*>

<*"So I heard."*>

They felt Pavel withdraw for a few seconds.

<*"Lord Orion would like you to separate. One of you should follow the trail as best you can while the other flanks at the same distance we are flanking you, but on the other side."*>

The Bavarian copied Cielo's flowing transformation, then rose up to squat on his heels sideways from her. <*"Good idea. I'd just as soon get away from the cat-stink, anyway."*> He used his fingers to wipe the remaining blood from around his mouth.

Cielo's lips curled in mock contempt. <*"Fine. I don't want to risk my neck with the way you blunder through the underbrush. They could hear you coming from half a kilometer."*>

<*"I'd better take the trail, your nose is useless for tracking."*>

The two comrades glared at each other, their scowls tempered by obvious good humor.

<*"From Lord Orion: I promised Alpha I would bonk your fuzzy heads together if you do not behave."*> Even quoting Steele, Pavel spurned contractions.

<*"Relax,"*> Cielo chuckled. <*"We're both paper-trained."*>

<*"Debatable. Harmonia shall be concentrating her perception on the fauna to our left and rear, while you two secure the right and center and I mentally*

take point ahead of you. Richard is launching his drone for an aerial view, so do not be alarmed if you perceive it.">

<"*Okay, we know what it looks like.*">
<"*Very good. We are ready to move out.*">
<"*Roger. Listening out.*">

Cielo converted, flicked her tail and was off. A moment later Walter snorted twice to clear his nostrils and again took up the trail, ears alert and nose questing the path.

CHAPTER 18

Thanks to the tracking talents of Doppelwulf the Corpsmen were making far better time than any other pursuing band, but they were dramatically outnumbered. The Ertainians were dropping random search parties all over the forest and were often too close for comfort.

Even more dangerous, the hundreds of ships crowded around the planet were sweeping the canopy with sensor probes. A few times Orion, warned by the detectors in his wristpad, was forced to gather his small team beneath a refraction shield of his own making to avoid detection.

The metamorphs were on their own.

Cielo crouched on her belly in the underbrush, a motionless shadow as her slitted amber eyes took in the tableau in the trampled clearing in front of her. The fur along her spine rose and she concentrated on an image of Steele, knowing he had a tracer on her mind.

Pavel was quick to respond. <*"Do you have something, Cielo?"*>

<*"Glad you called, man. I've got a big party right in front of me, pirates with guns."*>

<*"This is from Orion—hunters or trackers?"*>

<*"I don't know. I'm treeing until I find out."*>

Pavel sensed physical effort reflected in her mind, then he saw the ground far below through the panther's eyes.

She edged out onto a strong limb and stretched her neck to peer through the stippling leaves. Now knowing where to concentrate his telepathy, Pavel cut off the communication to search for the Ertainian minds.

<*"They are hunters, Cielo, and they are looking through the trees. Get out of there!"*>

<*"Too late—they're heading toward my tree. I'll climb higher."*>

Walter loped off the trail and circled in her direction. <*"How many?"*>

<*"At least twenty,"*> Pavel informed him. <*"Keep out of sight."*>

<*"They see me!"*>

Pavel sensed Cielo's violent effort, sensed her change. She had turned human in order to use her weapon. <*"Remain calm, woman, we are coming!"*>

Cielo ducked as a laser bolt flashed past her head, then leaned back out to snap off a double shot. The spheres gouged holes clear through a sapling and dropped a pirate. The Ertainians shouted and scattered, suddenly fearful as what they thought was a helpless target shot back.

Her effort was returned tenfold. The hunters spread out to surround the tree as she tried to keep the trunk between herself and the waving laser barrels.

Walter trotted up from the flank and crouched in a patch of bushes. He could see Cielo no more than ten meters up the tree and knew she was fatally trapped. In an instant the protective instincts of a pack leader took over. He scrambled to his feet and hurtled into the clearing, howling with all the feral fury he could muster.

The hunters shouted and screamed as the huge wolf tore into their midst, snapping inch-long canines and hurling his bulk full-speed into their smaller bodies. Walter closed strong jaws on a wrist, felt the hot blood on his tongue, the crunch of bone between his fangs. The hunter shrieked in pain and dropped his weapon, and Walter loosed him with a vicious snarl, knocked the next pirate sprawling with a whiplash charge and went for another.

Cielo took the respite of his attack to scramble lower, her pistol spitting deadly spheres of energy. She watched in horror as Walter took one laser bolt and then another, then she dropped her gun in the heat of savage frenzy and changed over. Walter fell to a third hit as she sprang, but he tore out a throat as he dropped.

The metapanther landed full on the back of one of the pirates. Her razor-sharp claws flashed in tandem with her ripping teeth and she bounded away, striking again before the shredded corpse had time to fall. Again her vicious claws swiped, nearly tearing a head off, then she felt a searing pain in her shoulder. She screamed in rage and spun toward another victim.

Suddenly she was no longer alone.

Richard cried out at the sight and snapped off a wild shot, missing her by the barest of margins and chipping the skull of a man beyond. His companion was far more effective. With the chilling calm of a professional, Pavel fired left and right, his icy grin growing with every hit. The Ukrainian crouched, feet wide set and gray eyes gleaming, and peppered the clearing with bodies.

And finally, Orion arrived. Carried by his personal sheath of force, he zipped through the treetops and came to an instant halt ten feet over the clearing, presenting himself as an inviting, if invulnerable, target. From his hands flashed two-dimensional slivers of mind-controlled lightning, guided through his first and middle fingers locked for accuracy.

Pirate after pirate blazed away at him, gaping in amazement as their lasers glanced off his shield, then felt the slicing touch of his fingers. In seconds the skirmish was over.

Pavel spun in a quick-stepping circle, questing with eyes and mind for any survivors. He raised one pistol and snapped off two shots that pierced the thick veil of leaves and dropped the last fleeing pirate. Rising to full height, guns up, he stood like a monument in the center of the clearing, proud satisfaction in every line of his frame.

Richard holstered his weapon and dashed toward Cielo, his heart pounding. She snarled and bristled, then recognized him and relaxed into his arms with a growl of pain. The fur on her shoulder was singed around the laser wound that pierced the bone.

Steele dropped to the ground and rushed to the whining werewolf. He fell to his knees and examined the three wounds, covering them with forcefields of reduced-speed molecules to cool and protect them until Sharon arrived, puffing from her run.

The biologist took a quick look and yanked off her pack to get at her medical kit. "Walter, can you change over? I can check you better in human form."

The wolf whined and clouded his eyes. With supreme effort, he ignored the pain and shock and concentrated his waning energies toward that special part of his mind. He became human, lying on his side in a drying smear of blood.

Sharon reached out and rolled him onto his back, then gasped in astonishment. "He's not hurt!"

Jander rocked back on his heels, stunned. "You know he was hurt!"

Walter sat up, running his hands over shoulder, waist and hip. "Mein Gott in Himmel!—here, here, here I was shot! But they're gone!"

Richard howled from across the clearing, "Cielo's all right! She was hit in the back, but she's okay!"

Cielo twisted and sent her smoldering amber eyes over her shoulder, showing smooth, unblemished dark skin.

Steele overbalanced backward and thumped to his butt on the ground. "Well, I'll be damned!" He gathered his feet and picked himself up, then meandered unseeing around the sprawled bodies covering the clearing.

The others watched silently as he paced, depending on his brilliant mind to discover the solution. Abruptly he spun and pointed, crouching like a fencer to drive his point home. "Lycanthropy!"

Walter looked confused. "Well, ja…"

Jander paced toward them, pointing arm shaking with excitement. "Walter, you're familiar with the legends concerning werewolves, aren't you?"

The Bavarian nodded ruefully. "My father used to frighten me with them when I was a child."

"How can a werewolf be killed?"

His eyes lit up. "Only by noble metal. Ordinary weapons cannot harm him."

"And I'm betting not even silver would work—unless the foreign matter remained in the body. These lasers leave nothing material behind to gum up the works."

He paced again, forming his theory in his mind. "Metamorphism," he continued slowly, "is a finite transmutation, limited to one form. There can be no changes not fitting the pattern. So, when you switch from one form to the other, the change is exact in every way. Your human form was not hurt, so it would not be injured when you changed back to it."

Jander stopped his pacing and frowned. "Question

is, have your wolf wounds been written into the blueprint?"

"Well, let's find out." Walter rolled onto his knees, steeled his nerves, and changed. He huffed in a breath, took a few tentative steps, then capered like a pup, tail wagging furiously. "Yip, yaroo!"

Jander laughed heartily. "I agree. How about you, Cielo?"

"She's all right!" Richard answered him. "She's purring!" He pulled the panther to him, burying his nose in her fur. Cielo moaned her pleasure and butted her head against his chin.

Jander beamed like a new father, arms crossed over his chest. "Well, well."

"Wait a minute." Sharon, the zoologist well-tempered by her education, thought on. "What about undigested meals... oh, okay. Enzymes would permeate the stomach contents and integrate the foreign matter with the consumer's metabolism. As a theory goes, I'd have to agree with you."

"Works for me." Jander extended both hands and helped Walter and Sharon to their feet as Richard rose with the nude Cielo firmly and naturally in his arms.

Steele braced his legs and clapped his hands together. "Well! Back to work. Walter, get back on the trail. Cielo, find your weapon and check these guys' back trail, check for pursuit. Richard, hop around on either side, see if this commotion drew anybody else. Sharon, see what the animals have to say. Let's go, people, get back in the groove! Pavel, let's have a look at these guns."

The variants scattered. Ford vanished, and the metamorphs dashed away, weakened a bit by shock and blood loss but glorying in their health.

Sharon, her training making her oblivious to the carnage, sat down with her backpack to a tree and closed her eyes, opening her mind to the impulses of the forest creatures. Pavel picked up a rifle and strode toward Jander, then slowed to a halt, intrigued. Steele moved to meet him.

"It is a laser, my lord, more powerful than anything we have developed. The trigger is a button parallel to the barrel rather than inset, I presume because they have but two knuckles in their six fingers to our three in five."

He raised the weapon to his shoulder, feeling the unfamiliar pressure of the Ertainian-designed stock on his human shoulder, aimed at a pseudo-pine cone and pushed the trigger. Nothing happened, and he lowered the weapon and looked again. "Ah, a double trigger, one on each side of the weapon. And here, on the underside, a three-way toggle switch at right angles to the barrel. I suspect the center position is a safety mechanism and the left and right positions select the trigger button."

"Which would imply they're left or right-handed, like us," Jander said.

Pavel pushed the toggle to the right, took aim and tried again. He was rewarded with a sizzling pop and a flash of red. The half-second bolt went high and to the right.

"Ouf!" How does one get recoil from a flashlight?"

He shouldered again and aimed more deliberately through the elaborate two-point laser sight, and this time hit the cone dead center.

Jander shooed away a scavenger, a bony ball of silky tan fur balanced on six prehensile appendages, and pulled the weapon from the stiffening object of its attention. He cleaned it off, sighted down the thick barrel through its laser sight and popped off a cone of his own. "It's a coherent wavelength of near-solid light. The visible is probably heterodyned for convenience, like the red coloration in the *Angel*'s weapons."

He crouched and pulled a small tool kit out of his pack. "The rear sight focuses a non-solid laser point through a range-finding circle at the business end. Very neat."

Pavel was briskly baring the tree of cones. "I like it. A weapon should have a kick—it makes you feel a part of it. This would not have the range of our guns, but it is more satisfying to use. And the sights are superb—we should reverse engineer them for our pulse machine rifles. That would take greater advantage of their longer range."

He swung his aim to a flowering tree a hundred meters away and fired again. A single blossom fluttered intact to the ground, cut off at the millimeter-thick stem.

Jander gave up trying to find a tool to unpin the

fasteners on the rifle and built his own from thin air. He removed the casing from stock to barrel and examined its innards, storing the information in his eidetic memory.

"Here." He pointed. "This provides the visible. Battery here in the stock, like ours, but it's voltaic, not rechargeable. You can see these guys are loaded down with disposables. They're probably dropping them all over the place while we're keeping ours. Okay, stimulation is here, here's the laser bulb, excitation here ahead of the trigger, focusing lens forward of that, here."

He waved a finger over the bulb. "Still hot, maybe it's always hot. That's why Walter's wounds were partially cauterized, though the deepest one still bled."

The Ukrainian followed his gaze. Pavel was no engineer, but he was well trained in the technology of modern weapons. A professional knows his tools. "This is something we lack, this insulated component. What is it?"

"You got me. Something to do with the stimulation, I think, that gives it the greater power without too much weight. That's the only way it could work without a supercapacitor." He discarded the gutted weapon and rose to search for another. "We'll take several with us for study."

"And for use." Pavel made a lightning move and popped three cones in less than a second.

Jander grinned and walked over to where Sharon

was sitting. A gecko-like lizard she knew was harmless crouched on her shoulder, long tongue flicking out to seize the mosquito-sized gnats that constantly dogged them. "Got anything?"

"Sure do. I found a huge predator who used to think of himself as king of the forest until he ran into a little green stick. Was Chelsea wearing green?"

"Wouldn't surprise me. Her favorite green jumpsuit would be comfortable under a pressure suit."

"It was Chelsea, then. This monster—mostly feline, but built like a bear—wanted Denny for supper. Chelsea ran him around in circles, punching him in the nose and not letting him get in any licks. She even kicked him in the genitals, which pretty much ended the fight, as you might imagine. Anyway, he's been avoiding every other biped he's seen like the plague."

"I don't blame him," he chuckled. "I've watched her move in spectral form—she's quick as a thought."

Richard popped up in front of them. "Coast is clear, boss."

"Good. Grab one of these rifles and practice a bit—if Pavel has left you any targets."

He looked around, unmoved by the bloody scattering of pirates. More small scavengers were already inching toward them from the underbrush, and bugs were starting to swarm. "Personally, I'm ready to get out of this graveyard."

CHAPTER 19

Denny lay on his back in the twilight, feeling Chelsea curled inside his arm with her head on his chest. They spoke little throughout the day, both overwhelmed with horror from the morning's fight. They simply pressed on after Denny had cleaned himself up in the stream and collected the weapons of his victims.

Chelsea stirred and snuggled closer, favoring her bruised ribs. Her firm if tiny muscles had protected her from any great harm. They rested now, neither able to sleep though they nestled in a luxurious bed of thick, soft moss that abounded in the shade of a richly scented spruce-like grove.

A cleared spot nearby held a crackling fire shrouded by the dense canopy above. The nights were turning cooler as they made their way toward the mountains to the north.

The titan sighed and finally broke the silence. "You know, honey, I didn't bust that guy up just because he was the enemy."

She smiled soberly and twisted her delicate fingers in the close-packed chest hair that peeked through his ruined shirt. "I rather didn't think so."

"I wasn't planning to kill him. I wanted to leave him alive to answer some questions. But when he used his strength against you…" She looked up and moved her fingers to his lips, but he shook her off and continued. "I lost it because he was doing just the thing that scares me the most, and that's hurting you."

"I know you wouldn't, Denny." Her delicate hand curled around his corded neck and brushed the skin beneath his ear.

"That's not the point," he sighed. "I'd never want to, but I might anyway. I can't turn my power on and off like the rest of you can. It's with me all the time. When I crushed him, I was taking out on him all my own fears and self-doubts. I…" He stumbled, at a loss.

Chelsea raised herself on an elbow and ran the back of her hand over the lengthening stubble on his cheek. "Don't you understand, we all feel that same way? Our powers are frightening, to ourselves as well as to others. What if something happens, some unconscious thought cuts in, whilst I'm taking a bit of a shortcut through you as I sometimes do? I could kill us both, and now we know I could blow the belly out of the *Angel* besides. And suppose Jander reaches for Vickie's hand and cuts it off? We all live with that fear. For all our knowledge, we still haven't much control over the human mind. One distracted thought or lapse in concentration, and any one of us could kill by sheer accident. You're not alone, Denny."

He digested that in silence. "I never thought of it that way," he said finally.

"Well, it's high time you did." She pushed against him in a playful attempt to cheer him up. "You're a big, bloody bruiser, and that's for sure, but you're just about the nicest bloke I've ever known. Not many chaps would do what you did today, for little me."

He smiled and caught her hand. "Little you, taking on a ton of mean pussycat. I hit that mother as hard as I could when I jumped from the tree and he didn't even blink." He sighed and squeezed his eyes shut. "I guess I proved today what you did then, though."

"And what's that?"

"That, uh... well, you know." He grinned crookedly.

She snorted and became transparent. He felt her weight float off, and saw her hair flip up, down and away to nothing. He sat up in alarm. "Where are you?"

The ghostly voice seemed to come from the center of his chest. "I'm a part of you..."

CAPTAIN Z'ZSCHOU OF THE *Rannz* stared bleakly at the forward monitor that displayed a panorama of the planet's night-darkened surface. Somewhere deep in the untamed forest, Meshzner's team had vanished without a trace. The dim-witted troll and his Ertainian escorts had ceased their periodic communication and all attempts to reach them or trace their rapid progress had been fruitless.

In another incident, a patrol of ground troops from two landing craft were slain to a man by a combination of military and feral force that had appeared and disappeared with no sign of their passage other than a minor spattering of alien blood.

From that skirmish site weapons had been taken, meaning their elusive quarry was even more dangerous now. Worse, the battle location and Meshzner's last known position were far enough apart to suggest separate enemies, the original two plus a number of aggressive natives that had ambushed the search party with unknown weapons. It was inconceivable that the pair from the gem-ship had been reinforced by their own kind through the fleet's deep line-of-sight blockade, so even though no signs of civilization had been detected, there must be a hostile force of planetary origin.

Or not?

The Captain tightened his thin lips. It was clear to him that the gem-ship possessed technologies far beyond the level Ertain had developed or even acquired through its commerce raiding. During the first fleet encounter, his squadron was placed on the very fringe of the sphere that englobed the gem-ship as punishment for not being able to capture it on first contact, and he had a distant yet terrifying view of the battle.

But even stationed so far away, he lost two of his ships—one was exploded from the inside out by a single massive fireball from an energy sphere, and the other was sliced in half by a rod of force that disrupted the inertia compensators and crushed it from bow to stern under its own drive.

Nonetheless, as one of the more intact squadrons remaining after the one-sided debacle, he was ordered to return to the scene and eliminate the debris, and had been humiliated by a tiny gunship that cost him the rest of his squadron and damaged his own ship. Now, having saved face and probably his life by running down the unarmed shuttlecraft, he was again buried deep within the combined fleet as his crew worked to repair the damage. With battle casualties and the loss of the three on the surface, he was down to thirty-four effectives in his crew.

He pulled his sleep-deprived mind back to his previous line of thought. The fact was, they knew very little about the stranger and his technology. But Z'zschou had seen the instant, near-magical change of positions the gem-ship had pulled off, and he knew without doubt the enemy had tricks enough to elude their cordon and slip a landing party past them...

"Admiralty call coming in, Captain!" his com officer called.

Z'zschou felt a chill. What now? "Put it through." He straightened his sweat-stained maroon tunic as best he could and squared his narrow shoulders as the surface view flickered off, to be replaced by the stern visage of his superior. The Admiral was looking down at his console and maintained a peevish silence for long seconds.

Z'zschou felt compelled to break the impasse. "Greetings, Excellency. Repairs to the *Rannz* are progressing and we should be fully operational in three days."

The Admiral pointedly waited another few seconds, then fixed the Captain with an iron stare. "Your search squad failed."

Z'zschou's jaw quivered but he tried to hold his voice steady. "They appear to have been ambushed, Excellency. At the time I was able to spare only three, and they were not up to the task." He paused, searching his exhausted mind for a positive note. "I was able to retrieve their landing craft."

The Admiral's eyes flashed. "You lost the fugitives!" he snapped. "You muddied the trail! You gave them warning that they were being pursued! You showed them who we are and what we want, and you let them go!"

He leaned his face within a few centimeters of the pickup, making himself huge in the monitor. "Your failure could not be more absolute! If you hadn't led us to that planet your life would already be forfeit!"

The Admiral leaned back, his glare undiminished. "When your repairs are complete you will proceed immediately under the escort of Squadron 8-03 to Ertain for evaluation. That is all." The monitor flashed to blank. The sensors officer hastily replaced the neutral gray with a view of their immediate volume of space. The rest of the Bridge crew was rigidly silent.

Z'zschou stared at the star-sparkled screen, which displayed the third squadron of Eighth Fleet retroing in to surround him. Its low number in the table of operations told him its commander was high in the Admiral's favor and would be unmerciful in his guardianship. His First Officer turned to him with an unreadable expression and waited for orders.

The Captain made a show of relaxing into his command chair, indicating to his subordinates that he was far from ready to give up. His situation was grim without question, but he still had hope. The Admiral said evaluation, not trial. He determined to work on his analysis of the enemy in the hope that he could bring forth some observation the high command might have overlooked.

Meanwhile, his crew, who were equally culpable under Ertain's brutal military law, could be relied upon to stretch the repairs as long as possible.

He oddly found himself hoping the mysterious enemy would find a way to surprise them yet again. He was not particular as to where his life-saving help would come from.

DENNY DOZED WITH CHELSEA NESTLED against his left side, sound asleep. Exhaustion, coupled with the luxurious moss bed, made him far more relaxed than he should have been on watch. They were both used enough to the constant bug traffic that the light touches of tiny feet were no longer noticed.

He awoke with a start to a different sensation. His eyes snapped open to the utter darkness of a cloudy night in the deep woods. The small fire pit they had cleared in the moss field had died down to glowing coals, making vision next to impossible. Denny stared upward and strained his damaged ears to locate the soft rustling that had awakened him.

Chelsea stirred beside him, and her soft grunt and moan warmed his chest. Her leg kicked with a light spasm.

Then Denny felt it. Something sharp pierced his calf just above his left boot, and an icy sensation spread from the contact.

Venom!

He kicked out with his left foot but was met with no resistance, just the squeak of a small animal scurrying away.

"Chelsea!" He nudged her shoulder, harder than he meant to.

"Oof. What the bloody—ow!" Something nipped through the jumpsuit covering her calf.

"Phase out! We're under attack!" Denny jerked his left arm from around her and scrambled to his feet. Squeaks and squeals by the dozen came up from the moss.

Chelsea felt something brush against her hand as she triggered her phantom form. With it came her psychic sight that needed no light, and she stared around her in horror.

The creatures were the size and shape of squirrels, with puffed tails but with much sleeker fur. The jaws were longer and thicker, with sharp incisors and long double canines far forward in their gaping mouths. Saliva dripped from their fangs as they encircled their prey, ebbing and advancing like a malevolent tide. Clearly, they could see in the near total darkness.

She felt the numbness in her calf despite her spectrality. "Denny, they're all around us!"

"I know that! I need light!" He groped around him for his spear. "Where's my stick?"

Chelsea located the spear for him, turned it spectral with her touch and released it to rematerialize close to his searching hands. "I'll stoke the fire!"

"Do it fast!" He found the spear, gripped it by the blunt end and scythed it through the moss. Most of the little hunters either ducked under or leaped over the flailing stick, but a few were knocked flying, stunned enough to be out of the fight.

Chelsea flitted over to their small woodpile and picked up a handful of kindling. She had to turn solid to stir the embers and blow life into the weak flames. That left her vulnerable to attack, forcing her to snatch a larger stick from the pile to defend herself. With her other hand she fed in more twigs, then larger sticks.

Denny saw the growing fire and backed toward it, sweeping the spear low around him. Stumbling from the numbness in his ankle, he did his best to defend a circle around the fire as Chelsea snatched up more substantial fuel and dropped it on the growing blaze.

As the fire brightened the little beasts gave ground, until they formed a chittering circle just out of reach of Denny's slashing spear. Denny drove them back enough to retrieve his javelins and his pack. He picked up one of the laser rifles he had confiscated, but discarded the idea of trying to use an unknown weapon and exchanged it for his spear. The cooked meat the couple had counted on for breakfast was gone, with only shreds of plastic sample bag to show it ever existed.

Gasping from their exertions, Denny and Chelsea sat back to back beside the fire, staring at the crowded ring of glowing eyes still uncomfortably close. Chelsea's first words were typically British: "Well, that was engaging."

"Are you all right?" Denny twirled his spear in the moss to clean off the toxic saliva.

"Well, let's see." She clicked on her psychic sight and examined her two bite wounds. "There's bruising about the toothmarks, but I don't see any swelling, or necrosis. I'm concerned about bacterial infection— these little gremlins haven't brushed in a while. We've been lucky so far with that, but this is the first time anything carnivorous has gotten to us. We should boil water and clean the wounds as best we can. Oh, let me check you out."

Without turning around, Denny crossed his left

leg over his right and pulled the ankle above his knee. Chelsea twisted to focus her fixed-reference clairvoyance on the damage. "It's worse than mine, but still not bad. Their little jaws must be pretty strong. The blood is clotting, so it appears the venom has no anticoagulant element. How does it feel?"

"Pretty numb, but it's starting to tingle. My metabolism heals quicker than most, so I'd guess the anesthetic is temporary. I'd hate to think what a dozen bites would do, though." He pulled over the pack and opened a compartment. "They left our water supply, so we're good there. But I'll have to take the purifier apart to get to the reservoir. That's the only thing we've got to use as a teapot."

"Och. Cruel of you to put it that way. I could use a spot right now." She added more fuel to the fire.

Denny got to work with his tools, keeping one eye on the gremlins. "They're thinning out. Looks like they're giving up. But from now on we're going to have to keep the fire going at night. That limits our choice of campgrounds, though. We'll need to..." He realized he was rambling.

Chelsea kept adding wood to the fire. "Earl Gray would be nice. Some people prefer a touch of lime with it, but I'm much more a puritan." She added more wood, one stick at a time. "But Earl Gray is rather strong, don't you know, so considering the time of night we're under perhaps a better choice would be something like..."

"Chelsea, stop!" Denny set down his tools and

grabbed the stick she was about to add to the scorching blaze. "The anesthetic has reached our brains. We're not thinking straight."

She cocked her head, her face expressionless. "Um...what?" She reached to the woodpile for another stick.

He took her by the shoulders and turned her toward him. "Look at me!"

She gazed up at him with vacant eyes and a slack-mouthed smile. "Oh, hello, Denny...." Her voice was starting to slur.

He shook her as gently as he could, fighting the buzz of numbness that scattered his thoughts. "Shake it off, girl,' he said urgently. "Think! Focus!"

"Aaahh...oh." She closed her eyes and shook her head, a bit of drool escaping from the corner of her mouth. She stared at the ground between them for a moment, then shook her head again. "We need to bottle that, mate."

He chuckled. "I'm with you. But for now, let's keep busy until it wears off. If we go down, those little guys will eat us alive."

"Oh, all right then. I'll make up the bed." She pulled away and started to pat down the moss.

Denny grinned and let her go for the moment. His far greater mass and stronger metabolism spared him the worst of the venom's effects, but he resigned himself to spending the next few hours keeping his loopy girlfriend from passing out.

WALTER AND PAVEL STARTED THEIR duty on the second watch, the wolf closer to the trail. Jander returned from his watch post and stretched out some distance from his sleeping comrades, Sharon, curled up in a neoprene blanket beneath a tree, and Richard, tucked away shirtless on top of his blanket with no regard for the coolness of the air or the bugs in his mattress of fragrant moss. So far, the traffic of four- to twelve-legged insects had not shown much of a taste for Gaean blood.

Cielo padded in from her post and located the teleporter with her keen cat's eyes. She glided over to him and used a claw to open the hook and loop of her weapons harness and let it drop to the ground. As silently as only a leopard could, she stretched out beside him, preening her back against his burly body.

He awoke with a start and rolled over, then discovered his companion. He grunted a greeting and wrapped his arm around her, stroking the short fur of her belly. She snuggled closer and began to purr like a contented chainsaw.

Richard ran his hands over her sleek coat, sighing as he rubbed his body against her back. He watched her claws slide out and retract in gentle rhythm, in time with her purrs of feline bliss. His breath came faster as he pressed himself against her, letting her know he wanted her.

He heard her moan again as her form moved under

his hands. In seconds he found himself caressing the supple skin of a beautiful and loving woman.

"I learned today that you cared for me," she whispered huskily, "and not just my human body. I know now that you love me in my feral form, as well. That is important to me, for I am both." She guided his hands over her, quivering at his touch.

"Yes, I need you," he breathed, "any way you want. All of you." He rolled her toward him and chuckled hoarsely. "And funny, I don't feel a bit like a pervert."

She gasped a tremulous laugh and twisted to face him. He met her open mouth with his, stroking her smooth skin with questing hands, then stronger and more urgent...

Jander smiled and got the hell out of their minds— he was no pervert, either. *Just checking, Vickie.* With any luck at all, they could come out of this with a lot of happy people.

VICTORIA STEELE WAS NOT THEN thinking of romance. Kurino called her away from the couch in her office down the corridor with her soft voice alive with excitement. Vickie glided onto the Bridge and looked around as Angela announced her. Mealla O'Hearne, an Irish former police officer with vivid coppery hair, bounced out of the command chair and resumed her armaments station. Vickie rested her hand on the back of the vacated chair. "What is it, Kitsune-san?"

"Look, Alpha-sama, see what we have found." Yukio, off-duty but still at work, pointed to the forward screen. Vickie pored over the picture, narrowing her eyes to find the distinction of this particular ship among hundreds. Arc lights illuminated several space-suited forms working inside a set of opened panels in the ship's retro ring while another group wrestled with a massive replacement engine floating nearby.

Yukio raised the magnification to pinpoint the cause of the damage, a straight-line series of punctures creasing the belly of the ship like holes in a belt. "We noticed her because communications detected a long-range transmission to her, then another group of ships broke formation to surround her. Perhaps for repair assistance?"

Vickie's jaw tautened. "Scatter to the Bridge," she ordered, and Angela fired the command to Nwoye Lam's quarters.

"That's the *Rannz* we heard about, isn't it, Yukio? I can see the damage from the Banshee fire."

"It is, Milady. What will we do?" The Japanese glanced around as Lam entered, shirt unbuttoned and stifling a yawn. His relief skimmed out of the helm chair and took her post at the backup station facing the bulkhead beside his console, watching her monitor for every move her gifted mentor made.

"First, I want to get a better look. Scatter, see how close you can get us to that ship." Lam nodded and settled into his chair. Vickie slipped into the command chair, never taking her eyes off the target. She pondered in silence, then shook her head. "I'd like to, Kitsune, but Lord Orion ordered that we take no offensive action until he gives the word. We have to let them go."

The ghost settled her unblinking eyes on her superior. "We have giri, Alpha-sama."

Vickie understood the Japanese word. They had a manifest obligation to exact revenge.

She narrowed her eyes as she considered options. "You're right, Yukio. We may never get another meaningful opportunity. Angela, call Tenome to the Bridge level teleporter." She tapped a button on the arm of the chair. "Armory. Prepare a two-kiloton package bomb and deliver it to the 'porter on Bridge level." The speaker in the command console murmured acknowledgement.

"Twelve thousand kilometers, Lady Alpha," Lam reported. The intensity in his deep black eyes, the sharper clip in his Nigerian accent, displayed his own grim resolve. Freddie Soames had been a close friend and drinking buddy. "It's too crowded in here to get any closer."

"Very good, Nwoye, hold us steady." Vickie rose and left the Bridge for the teleportation room halfway around the circular corridor surrounding the command center. Arai Osamu, Corpsman Tenome, was already there.

"Osamu, take a look in that direction." She pointed to a spot on the deck just below the bulkhead.

Arai clicked on his second sight, squinted in concentration to the limits of his range, then frowned and nodded sharply. He, too, was Japanese; he needed no further instruction. His hands flashed over the keys of his console, locating the *Rannz* through sensor data and calculating angle and distance.

When he had it zeroed in, he turned to a small freezer and pulled out a cube of dry ice, which immediately started to steam. He set the cube in the center of the small 'porter platform and returned to his console, then triggered the jump. With his clairvoyance he watched as the cube materialized a dozen centimeters off the deck in a back corner of the work area, behind and out of sight of the repair crew. It dropped through the artificial gravity and smashed in a puff of vacuum-frozen carbon dioxide.

Osamu adjusted his controls to compensate for the vertical error and locked them in. Angela would do the rest; no matter how much either ship pitched, the target would remain constant. "Ready."

"Just in time." Vickie turned to watch as two technicians wheeled the small oblong bomb from the elevator and wrestled it toward the platform. She took it away from them and floated it the rest of the way with her telekinesis.

Osamu again shot power through his controls and set the bomb flat onto the deck of the distant ship. "Set to go, Milady."

"Thank you." She returned to the Bridge through the front hatch next to the armaments station and waited as the fully informed O'Hearne set the tachyon impulse trigger. In short order the redhead stepped back and nodded, teeth bared in what was not quite a smile. Vickie, well aware of her commander's orders and assuming full responsibility for breaking them, reached for the board.

"Alpha."

She looked behind her to the main hatch. A brown-haired woman dressed in black took a tentative step forward. A glance at Yukio's deadpan expression told her who issued the summons. Vickie smiled sober encouragement and stepped away from the console.

The woman slipped forward, staring red-eyed but unblinking at the monitor. The silence of the Bridge was almost painful as she moved without hesitation to the armaments station. Slowly, savoring every second, she found the command key, then returned her glare to the screen, placed her left ring finger on the key, and pressed it in.

The monitor caught a small, almost insignificant flash from inside the retro ring of the *Rannz*, then the bomb exploded with an instant but blinding blue-white flame. The massive spark imploded the nucleonic fuel generators behind the retro ring.

The air within the ship flared, spreading the inferno throughout the ship. The cruiser bulged as the tensile strength of the nanosteel hull tried to contain the explosion, then the hull released, violently tearing the ship to incandescent fragments that hurtled outward in all directions. The surrounding squadron staggered under the white-hot debris and hastily powered away, leaving behind nothing but a cooling field of dissipating gasses.

Thus Ann Whitney put an end to her husband's killers.

CHAPTER 20

Chelsea recovered from her giggle trip from gremlin bites in half a day. While she regained her senses, Denny nailed a dorse with a javelin and harvested both the meat and the hide. Thanks to his backwoods training, Chelsea was now wearing an odorous stone-washed vest of soft skin with the fur side in to warm her through the increasingly cool nights.

Through the next day they worked their way through the forested uplands and climbed into the higher altitudes, leaving gremlin territory behind. The occasional cold showers accompanied by chilling winds added to the misery of their trek through terrain that became more rugged with each passing mile. Their progress was now impeded by ravines and ridges, dense underbrush and swiftly cascading streams.

And pirates.

Chelsea wafted through the trees still damp from a sudden deluge that had the benefit of obscuring their tracks and slipped into Denny's hiding place. "They're all over the place," the ghost reported. "They seemed to have learnt we're heading for higher ground. I rather doubt we can dodge them all."

Denny glanced up from where he was studying one of the lasers on the rough stump next to the log he was straddling. The cooler air was not biting enough to penetrate his dense skin. "Did you find us a good fort?"

She pointed. "That way about eighty kilometers, and up a thousand meters or thereabouts, I saw a plateau with a rockfall in the middle—actually, a gaggle of rock needles that eroded more slowly than the surrounding rock and eventually collapsed. It's a good place to make a stand—nice field of fire, isolated. It has a spring, too." She sat on a wet rock and stretched her fatigue-stiffened legs. "But we'll have to contest it. There's an entire pride of smileys in residence."

"Sweet." He frowned. "These guns we took from those two pirates are okay, but they cauterize the wound when they hit. I'd rather have a cannon for those monsters."

"You have me." She cocked her head and smiled pertly.

He grinned back and nodded emphatically. It had taken only one demonstration to convince him of how insuperable his little girlfriend was. He was certain that in head to head battle against the power of a living phantom, not even Orion could stand. "Okay. When we're ready you can scare them off. But we'll leave them alone for now, so the pirates won't occupy the spot." He considered that problem. "We should get through okay, if we keep our eyes peeled. We're surrounded, you say?"

She nodded "Scores of them, possibly hundreds—I've no doubt I've missed some. But there seem to be relatively few of those ogres, one in fifty perhaps."

"That's plenty." He finished putting the laser back together and returned his tools to his battered pack. "Lots of possibilities in these things, if I can find the time to operate on them. Well, let's go." He grunted to his feet, scanning the surrounding forest, seeing nothing he had not become accustomed to. "When was the last time we had a decent night's sleep?"

"The day before we first met." Her eyes gleamed with not-so-hidden meaning. He grinned and stroked her matted hair.

PAVEL LET OUT HIS BREATH WITH a whoosh and glanced at the larger man walking the trail in front of him. "Still nothing, sir. We should be close enough to locate them, but there are too many pirates in the area for me to discern even variant targets. And Denver and Chelsea have enough else on their minds to make contact difficult." He resumed his mental scan of their more immediate surroundings.

"Don't feel bad. I can't find them, either—and they're the only ones in the forest I can detect." Steele pursed his lips and brushed aside a branch over the game trail they followed. A scratch left by

Walter's claws every dozen meters or so led them on. "I never thought of my power as directional, but then I've always had an idea where the target mind was. I guess every sense has to be focused..."

They were single file on a game trail. Their pace was slower because the rains obscured the trail almost beyond even Doppelwulf's detection. They were forced to abandon their parallel tracking as the surrounding undergrowth became much denser. Pavel was at Jander's left shoulder. Richard, whose drone had fallen victim to a four-winged flying lizard that thought it looked edible, was ahead on point. Sharon followed them, keeping a mental eye on their back trail.

Far ahead of them, to the north, sounded a low, haunting howl, starting on a rising note and held for several seconds on a slowly decreasing scale—the assembly cry of the wolf.

"Link with him, Pavel. What is it?"

The werewolf's mind was clouded with horror. <*"I believe I have now seen a Lievan—in pieces."*> He displayed a mental picture of Meshzner, foggy with his emotions. The wolf's eyes saw no red or green colors, but the carnage was nonetheless plain to see. The reek of putrefaction and the motion of foraging insects were emphatically graphic.

"We'll be right there. Come on, people." Pavel passed the message and the four humans moved forward; Cielo glided toward them from her flanking position.

They burst into the clearing and stopped cold. "Holy mother of pearl," Sharon muttered.

Walter stood erect, unmindful of his nakedness, staring at the mutilated corpse. "From the spoor, I know that Denny did this terrible thing."

"Denny couldn't..." Jander swallowed and turned away. He turned right into the sight of another body, impossibly folded in half with broken bones already bared of flesh piled under a blood-darkened tree.

Cielo shouted from the edge of the clearing, waving a red-streaked, bug-covered round object at the end of her arm. "Here's his head!"

Richard was stunned by her composure. He was suddenly struck by what it was going to be like to be in love with a predatory cat.

Jander shook his head as he approached the scavenger-ravaged Lievan. "I can't imagine what could drive him to such a thing. I'm all in favor of wiping these pirates out of business, but this I can't understand. This guy was killed a dozen times." The unforgettable stench of rotting, bug-infested gore, blood and feces drove him back.

The icy Ukrainian, who everyone would have sworn did not have a romantic cell in his body, broke the silence. "Tell me, my lord, how would you react if someone threatened your Victoria?"

Jander's eyes hardened at the thought. "You're right, Pavel, I would have turned him into hamburger. That must be it."

"And if I may be allowed to speak as a professional,

I can tell you that only when combat is considered on such a personal level can it be understood—and justified." He left the others to their thoughts and circled around to examine the smaller bodies. "Do you also notice that none of them have weapons? It is safe to say that our comrades are now armed."

Jander grunted, "A good thing, too. They're walking into a nest of fire ants."

Walter added, "I found a couple of backpacks a while back. I'd guess the two smaller Gefährten dropped them before they joined the fight."

"And ran from it, by the looks. Can't blame them for that. I'm leaving, too." Jander swiped at his tormented nose with the back of his hand and headed for the sound of a stream to the north.

"THIS IS GETTING MONOTONOUS," Denny muttered. As they moved closer to their target refuge, they were forced to zigzag through increasing opposition. He was belly down behind a rock-strewn ridge that gave him little cover save for its slope, his toes dug in to keep from sliding backward. The air was filled with cold mist from the lingering fog that was rising to form a low ceiling of gray, chilling his already taut muscles under his tattered shirt. Chelsea escaped the discomfort by staying spectral along with her vest and jumpsuit.

Their travel was not without conflict. Twice

Denny fought his way through small squads of pirates, using fists, feet, spear and confiscated lasers to dispatch the enemy determined to capture him alive and dying for their efforts. On three other occasions, Chelsea caused small explosions to divert the attention of search parties and give Denny an avenue of escape. She had yet to take a life, but she was learning to calibrate her blasts by varying the mass of the catalysts she released in solid matter. Now, after an uncomfortable night huddled together in a gully, they found that their circuitous trek to the north had led them into a deep valley that allowed them little room to maneuver.

The decline in front of them dropped into a broad, rocky meadow formed by the seasonal flooding of the river that rushed by to their left. To the right was a thicker glade that stretched upward through a series of terraced ridges that would be difficult to climb. Beyond the shallow vale ahead of him the ridges sloped more gently, though their sparse trees provided little hope of cover for a man of his size. Their only path north would be across the floodplain and up through that open terrain.

Unfortunately, the area was already occupied. Denny peered across the sparse grass at the large group of Ertainians scattered in the fragrant conifers on the other side, chatting like soldiers everywhere as they wolfed down their morning rations. "How are we going to get around this bunch?"

"Suppose I divert them?" Chelsea whispered from

her position inside a squat conifer. "I could make an appearance up on those terraces to the east, perhaps half a kilometer away, and lead them a merry chase indeed."

"Lady, you're terrific. Go ahead. I'll follow the river upstream until I find cover." Chelsea winked and sank into the ground.

Moments later shouting rose up far beyond the stepped ridges to his right, followed by the snap of laser fire. The men across the clearing spun to their feet, dropped their trash carelessly on the virgin ground, grabbed their rifles and rushed toward the disturbance. They scrambled up the ridges with a clatter of loose stones and were soon charging into the trees without looking back.

Denny rose and stepped cautiously into the meadow. He scanned for a path through the ankle-turning ground, then moved in a crouch toward the bush-covered ridge on the other side.

He was halfway across when he heard a yell behind him and whirled to face it. A wide-eyed pirate scrambled over the edge of the ridge he had just vacated and swung his rifle to bear. Denny cut him down with his own purloined laser and spun toward the river, running smack into three others climbing up its steep bank.

Mindful of their orders to take the engineer alive, the three pirates clubbed their rifles and started swinging, not knowing they were playing the titan's game. With twice the speed and ten times the power of any of them, he smashed left and right. The first had his skull fractured with one sweep of a massive backhand, the second followed with several ribs caved in by the laser's butt, the third felt his hip dislocated by a mighty kick.

Seeing more pirates downstream, the giant whipped to his right, skidded to a stop as the turf ahead was scarred by a laser bolt, and double back-flipped a full five yards to flail into another attacking squad. He spun around, searching again for an avenue of escape.

Pirates by the dozen rushed toward him through the trees and up and down the river's edge, until he was under the guns of a full company, all of them shouting at him in Ertainian that his wristpad's translator squawked in a meaningless jumble.

He was surrounded. Recognizing the futility of further resistance, he stood to his full height, spread his arms wide and let the rifle drop. Adopting an almost comically contrite expression, he raised his hands over his shoulders.

One of the pirates, obviously an officer, holstered his gunpowder pistol and swaggered forward. "So, killer," he smirked in his own language, "we have you at last." He ignored the three sharp sticks strapped to the pack on the titan's back as inconsequential.

Denny listened to his wristpad's interpretation and his eyes widened in genuine surprise. "You're calling *me* killer?"

The officer stopped well out of reach, looking the

giant up and down with a contempt that did not quite hide his apprehension. "Do you deny that it was your ship that destroyed the Fourth Fleet? And isn't it you who has killed so many of us in these forests?"

"Hell, I'm proud of that. You butchers have had it your own way far too long." The titan glowered down at him. "And you won't have me for long at all. My partner will be here any second."

"That useless female? She will never come," the pirate sneered. "I saw her shot myself."

Denny's heart leaped, but he dismissed the thought. "You'll find us not easy to kill."

"Indeed." The entire company turned at the hollow voice. Chelsea dropped from the low clouds and drifted over their heads, floating with one leg bent in a classic hovering pose.

In an instant several startled pirates blasted away at her. She did not move, allowing the bolts to pass harmlessly through her and chip twigs off the trees on the ridge beyond.

Seeing that her theatrics had the desired effect, she unfolded and swooped to ground level. She touched the rifle of one of the pirates, rendering it ethereal, then reversed it and shoved it halfway into his body.

The pirate shrieked and bolted away. Chelsea kept up with him easily, keeping the gun steady within him. In her loudest and most ghostly voice, she screamed, "Stop!"

She was close enough to Denny that his wristpad

picked up her high-pitched shout and repeated the command in Ertainian. Everyone in the glade froze, including her terrified victim.

In bell-like, Shakespearean tones, the awesome phantom continued, "Do you know what would happen if I released this rifle? It would materialize in an instant. You may recall that in the past few days there have been explosions in the forest. To cause that, I released the merest pebble inside something larger. One crater was four meters in diameter. Imagine the damage if I release this gun!"

Apparently her unwilling subject had a good imagination. He loosed a tremulous wail and sagged to his knees, huddled with his arms clutching at his body.

Chelsea kept her position above him so that the gun tilted downward to trace a line between his nose and his midriff, the stock an inch in front of his left eye and the barrel deep in his gut.

Most of the other pirates edged away in alarm, but the officer stood his ground. "If you do that, you will kill your man."

Chelsea gritted her teeth and bluffed it out. "He survived the other explosions, nearly at ground zero. His strength is many times that of those grotesques you call giants, and his skin is as tough as a battleship's hull. He would live. But you, all of you, would die. Let him go!"

One by one, the pirates lowered their weapons. Those at the edges of the clearing were already melting down the riverbank or into the trees.

The officer looked around at his eroding support, then gave up. "You win, phantom, this time. But there will be another." He signaled the remaining pirates to lower their weapons and back away from the captive.

Chelsea stayed with her captive. "Take off, darling. I'll hold them here until you're clear."

Denny nodded and trotted for the shrubbery-covered ridges to the north. Eyes darting to find the easiest path, he increased his pace up and over the rocky slopes until he was sprinting at a speed to be envied by a thoroughbred stallion. Skimming past trees and boulders and hurtling over bushes and fallen logs, he reached inside for all the power he could muster, and held it.

One minute, two, the awkward silence held. When Chelsea felt his lead was great enough, she pulled the rifle out of the sobbing pirate, snatched another for Denny, and soared aloft.

The officer barked commands. In seconds the ghost was suffused with spears of energy as the larger group of pirates started after the titan.

"You had your warning!" Chelsea shouted, and flashed back down to the ground.

The Ertainian in her path fell flat in a futile attempt to escape. She followed him down, shoved one of the rifles lengthwise into the ground beneath his prone body, and let it go.

The glade instantly ceased to exist.

THE CLOUDY SKY FLARED ALIGHT to the north and a bit west. Seconds later a distant but still stunning concussion wave struck them, and soon after that the ground heaved under their feet. Jander, Richard and Pavel looked at each other and spoke at exactly the same time. "Chelsea."

Jander faced in the direction of the blast and closed his eyes, pushing outward with all the power of his prodigious mind. With a jerk of his head, his eyes flew open. "I have Denny! The thoughts are not too coherent—he was just over the edge of a ridge when the concussion wave came and he's pretty stunned—but he's running like hell toward the place they've chosen as a redoubt."

He pointed, and watched as Pavel concentrated. Doppelwulf trotted up panting from his run, and seconds later Raankhak slinked out of the bushes and flopped on a soft patch of matted leaves, ribs heaving. Sharon moved in from their back trail.

The Ukrainian was silent for several seconds, then sighed and shook his head. "I believe I touched him, but my general call would only be another stab of pressure to him. He must recover first. I cannot find Chelsea."

"Neither can I. Either she's now in a different area, or..." He could not finish. After all, they had no certain proof that a ghost could not be killed.

Richard caught his arm. "Let me go after him."

"Negative. You might land right in the middle of a campfire. Believe me, there are pirates out there."

Jander paced a few steps, head down. "Here's what we'll do. You and Pavel together will take short hops in that direction, always landing where you know it's safe. But be ready to hit, hard. I'll take Sharon with me in a bubble, flying over the trees. The metas will run on alone—they'll keep up, I'm sure. You can take offensive action, but be certain you can get out unhurt."

Walter bared his teeth with a snort and waved his tail. Cielo sat up, blinked her bright amber eyes and raised a paw flashing two-inch daggers.

Richard dropped his pack and rifle and started peeling off his shirt. "No sweat. We'll link both body and mind, back to back. Okay, Pal?"

Kalanev took the invitation to telepathic contact and smiled. "That is an excellent idea, my friend." He shouldered out of his pack, pulled off his own shirt, and handed his laser rifle to Gibson. "I will use the pistols."

"I thought you liked the rifles." Sharon automatically checked the weapon's charge indicator. The Corps' basic training, designed and governed by a transitioned U.S. Marine, made the action spontaneous.

"One uses the proper tool for the job. We strike hard and fast, no time for niceties." His grin chilled the air for yards around. "I am more than ready."

"Okay," Jander said, "but remember, without your shirts you don't have the nanosteel weave to protect you. Be careful!"

"Hell, my middle name is careful." Richard tied his shirt around his waist and set his burly shoulders to the Ukrainian's whipcord back, then quickly stepped away. "Oh, boss, can I have the double holster?"

"Sure." Jander unbuckled his gun belt with its attendant score of charged batteries, knife and canteen, and accepted Richard's single rig in return.

A few seconds for adjustment, then Richard again settled his back against the Ukrainian's, shook his arms to loosen his muscles in the cool air and said, "All right, King Cobra, let's see how well you trained me to bite." Kalanev nodded shortly, and the black and white killing machine disappeared.

"Take off, critters. Ready, Sharon?"

The woman nodded and slung Pavel's rifle over her left shoulder, careful not to tangle the strap on the hilts of her daggers, and laid Richard's on the pile of packs. Walter and Cielo separated and took off through the trees. Moments later Jander gathered the packs into a bubble of gravitic force, and he and the biologist lifted off the forest floor and wafted toward the mountains.

It was on.

CHAPTER 21

Connors ran all day and through the night, fighting his way through the headache from the blast concussion as he pushed his battered body further from ground zero.

During the first few hours, he managed to furnish himself with plenty of rifles and batteries from pirates killed outright by the detonation. Not knowing their metabolism, he dared not try their rations; nor could he stop to roast one of the many animal bodies he saw because he knew the area would be under heavy surveillance.

That added hunger to his misery.

Struggling up yet another tangled ravine, he tripped over a root and fell heavily, gasping for breath. He lay where he had fallen, trusting the shadows of the deep gulch to grant him a moment's respite.

During his previous rest stops, he learned to rewire the lasers to release all their energies through the exciter in a split second, turning fine weapons into heat-concussion bombs. His back trail was studded with trip sticks, pressure mines and spring traps.

Behind him, in a zigzag line through the ridges, lay dozens of burned and broken pirates stiffening or groaning under the heavy gray sky.

He had not seen Chelsea since he left the glade, but he was able to follow her progress. There were no more massive explosions, but the thunder of smaller blasts had met his still-ringing ears, coupled with the crackling fall of forest giants or the rumbling groan of avalanche. He knew that in the glades and ravines all around him, pirates were fleeing for their lives.

He struggled to regain his feet under the thick dawn sky. His chipped and bloody spear, slung by a knotted vine behind him next to his pack, snagged on a creeper protruding from the ridge and caused another stumble. The javelins were long gone, drilled through Ertainians who had the misfortune to catch him with his lasers low on power. The environmental pack, perforated by several hits and rendered useless, nonetheless still guarded his back.

A long, six-legged ferret-like creature with half-inch fangs too much like a rattlesnake's fearlessly eyed him from a nearby rock as he righted himself. He shifted his spear to a more comfortable position, then set off at a ground-eating trot. Without the sun to guide him and with his wristpad ruined by a laser that had burned a deep groove in his forearm there was little chance that he had kept his line, yet he kept moving uphill, whipping from one rugged ravine to another, bloodshot eyes on swivel. Clutching twin lasers like pistols in his big hands, he pressed on.

Chelsea settled herself above a high tree limb and materialized, dropping the centimeter to the branch and steadying herself against the trunk. The stink of her uncured vest wrinkled her nose as soon as she gained solid form, and the flying insects descended on her in a three-dimensional stampede. She wiped her smudged forehead with an already soggy green sleeve.

She had long since stopped caring about appearances. The tremendous mental peak she had sustained for the last few days was taking a toll on her concentration, adding the danger of unintended explosions to everything else on her weary mind. She shook her head and focused her bleary eyes through the wind-rattled foliage, staring over the nearby conifers to the high plateau ahead.

Searching the edge of the mesa for her giant lover, Chelsea tripped her clairvoyance. She still could not find him. Again she shook the cobwebs from her brain and triggered her spectrality, then floated east toward the small groups of milling pirates. She would work the area around the plateau, hoping to attract Denny's attention and guide him in.

Jander and Sharon floated invisible a thousand meters over that same plateau, studying the movements of the pirates to the south and west.

"Sharon, I'm going to set you down in that rockfall, where I believe Denny is planning to fort up. It's good ground."

The oval mesa was a leveled limestone ridge that extended well over a kilometer east and west, mostly barren and rocky, and tapered to brush-covered downward slopes toward the south and upwards to the west with sheer drop-offs to the north and east. A stretch of undulating surface spanned about five hundred meters from the south lip of the mesa to the rockfall, then another three hundred meters to the drop-offs. The eastern cliff glistened with water seeping from an artesian source.

"I love this field of fire. You might be able to help him through the approach when he reaches the plateau."

"Can't you just find him and get him out?"

"I have him in mind, but his memory doesn't have anything we've seen. I can't pinpoint his position without a reference point. It would take too long to search under every bush in the area."

Jander pointed toward the north-south ridges ascending toward the mountains to the west. "I feel I'd be better used if I hit that concentration over there, where all the landing jets are. I wonder why they haven't taken over this plateau? It's flatter than anything else around."

Sharon smiled. "I can tell you that. There's a whole pride of those giant cats in residence. They're in a big den under that pile of rock needles on the eastern side. Drop me off and I'll see what I can do."

"You mean, recruit them?" Jander's eyes gleamed at the idea. "If it works, we'll have the best ground troops money can buy."

"If I can control them. I can influence animal minds, but these brutes don't give me a whole lot to work with. I'll need you to stick with me while I try it out."

"Can do." Jander directed his sphere of force toward the rockfall. Since he had altered its composition to refract light and sensor waves, they were undetectable. Thus Chelsea stared right at them and did not see.

They settled in the center basin of the rockfall and Steele dropped the shield. He could hear the tinkling of a spring nearby, which explained the place's popularity for the cats. He found an overhang caused by a domino tumbling of monoliths and deposited his load of packs, rifles and provisions under it. The weathered columns of rock lent an almost Stonehenge majesty to the place, but scattered piles of large bones and cat scat brought them back to reality in a heartbeat. They were literally in the lion's den.

Sharon took a deep breath to calm her spiking nerves and broadcast her incontestable mental snare. A scream of bestial rage thundered through the boulders, and the first of the tigers leaped into the clearing, the huge double canines bared in a terrifying snarl. He was followed by another and another, until the two Corpsmen were surrounded by an even dozen fearsome monsters.

Jander stared at them wide-eyed. "Chelsea beat one of these things? They make a tiger look like an ocelot."

"Don't show them any fear," Sharon said through clenched teeth. "I can't control them without an object lesson, They're hungry—the pirates have driven off the brush grazers that are their main prey. If we're not careful, they'll be snacking on us."

Jander smiled tightly, his mind firmly within hers to coordinate their efforts. "Let 'em come."

One giant cat after another started forward, fierce eyes intent on the easy kill. Sharon juggled her mental forces to push them back, succeeding by the barest of margins.

Suddenly one of the tigers charged, roaring a challenge that would have frozen any other creature with panic. But not these creatures.

Steele leaped into the monster's path and back-handed the beast across the snapping jaw with his entire forearm, then slammed into him with his shoulder. The power of his forcefield anchored and amplified blows sent the cat spinning, knocking him into two others.

All three regained their feet in a snarling scramble and pounced together. Again Steele whipped forward, shouting and kicking, driving the beasts back physically as Sharon drove stabbing commands into their feral brains.

Back and forth the man and animals struggled, Orion using a vibratory screen to roar as loudly as the cats, pushing himself and his bag of tricks all out to beat them into submission. Harmonia, with her back pressed to a boulder, sped her overwhelming bolts of mental influence, demanding obedience, battling for mastery. And slowly, reluctantly, the monsters submitted to her uncanny gift.

Jander crouched, gasping, meeting the tigers stare for stare. Very few of them looked away for long. "I think we've got them. But whether they'll stay got when I'm gone, I couldn't tell you."

"They won't, I know," Gibson said through gritted teeth. "It's you, more than me, who is controlling them. They'll obey me under fear of punishment, but not of their own free will."

Jander paced back and forth, pondering solutions. "I'm going to disappear, but I'll still be here." He vanished.

Startled, the cats shifted back, then, as they realized the woman was alone, they circled forward, growling. Suddenly, a wiry female snarled and leaped for the unprotected woman.

Sharon kept her cool, shouting harshly and shoving her arm out like a traffic cop as she fired a mental command. The cat stopped cold, flattening face-first as if she had struck a wall, which, in essence, she had. Steele, invisible, had thrown a forcefield in her way.

The process was repeated by another cat, then two more. Another, an enterprising youngster, scrambled onto Sharon's boulder and swiped down at her. She threw up her arm, and Steele acted as her extension to yank the tiger off the boulder and hurl him halfway across the basin. The young cat twisted and landed on its feet, still full of fight.

Somehow Sharon maintained her composure,

stamping her feet, shouting meaningless words at each cat that dared to meet her eyes. At last, after long moments of false lunges and defiant snarls the pride settled down, growling in frustration but keeping a respectful distance and no longer glaring their direct challenge.

Sharon swiped at her forehead with an equally drenched sleeve. The nanosteel-laced fabric wicked away the moisture but was not the least bit absorbent.

"I think they're convinced," she panted.

His voice answered from empty air. "I'll stay a while longer. It's not enough to hold them off. You've got to use them."

She nodded. As if to prove her trust in her namesake goddess, Harmonia of the Corps tested her mastery. She took a deep breath and tried a gentler tone of contact.

The restless cats growled and paced, glowering askance at their camo-clad controller as she stepped toward them. She waved one hand in front of her and sent a calm command. One of the cats snarled in confusion, then clambered onto a tumbled slab. Another followed, and a third, standing shoulder to brawny shoulder. Then the youngster, no more than a third of a ton of rippling muscle, leaped onto their backs. The tigers shifted and moaned but held steady.

They were under new management.

"Well, if it isn't Dr. Doolittle."

Sharon spun, wide-eyed. Nebula perched on a finger of rock with her dangling legs crossed at the ankle, looking filthy and haggard but still irrepressibly grinning.

"Chelsea!" she cried, and scrambled toward her. The tigers snarled and leaped off the boulder, but at a commanding thought they stopped cold and glowered morosely. The two women met in a tearful hug.

"Well, the prodigal ghost returns," Steele dropped his shield and opened his arms.

Chelsea cried out and flew into his chest. "Oh, Jander! Denny's alone out there! I can't find him!"

He gave her a strong, brotherly squeeze, gallantly ignoring the reek of her uncured vest. "Neither can I, exactly, but I know he's all right." The blonde sobbed with relief and clutched at his shirt. He unhooked her fingers and pointed with his chin. "He's over in that direction. I wish I could take the time to find him, but the pirates are bringing more men into the mountains all the time. I've got to disrupt that."

She ran her arms down his chest and gripped his hands as she stepped back. "Why? Why can't we just leave this awful place?"

"Because it's not an awful place. I have plans for this world, and I want the pirates off. Just escaping from them isn't enough for me. I want them to treat this planet as taboo."

He released her hands and swept his arm toward the south. "Cobra and Hermes are around here somewhere, doing their best to depopulate the place. Raankhak and Doppelwulf are on their way, too. They should be here soon. I've got to get going." He slipped his hand around her neck, smiled in encouragement, then rose into the air and faded to invisibility as his form-fitting personal shield built up around him.

The two women shared a look. "He doesn't miss a trick, does he?" Sharon remarked.

Chelsea quirked her lips and turned to other matters—twelve of them. "What are you planning to do with these buggers?"

"Scare the devil out of a lot of pirates, I hope," she smiled. "When Kodiak makes his break, these guys will run interference."

Chelsea considered. "I'd better find him, then. I know what he'll think when he sees them—he wouldn't stop running until he found Godot." With that, she turned translucent and whisked away.

Sharon commanded her troupe to settle down to rest, then started scanning the area to find them some prey. As much as she hated sacrificing other animals, she had a responsibility to feed them if she wanted them to stay.

CHAPTER 22

The little dorse trembled in the ravine, her soft ears quivering to the sounds of battle. What had happened, that this familiar land had suddenly sprouted these mighty two-legged killers? It was bad enough to have to hide from the great cats and the other hunters. But these monsters that killed without reason from a distance were enough to terrify a far braver creature than she. The ordinary dangers of natural forest life were nothing compared to them. So she trembled, alone and afraid.

She heard a rustling behind her and knew she was no longer alone. A monstrous multi-colored creature fell apart, becoming two of the upright destroyers. One of them stared at her, then waved its free upper appendage. The dorse galvanized at the motion and bounded down the ravine, blindly amazed that she was still alive.

Kalanev watched the six-legged creature go, his ice-gray eyes showing no interest. "Let us rest a moment."

"I'm all into that," Ford said with a sigh. He unwrapped his shirt from around his waist and mopped his forehead, then shrugged into it to allow himself a momentary respite from the cool air. "Man, those Lievan dudes are *mean*. I musta pumped twenty shots into the last one."

Pavel sat down on a rock and pulled out his canteen, seemingly unmindful of the chill. "Aim for the eyes. The skull is not so thick there." He took a deep but single draught and swished it around his mouth before swallowing.

"Yeah, you can say that. You can knock a flea off a mouse's nuts at a hundred yards." Richard sighed again and reached to change the batteries in his guns. The basic task helped to skim the cold frenzy of life and death from his mind, and he sighed again.

"What is this thing, brother?"

The Ukrainian regarded him curiously as he passed him the canteen. "How do you mean?"

"How many men have we killed today, dozens? Fifty? Maybe more than that, and we'll ice a lot more before we're done. And it doesn't hurt. I mean, I can kinda explain it by Cielo almost gettin' blown away, but I should feel something, shouldn't I?" He too took a single pull from the canteen and returned it with a nod of thanks.

Pavel's smile was entirely different from his battle mask. "Why? We are not killing men, not by my definition. Men do not prey on the weak, as they do. Real men, like you and me, and our lord Orion, protect those who cannot protect themselves. These pirates are not men; they are vermin. They should be eradicated like vermin."

He shrugged and stowed the canteen. "If there were some good in their actions, some civilized reasoning to redeem them, perhaps we would not feel this way. But I have seen their minds. Do you know why they are here, Richard? The want the knowledge in Kodiak's brain, so they can be stronger and pillage more efficiently. They are so callous that they do not even crave revenge for their reverses. They have no respect for the fallen warriors of their own species, no use for the dead. They want our secrets, nothing more. We must see that they do not succeed. To that end, we must combat their threat any way we can, including killing them en masse."

"Doesn't it ever bother you?"

Pavel was silent for long moments, until Ford thought he would get no answer. Then the Ukrainian spoke, his voice bitterly reflective. "I am a killer, Richard, by training and by trade. Before I joined the Omega Corps I killed for pay, for a fine car and a handsome dacha in Crimea. Often I killed in cold blood for the glory of the Soviet, seemingly without conscience. Many of those I killed were good men, and women, those who should have been friends. And more than once I was nearly killed myself, all in the line of perverted duty. Even after the Soviet fell apart and I walked away from that life, I had to remain on constant guard because of the long memories of my erstwhile foes."

He drew his guns from their holsters, holding them loosely in his slender hands as he stared into the distance. "When I first met Lord Orion I doubted him, thinking him only another power-hungry demon in human form—another demon like myself. I realized in short order that I was mistaken. A demon such as the Minister who controlled me before my country regained autonomy would never have risked his life to save mine, as Orion did. I am still a killer, yes, still under the command of a powerful leader who tells me when and whom to kill. But for the first time in my life I feel myself to be a man, a *good* man."

He examined the pistols in his hands and sighed. "No, it does not bother me anymore. For I am exorcizing all those demons buried within me, by ridding creation of those who prey without conscience upon the innocent. I am repaying my debt, to myself, to Orion, and to mankind."

He leaned back and stared pensively at the heavy gray-green clouds. "Some would tell you that what I am feeling is the pride of righteousness, the power and glory of successful conflict. But there is no glory, save that of good, no power, save that of justice. How a man reacts to killing depends entirely on the cause he is serving. We are serving a good cause."

Richard absorbed his words in silence, then nodded. "It is a new way of thinking, yeah. I never dreamed of any of this when I was driving a cab. The Corps is all about second chances, Pal."

"Indeed." Pavel watched the thick clouds a while longer, then flexed his shoulders and stood. "We have wasted enough time, my friend. I am ready."

GRUNTING SOFTLY, DENNY FLOPPED on his stomach at the edge of the woodland bordering the plateau. A mouse-sized insectivore with kangaroo-like legs sprang over his outstretched arm and vanished into a spray of tough grasses. He studied the layout of the rockfall five hundred meters ahead, waiting for the blasts that would signify that the place was cleared for occupancy.

Instead, he was aware of explosions to the left of the mesa, far away from his position. Had he gotten so turned around that he had completely circled the area?

Then his eyes lit up. Chelsea was just then lifting off from the rockfall. He took careful aim with one of his lasers and fired three quick shots past her head. He watched in relief as she heeled over and dove for him.

Her happy grin turned to alarm as she set down beside him. "Darling, you're hurt!"

He flexed his wounded left forearm and grimaced, "Just another puncture for my collection. These guys have never gotten used to my speed, so this is the only real hit they've managed. And like I said, these lasers cauterize as they wound. Which reminds me, how about those cats?"

Chelsea examined the long, blackened groove with her clairvoyance, relieved that the bone was not hit. "As long as you see a medical transmutator soon it shouldn't become bothersome. Harmonia has the cats under control. They'll be on your side."

He grinned and slapped the ground. "You mean, Orion's here!"

"In the flesh. Those explosions are his. He's dive-bombing the pirate encampments to the west of us. Some other Corpsmen are coming on their own hook, but they haven't arrived yet."

"Says who?" The words were more growled than spoken; Raankhak did not bother to change over in order to speak. Denny whipped his rifle around but recognized her in time.

"Don't sneak up on people like that. You could get your tail singed," he chided her. "It's great to see you, little sister. Who else is coming?"

The vocabulary necessary was too much for her feline jaws, so she transformed. Denny gave her a twice-over, then guiltily looked away.

She genuinely did not notice. "Doubledog should be along in a few minutes. He got tied up with a couple of Lievans. I let them go right past me, but he's too clumsy to sneak off." She dazzled them with her teeth, then, shivering a bit in her naked human skin, switched back to cat.

"Lievans are the big guys?" Denny asked, and got a cough of concurrence from the panther.

Chelsea added, "Cobra and Hermes are out there, too, hopping along killing people. If I know Pavel it'll be a bit before they break off."

Denny grunted, "We'll wait for Walter, then." He stretched out and relaxed for the first time in far too long, trusting the keener senses of the panther to keep guard.

Chelsea sat on his stomach. "Did you have much trouble?"

He poked his chin in the direction of the slopes and terraces below. "Ask them. I left a trail of destruction from here to your blast site. By the way, how much damage did you cause?"

The panther flowed. "I can answer that. You could hide the *Angel* in that hole. It diverted a good-sized river and is on its way to becoming Chelsea Pond. What did you do?" Again she morphed.

Chelsea told her, as briefly as possible. "Since then I've been using little things to fuel the reaction. I don't think my sanity could survive another muck like that."

"I couldn't, either," the titan averred. "I was a full kilometer away and it still flattened me." He saw Cielo prick her velvet ears toward the back trail and sat up, shifting the ghost onto his lap. "Here comes the mutt."

Walter trotted up, tongue lolling from his long run. Seconds later he was shaking hands with the giant. "Good to see you, old friend." He smiled his greeting to Chelsea, still cupped in the crook of the giant's arm. "Whoof, du stinkst, Mädchen." He shared a glance with Cielo, whose eyes also acknowledged the change in the couple's status.

Chelsea gave him a rueful grin as she brushed her knuckles down the filthy skin of her vest. "What? This is the absolute height of colonial fashion. You should be so lucky—your fur is on the outside."

"We'll have to save the reunion for later, guys," Denny said. "Right now, let's worry about getting to those rocks. Chelsea, you'll be our air support. Soften them up on this side, then hit the west hard, decoying them while we make our dash."

The ghost nodded, selected a handful of tiny pebbles from the rough ground and soared aloft. "Let's get ready, people."

He grinned at the thought; he was now the only "person" present.

CHAPTER 23

The northern mountains of the planet's largest continent were formed by the convergence of two vast tectonic plates that had been grinding toward each other for eons. The southern plate splayed east and west as it pushed northerly, tearing the terrain into north-south ridges, while the larger northern plate splashed southward to form ripples of granite and limestone like waves against a shore.

In between, at the line of convergence, an eleven hundred-kilometer range higher than the Himalayas stood like shattered stalagmites against the sky. Frigid gales from the polar region swirled south to meet the mountains and form cold fronts on the northern side, creating violently turbulent air masses under which little more than mosses could survive.

Now, in the early autumn when the polar oceanic air stream was most vigorous, the increasingly foul weather often gained enough force to push through the mountains and rush downslope to meet the southerly warm fronts, resulting in thunderous blizzards of hail, sleet, cyclones and icy gales.

Such a front was headed their way, and even though the altitude of the Corpsmen's chosen refuge was less than a quarter of the climb to the highest peaks, the storm promised to be fierce.

If the Ertainians were aware of the impending threat, they chose to ignore it. While Denny and Chelsea were forced to the east by the terrain on their overland trek, their pursuers had taken an aerial route from the Sprite's crash site directly toward magnetic north. Their rally point was a weathered area to the west of the plateau, south of a deep notch in the mountain range that would place them right in the funneled path of the storm.

Their chemical-fueled landing ships were scattered over the broken terrain wherever they found room, sitting drive engines down on the scorched and denuded rock with their laser-turreted noses pointed skyward. Each of them disgorged from ten to thirty invaders, who swarmed over the landscape in undisciplined squads with no apparent battle command. Junior officers gathered them up and started them eastward up and down the washboard ridges in unruly clusters.

It was clear that they knew where the fugitives were, and equally clear that they still intended to take Denny alive. Chelsea, on the other hand, had been shot through so many times, it was obvious they cared nothing for females.

Orion swooped down from the gray-green clouds six thousand feet above them and circled to look them over. He imbued his form-fitting personal screen with the colors of the Omega Corps dress uniform, comprised of a gold-trimmed crimson turtleneck under a flare-shouldered sleeveless jerkin of silvery nanosteel blue, black slacks and matte black boots, and topped by a flat cap the same color as the jerkin. His ostentatious entrance drew increasing laser fire as he casually toured the area. None of the bolts came close at that extreme range, but they did serve to draw the attention he wanted.

As he flew overhead, one of the shuttles joined in the defense, its larger-caliber lasers and superior targeting managing to splash the flying figure with powerful bolts of crimson fire.

Steele deflected the assault with no great effort, but this time chose not to ignore it. He stopped in mid-air, focused his attention on the offending ship and spread his arms. From his shoulders outward, he flared shimmering two-dimensional sabers of silver energy thirty meters long, then kicked into motion and dove on the still-blasting ship.

As he neared it, he crossed his sabers in front of his plummeting form and went in for the kill. The twin lances scissored into the hull as he swept his arms wide at opposing angles, low to high, careful to avoid sections where he believed the internal energy reserves were housed.

The big lander shrieked its metallic death knell as it was cut into four pieces. The cheese slices of the sides squirted outward and crashed into the rocks below, and the nose section, now a wedge of raw nanosteel, scrubbed down the wedge of the tail section and slid shrieking to the ground. No explosion occurred to contaminate the area, but the ship was reduced to steaming scrap.

Jander floated lower and looked over his handiwork, momentarily untargeted as the pirates stared in stunned silence.

Then one of them tried his luck with a laser again, and others quickly followed suit. Their target rose higher in the air, created what could be called a gigantic cricket bat out of thin air and started slapping at the slopes of the ridges. The disorganized squads abandoned the high ground to seek cover in the gullies between, slowing their advance and buying the three ground-bound Corpsmen time to try for the rockfall.

The trio still had plenty of antagonists in full pursuit through the forests behind them. They made it about halfway across the gap without much opposition, but now pirates by the score were pouring out of the forest and onto the brush-covered fringe of the plateau.

Denny zigzagged along his chosen route, no whit slower than the metamorphs racing on either side, then dove into a depression as the laser bolts trying to cut his legs from under him became too close and frequent. He aimed a rifle he had rewired for continuous fire and squeezed the trigger, mowing down the front line.

Only a man of his strength could have kept the vigorously bucking weapon on target; only one with his dense skin could have withstood the searing heat. It burned out the exciter in a few seconds, but it bought the time for his companions to find their own cover.

They quickly converted to human and added their pulse pistols to the firing line. Denny discarded his glowing jury-rigged laser and yanked another from the captured arsenal under his arm. As he raised it over the lip of his shallow foxhole, he saw Chelsea skimming a weaving path through the deeper ranks and shoving pebbles barely larger than sand into the center of bigger rocks.

The molecular fusion created bone-jarring thuds and sent a storm of stone shrapnel for meters in all directions. Having relieved the immediate pressure on her mates, she arrowed deeper into the ranks to disrupt the reinforcements.

Kilometers to the west, Steele found a resting spot on a boulder overlooking the landing area. He had cheese-sliced a dozen small ships and scattered hundreds of pirates, yet his goal of total confusion was not reached.

With the stolid deliberation of automatons, the soldiers of Ertain suffered his worst and kept on pressing forward. The Head was an absolute dictator, and his admirals felt the pressure of his wrath and passed it to the lower ranks. They would not, could not quit.

Steele sighed, then turned as another set of explosions echoed through the canyons behind him. He focused his mind and received the concentration with which Chelsea was adhering to her task, then found the reason for her efforts. He took to the air to help.

"We can't stay here," Denny shouted over the snap of their weaponry. "They'll overrun us in a matter of minutes. But they're getting too damned accurate for my taste."

Walter sat up and pointed. "Here comes the Luftwaffe!" Then he howled and fell back, staring at the blackened hole in his shoulder. Grimacing away the pain, he changed to wolf and back to human. Whole again, he picked up his pistol and fired away.

Connors stared. "That's some trick," he called.

Walter grinned and again pointed aloft.

Orion came in low, fast and conspicuous in his Corps uniform sheath, and quickly drew fire from the pirates. He slowed, spiraled up to twenty meters and halted in mid-air, hands on hips and glaring haughtily. Denny grinned in appreciation, then motioned his companions to move again. The three sprinted toward the rockfall.

Jander watched them go, content to be the target for the moment. He had taken the time to analyze the exact wavelengths of the laser weapons and constructed an economical shield capable of handling almost any amount of both laser and projectile fire. The visible frequencies he allowed to strike him, giving the astounded pirates the impression that he was absorbing the blasts. At times he was almost inundated by the silver-red light strobing from a hundred weapons.

When some of the pirates returned their attention to the speeding fugitives, he took action. He soared high in a reverse swan and circled back toward the advancing line of soldiers. He leveled off at chest height and sped in. From each of his widespread arms flared ten-centimeter cylinders of shimmering silver energy five meters long, huge pipes of force spaced one hundred fifty centimeters off the mesa.

The pirates gave back as he whistled in, but few were quick enough to evade. Straight through the close-packed troops he bulleted, clubbing those within his twelve-meter wingspan into the rocky soil, leaving an avalanche of shattered bones in his wake. Those who tried to duck were knocked senseless or worse. Others who tried to leap over the speeding cylinders crashed to the ground with shattered legs and skinned faces.

Only those who fell flat were able to escape, and they were pummeled by the broken bodies of their unlucky fellows. Grimly efficient, Orion looped into the sky and wheeled toward another concentration of pirates, leaving the survivors to crawl back to the shrubbery or to be pulled back by their crewmates.

Jander's tactics were concocted more to intimidate than to kill. His pipes could just as readily have been blades, but he could not bring himself to the wholesale slaughter of common soldiers. Unlike his more vulnerable companions whose weapons were meant to kill, he struck to disrupt troop formations and tie up the survivors with rescue missions. He still had hope that the enemy would see the futility of their cause and withdraw on their own.

Chelsea had reached a point beyond such mercy.

On the western side of the plateau, Nebula glided through the air toward another group, who fired through her and fell back in panic. Chelsea drifted in their wake, then flipped over and dove, shifting a tiny, immaterial pebble from the supply in her left hand to the fingertips of her right. She flashed through one of the pirates and released the pebble, inundating her ethereal form with a booming crimson gusher of bloody shredded flesh. Untouched, she emerged and floated away, leaving a shallow red-splashed crater surrounded by unmoving forms, stunned or dead. Dozens of other pirates fell away from the spot dazed and deafened by the concussion.

Suddenly the space was no longer vacant; the deadly team of Kalanev and Ford had at last made the scene. The brawny African-American and the wiry, sandy-haired Ukrainian stood back to back, blasting away with lethal accuracy.

So stunned were the pirates that Kalanev, much the faster of the two, had time to reload before the Ertainians reacted. At the first sign of return fire the two comrades vanished. The bolts of energy meant for them zinged through the empty air and bored into the pirates beyond, multiplying the physical and psychological damage even more.

And at another place, far away, was another flash

of chocolate and cream, another half dozen dead. Steadily, inexorably, the toll mounted. And no two survivors could agree which was more frightening, the frenzied, snarling menace of the black man, or the cold, calm mockery on the face of the lean assassin.

Denny and the two metamorphs made it untouched to the redoubt and scrambled to places of defense. Incredibly, the surviving pirates kept on coming, through the hell of the four untouchable ambushers in their midst and into the murderous fire of the three defenders.

Sharon distributed extra batteries to the metamorphs and returned to her spot in the center of the area, struggling to retain control of her savage charges stationed along the perimeter. The few pirates who managed to reach the rockfall were torn to pieces, their companions falling back in abject panic as the mighty beasts roared their challenge through dripping double-fanged jaws.

The last of the pirates fell back to the woods below the plateau, pursued by Jander and Chelsea until the cover thickened. Orion turned a few triumphant loops and glided to the fortress, settling beside his best friend. He retained his shield in order to survive the titan's ebullient welcome.

Richard and Pavel, attracted to the redoubt by the sudden cessation of combat, popped in to receive similar greetings. The pathport team, so dubbed by Rosenberg in a moment of un-German brevity, found their packs and pulled out their camo pullover jackets to drive the bone-deep chill from their bodies.

The starving tigers got their feast. Sharon allowed it, queasy but glad that she did not have to sacrifice innocent prey animals after all.

"You and Chelsea don't have to stay," Jander told Denny as he stepped back from the reunion. "The rest of us can take it from here. We have extra wrist-pads that'll take you both back to the ship."

Since the pair had not reached the surface through the *Angel*'s teleport facilities, neither could have used their own multiplex wrist instruments to trigger their return, even if Chelsea hadn't lost hers with her pressure suit. Denny had discarded and slagged his own ruined unit.

Denny grinned and thumped his much-scabbed chest with his blackened arm. The deep bruises from the crash landing had faded thanks to his rapid-healing metabolism, but it was clear that radiation from the solar flyby in the Sprite had taken its toll. A pinkish rash mottled his skin and almost certainly made him itch, but he retained his determination in spite of it. "I'm feeling fine, Chief. I want to be in on the end."

Chelsea alighted on his shoulder and nodded her agreement.

"I thought you'd feel that way. I'd like to keep you around for appearances sake, for the same reason I don't want to bring anyone else down from the *Angel* because I want to show these guys we don't need any help to handle the likes of them. All right, but let's relax for a minute."

The weary warriors flopped in the center of the redoubt, guarded by a dozen very ferocious sentries. But the rest was brief as their dedication to duty compelled them back to work.

Richard followed his ears to the spring that had attracted the big cats and gathered canteens while Chelsea borrowed Sharon's medical kit and went to work on Denny's arm. Her paramedic training made her better suited for the task despite Sharon's far more extensive education as a zoologist.

The ghost pressed hard with a needle to deliver a topical anesthetic through his thick skin, then gently scrubbed the long groove gouged diagonally across his forearm. As the wound was already cauterized, she contented herself with cleansing the area and wrapping it with an elastic bandage.

Next checked were the innumerable punctures, scratches and scrapes on Denny's ironbound torso. The titan tore away what was left of his shirt and Chelsea settled down for a lot of work. Sharon contributed by unwrapping and feeding him energy bars that disappeared as soon as they hit his hand.

Meanwhile Walter unshipped the solar accumulator, which was sophisticated enough to ignore the thick cloud cover, and collected spent batteries for recharging. Pavel crouched high on a weathered rock to keep watch while Cielo prowled the perimeter, casually ignoring the native beasts that outweighed her fifteen to one.

Jander fired up the cookstove for warmth and added a collapsible pot to brew some freeze-dried coffee. He shook his head in sympathy as Chelsea spotted hole after hole through the titan's tough hide, tweezing out a motley collection of foreign projectiles and painting the raw flesh with a cut-knitting gel. He guessed that the big engineer had lost a good seventy pounds from pushing his mighty frame through their limited diet. "Have you decided what we're going to call this planet?"

Denny looked at the ghost and shrugged. "I haven't really thought about it, have you?"

"Now that you mention it, I'd like to call it Arcadia." She dimpled. "It fits what we've found here."

Jander did not bother to probe their thoughts, He saw their expressions, and had seen them echoed in the faces of Richard and Cielo. "Indeed it does. Welcome to the land of peace and plenty."

He looked up to the roar of an Ertainian shuttle as it came into sight from the west and flicked out a forcefield plane to slice it down the center. The disintegrating halves smashed jarringly into the plateau a few hundred yards east of the rockfall.

"Unfortunately, we have no peace and plenty of pirates," Pavel the Heartless called down from his post. As if in emphasis, a rumble of thunder rolled through the thick clouds from the direction of the higher mountains upwind. "I presume we are not leaving this warrior's paradise to the Ertainians. What are your plans?"

Jander grinned. "I want to surprise you. I'll tell you this much: Assuming I have the brainpower to pull it off, it'll be the biggest show since Zeus took over from his old man. I'm going to do some tricks with mirrors."

"Mirrors." Pavel narrowed his eyes; then, like the loyal soldier he was, shrugged and dismissed it.

Richard, however, was not in awe of anyone. "You're crazy, boss. Why don't we just call in the *Angel* and waste 'em?"

"Because the *Angel* is an understandable phenomenon. As I told Chelsea, I want to make this planet taboo. That calls for something a bit more… ostentatious." He smiled, then called to Kalanev, "Let's see if we can get in touch with Vickie."

Pavel took a long look around, waiting for Cielo to take his place on watch before he dropped down from his perch. He pressed a button on his wristpad, said, "Bangle, pulse to Angela," then opened his mind. Seconds later a stupendous aggregation of telepathic power drove into his brain from the invisible *Angel* keeping pace with the third moon. He counted at least eight individuals in the team, Tsin among them, joined together to bridge the tremendous distance from ship to planet.

<*"Finally! I was getting worried,"*> Vickie's relieved thought barreled in, her crystal-clear intelligence overpowering the others with ease. <*"Is everybody okay? Is that you raising hell in the mountains? Was that Chelsea creating a lake? Is…"*>

Jander raised a hand in defense as he spoke aloud, trusting Pavel to relay the words "Easy, lady. Yes, that's us. I told you it might be quite a while before we got back to you." He gave her a brief resume of the week's worth of action so far. "So, I'm going to blow the lid off in a couple hours. I'll make my appearance— believe me, you'll know it—at the height of the battle down here. The end of my show will be your signal to go into action. Start from just above us and work your way outward. Keep the baffle screens tight, and send some Banshees to the savannah concentrations and wherever you can spot them in the forest. Have the gunners remove the visible from all weapons, and never keep the *Angel* in one place more than a few minutes. Real mysterious—the more impossible it looks, the better. When we're through with them they'll be glad to sit on Ertain until hell freezes over—or until we find Ertain, at least. All clear?"

<*"Not exactly, but you're the boss. We'll hit 'em high as soon as you're done hitting 'em low. I still don't know what you're going to do, though."*>

"Neither do I, to be honest—it'll take more power than I've ever dreamed of putting out before. But if I do pull it off, this place will be ours forever. So grab yourself a sensor and watch. I'm gambling that the pirates will. They'll be more receptive if they see it for themselves, rather than hearing about it from whoever manages to escape from down here."

<*"But the visibility's pretty iffy right now. You've got heavy cloud cover for a hundred klicks and it's*

getting worse.">

"That's part of my plan. Visibility's no problem with the sensors they've got, and the storms are necessary for my show. Should be fun."

<*"Yeah, you said that about the Fourth Fleet just before we pulverized them. I'll watch, believe me!">*

"I need you to do more than that. Once I get going, I want you and Pavel to connect again and stay in touch. Keep the sensors as active as you can so I can see what's going on through your eyes—I'll be blind otherwise. Link with Yukio, too. I'll keep a solid tap so if anything goes wrong, we'll all know about it. That way I'll have you to cover me if things get too sticky."

<*"Now you're making sense. We'll sneak up as close as we can just in case.">* Pavel shied away from the emotion inherent in her next thought. <*"Be careful, darling.">*

"Right back at you, luv. See you later." The link was broken. "What's the word, Sharon?"

"The animals indicate they're building to rush us. There's a tremendous force still arriving from both the forest and the mountain camp. They'll charge us pretty soon. Apparently, their orders are still to take Denny alive."

"Sheesh, they're persistent," Denny groused. "If I'm that damned valuable, I want a raise."

"Just be ready." Jander did not rise to the humor. It was obvious he was already working on his game face.

He looked up as another deep bass roll of thunder rumbled through the heavy clouds overhead. "Perfect conditions. All right." He turned to the others. "Kodiak and the metamorphs will defend here, with Harmonia and her cats in tactical reserve." He met the zoopath's eyes. "Sharon, I know this will be tough for you, but your tigers must be expendable. If using them for our defense means their lives for ours, I'm trusting you to make the right decision."

She took a deep breath, then nodded. "You know I'll feel every hit, every death. But you also know I'm a Corpsman. None of us will let you down."

"I know that. Thank you." He held her steady eyes for a time, then turned to the others. "The pathport team will continue their hit-and-run tactics, with Nebula as close air support. I'll make my entrance between here and the mountain camp to the west. As soon as you see me, get back here and duck, so I don't trash you by mistake. I'll do my best to shield you, but I'll be pretty damned busy."

He rose to his feet and rotated his head to loosen his neck. "I'm going to get ready—this will take more concentration than I've ever needed before."

Richard snorted. "This from somebody who once moved an eight hundred ton slab of rock a thousand yards."

Steele unbuckled his gun belt, detached the canteen and handed the rest to Connors, who still had twin lasers at his side. "Meters, actually. But that was dead weight. What I'm hoping to do will take a lot more." His smile was grim. "See you later." He leaped into the air and zipped over the rock wall, turning undetectable as he rose.

Denny shook his head. "I can't wait to see what he's cooking up. From the sound of things, it'll make Ragnarök look like a spelling bee."

He buckled on the gun belt, needing the last hole despite his weight loss, then pointed at Pavel. "You're the pro. I'll turn tactical over to you. What'll we do?"

The Corpsmen grouped around a thin dusting of sand, and the Ukrainian sketched out the defense of their redoubt.

CHAPTER 24

With the hesitation of those unused to ground action, the Ertainians and their Lievan drones massed at the edges of the plateau. The Head was adamant in his demand that the presumed engineer be taken alive, despite their enormous losses so far.

The Gaeans contented themselves for the moment with long-range sniping with the powerful pulse pistols, waiting for the mobilization to be almost complete before venturing out. Ford and Kalanev made a hit on what the telepath perceived to be a group of officers, while Chelsea made several uncontested and devastating raids to gather laser rifles for the defense.

Richard, a competent mechanic in his own right, took a quick lesson from Denny and busied himself rewiring the lasers for rapid fire. Denny shifted boulders to build a series of strongpoints along the south wall and stocked each of them with the modified weapons.

The plan called for him to anchor the defense, changing positions when the opposition zeroed in on him. Walter would flank him on the eastern end while Cielo, a well-seasoned warrior, would cover the narrower but busier field of fire that sloped upward to the west. Sharon held a sniping position higher in the rockfall with a clear view from which to direct her cats, who were concentrated along the north and west walls to guard against any attempt to flank them.

Cielo leaped down from her high watch post and changed over. "They're about ready," she reported, then pulled on her briefs, grabbed a blanket along with a fistful of pistol batteries from the recharging station Walter was running full speed and headed for her battle position. Sharon's tigers glared at her, more wary of the relatively tiny changeling than they had ever been of Orion.

Chelsea returned, burdened with a full case of laser batteries she purloined from a supply site she had then destroyed.

Pavel called Richard over to join them. "Nebula, you will cover the west approach, as planned. Be certain that any larger craters you cause are out of laser range; they could use them for cover. And keep an eye toward the cliffs behind us as well. Use your own discretion; you are the strongest of us." Chelsea beamed and inclined her head. "Richard and I will attack the mass of pirates in the ravines to the south, with a few incursions to the west. We will begin now."

The ghost threw him a mock salute and dashed off to say goodbye to Denny. Seconds later she rose above the rocks and circled the area fully visible, then dove underground to keep the pirates guessing. The two gunmen, again bare to the waist and leaning back to back, raised their weapons and disappeared.

JANDER, SEQUESTERED DEEP WITHIN a cave, felt and heard the rising clamor of battle. For a few seconds he allowed himself to wonder if he was doing this the right way. As he had told everyone, Spart included, he was very much against sensational publicity for himself and his group. But after long and intense conversation with Vickie following the Sforan incident, they decided that secrecy was impossible, even detrimental to their cause. Thus he attacked the staging area in the image of their uniform, and he was about to put the Omega Corps on the galactic map in a big way with an unforgettable display of power.

Still, as an integral part of his plan, he wanted to make it appear that the Corpsmen only might be responsible for the spectacle. The Sforan operation was bound to make the Corps' name and its people public knowledge; the Confederation media were just as ferretous as their Gaean counterparts. The Ertainians, with their efficient espionage, were certain to recognize that the quarry here were components of the super-powered Corps.

But the upcoming visitation Steele was planning would be unlike anything ever imagined of any mortal, however fantastic. He hoped he had the strength to carry it out; any sign of faltering would negate the entire performance.

He cleared his mind of those useless thoughts and bent his full mental capacity to the purpose of digging for and harnessing the last, least dregs of concentration within him. He would need it all.

THE PIRATES ADVANCED IN RAGGED, uneven groups, preceded by their wide, powerful Lievan fodder. Chelsea concerned herself mainly with those, since the guns of either type could hardly stop them. She soared down the line, materializing a pebble in every fifth giant as she passed. Behind her a long, snaking row of mutilated corpses left the following Ertainians open to the withering fire of the defenders.

Behind her from the redoubt, Denny's lasers cut wide swathes in the forward ranks, while Walter and Cielo, and Sharon from her sniper position, added to the score with their far more powerful pulse pistols. Outnumbered and outgunned, only their superior marksmanship kept them from being overrun.

Richard and Pavel concentrated on the rear areas. They took the pirates completely by surprise time after time, appearing in their midst from out of nowhere and blazing away with all four guns. Dozens died without knowing how; scores saw the pair but did not live long enough to react. Those who could react found themselves killing their own comrades as the twin marauders disappeared.

Then, inevitably, their luck ran out. Once too often, they materialized in a large concentration of troops. They took their toll, but an officer who was the slightest bit faster than anyone else raised his projectile pistol and fired once before he died. Richard grunted and slid down Pavel's back, forty grains of expanded copper lodged near his heart.

Pavel cursed, feeling the shock of the hit in his own nerves through their mental link. Hurriedly he holstered his pistols, spun and wrapped his arms around his shocked and fading friend. Then he accomplished something that everyone, including Orion, would have sworn was impossible: he used his rapport with Richard to trigger and control the teleporter's ability. There was the familiar wrenching twist of probability, and the two were within the redoubt.

Sharon gasped and started to move toward them, but Pavel waved her back. "Stay with your animals." He touched the keypad on his wrist to alert the ship.

Cielo heard him and turned, gave an inarticulate cry and leaped toward them.

Kalanev barely glanced at her as she rushed in. "Get back to your post."

The Sudanese ignored the order and kept coming.

Cobra whirled with a snarl and whipped out a pistol. "Get back to your post, Kiaga!"

Cielo halted, stunned by his harsh tone and

deadly menace. She glanced from him to her man, the bulging puncture pulsing on his bloodied chest, then froze her eyes on Pavel's icy stare. He made it crystal clear that he meant to enforce his discipline.

She hesitated, feebly extended a hand, then slumped. Swaying, she turned and staggered back to her position.

<*"Yes, Pavel?"*>

"Alpha!" He spoke aloud to better drive his thoughts home. "We have a medical emergency—Hermes. Prepare to accept him via 'porter and have a replacement on hand."

<*"Roger, Cobra. We're under way right now. Prepare to trigger in twenty seconds."*>

Pavel glared at his wrist, hand poised over the tiny keypad. When the seconds ticked off, he tapped in his automatic recall code and stabbed the execute.

In a blink he found himself staring into Vickie's eyes. He shook off the sudden change in sight, sound and atmosphere and hopped down from the platform to make room for Dr. Kirkland's crack triage team. Seconds later his teammate was on the high-speed elevator and moving toward the sick bay eleven levels below.

"Where is the replacement? I must return immediately." Cobra's icy eyes were filled with a raging fury that only the loss of a brother could trigger.

"Coming now," Alpha told him. "I've called David Malloye as best for the job."

"Mal—" Pavel stiffened, then narrowed his eyes

as the Israeli flashed into being in front of him, still buckling his twin gun belt. The teleporter stopped short and returned Pavel's glare with compound interest. "Hello, Cossack."

Kalanev bared his teeth. "Well, pig-eater. Can you shoot someone head-on, or must they turn their backs?"

"You should talk, you baby-killing—"

"*Stop it!*" Vickie's voice was no less heated than theirs, her bearing no softer. Her fists balled at her sides. "You are both members of the Omega Corps. Your encounters in the past mean nothing here. You have your orders and you will carry them out, or you will answer to me!" Hazel eyes blazing into theirs of gray and blue, her muscles taut with inborn power, she stared them down.

Pavel relaxed his knife edged stance with obvious effort and turned back to the platform. "I beg your pardon, Lady Alpha, I am under stress." He jerked his head to the sabra. "Come."

Malloye met Vickie's eyes and moved shoulder first toward the Ukrainian. "By your order, Lady Alpha."

"No! For the Omega Corps, and for your brothers and sisters below who depend on your skills. If any of them die from this delay, I swear you'll both join them!" She savagely chopped a signal as she headed out to return to the bridge, and the wide-eyed Arai punched a key to send the two antagonists to the surface.

They materialized in the rockfall, glaring at each other. "Well, back-stabber, let's see if you can shoot," the Israeli sneered as he tore off his shirt.

Kalanev unlimbered his pistols. "Just be very certain you *do* stay behind me."

With equally murderous expressions they linked minds, steely psychic wires snaking through a solid wall of enmity. Back to back, they flashed into battle to take out their hostilities on the Ertainians.

In the interim, with only Chelsea in the field, the pirates came close to breaching the shallow defenses. Now hundreds were crouching nearby, slithering forward as close as thirty meters to dash for the rocks.

Denny took a beam through his right calf as he dashed between positions, but kept on fighting. Cielo sustained a head wound that barely left her conscious; only her catlike stamina gave her the strength to convert and heal herself.

Into the temporary breach Sharon sent two of her cats, meeting the incursion with teeth, claws and fury. The few pirates who managed to invade the redoubt were torn apart.

Still, the momentary penetration emboldened the pirates, and they pressed their numerical superiority with no thought to casualties. The weary Corpsmen escaped further damage by the barest of margins. They were close to losing the battle. Then three things happened at once:

Kalanev and Malloye appeared in the Ertainians' midst, the feuding veterans doing even more damage than the previous team.

Chelsea pulled out all the stops and started grabbing larger stones for her catalyst, hitting the rear areas with explosions comparable to quarter-ton bombs.

Sharon drew one of her daggers to supplement her pulse pistol and joined the perimeter herself, and loosed her tigers into the nearer ranks of the pirates. The two thousand-pound cats charged with terminal velocity into the Ertainian lines, striking with claws longer than fingers left and right, shearing off heads and snapping spines with one sweep of massive paw or doubled fangs.

The pirates fired wildly, killing their own as they tried desperately to slow the savagely twisting cats; and when they did hit them the rage of the behemoths was redoubled. The pinpricks of the lasers did little but make them even more furious. In a matter of minutes the only creatures moving in the area were on four gory legs.

Then, one by one, the cats dropped. Ertainian officers screamed hoarse commands and sharp-shooting Lievans stood stolid as the tigers bore down on them, waiting until the last second to fire and leap aside. Fewer than half made the leap in time, but the rest survived to die later.

At last the zootelepath felt compelled to withdraw her five remaining wounded cats, saving them for the defense. Thus the battle turned again, and the mesa became increasingly littered with moaning bodies, and others that would never speak again.

Gradually, so insidiously that it was almost unnoticed, the gray-green sky darkened and the wind increased to gale-force gusts. Abruptly, above the piercing hiss of the lasers and the pop and crack of projectile pistols and pulse guns, even above the bone-jarring thump of Chelsea's explosions, resounded a tremendous roll of thunder, a mighty rumbling roar of unrestrainable nature.

Then, far to the west between the plateau and the Ertainian landing field, a massive funnel sliced from the roiling clouds, growing half a kilometer wide as it spun its way to the ground, hurling uprooted trees and boulders as big as houses far from its path.

But this was no tornado such as anyone had ever before seen; powerful cyclonic winds blasted through the battlefield, flattening Ertainians and even staggering Lievans, yet the cyclone itself stayed in place and cratered its anchorage as if tethered to the mountainside. In small groups, the pirates ceased fire to dive for cover and stare at the phenomenon.

The sounds of combat died away as the Gaeans rushed to reach the den in the depths of their sanctuary, where they huddled behind the frightened cats. The Ertainians sought shelter of their own as the winds increased to hurricane intensity. The roaring funnel widened, then split in two and began to rise from the ground, leaving a pair of titanic pillars behind.

As the freakish tornados rose slowly upward

to rejoin the clouds, the towering pillars remained firmly anchored on their long, narrow foundations, seemingly reaching clear to the rumbling sky. The pirates cowered deep in their cover of craters, trees and rocks as the twin columns were dramatically revealed for what they really were.

They were legs.

CHAPTER 25

Faster now, the tornados continued to disperse, leaving whipping gales in their wake. As the clouds thunderously roiled and parted, the rest of the mighty form slowly emerged from the lightning-pierced darkness.

It was a hominin figure of painful black, glittering ebon with silvery highlights from its smooth head to the sturdy tendons of its feet, save for the fiery-red, lightning-laced eyes. It stood at least a thousand meters tall, the skin of the torso undulating to the stresses of the massive musculature beneath shoulders two hundred meters wide.

The Colossus swept its awesome eyes over the battlefield below, from the savaged mountain landing site to the bloodied and rain-drenched plateau. The crimson eyes flashed fire as the right hand raised from its side to form a massive fist.

Two Ertainian landing ships approached from the west, spitting bolts from their large-caliber lasers into the massive figure. The blasts were absorbed with no effect whatsoever save to attract the great being's attention. The right arm extended, rising to point a finger at one of the ships. A blinding slash of gilded lightning blazed forth to utterly consume the twenty-meter long vessel. The other ship sheered off and tried to escape, but came much too close.

The Colossus reached out the other hand and snagged the shuttle in mid-air, smashing it to a stop with no apparent effort, then brought it close to its blazing eyes. It glared at the ship with contempt, then threw it down onto the rugged mountain below. The small ship exploded in a brilliant fireball of chemical fuel almost at its feet, and it did not spare it another glance.

And then the Colossus spoke.

"I... AM... ANGERED."

The deep voice rumbled outward, gathering volume from the seething air, as audible as the rolling thunder from kilometers away, deafening close up. The Ertainian words themselves would have been inane from a lesser being. From the Colossus, they were dreadful.

It spread its arms, encompassing the very horizon with its presence.

"THIS WORLD IS MY HOME. ALL WHO SEEK SHELTER FROM THE STORMS OF UNJUST FATE ARE WELCOME HERE. ANY WHO COME SEEKING TO FORCE THEIR WILL UPON OTHERS SHALL FEEL THE BOUNDLESS MIGHT OF TRUE JUSTICE.

"YOU OF ERTAIN, YOU OF LIEV HAVE COME TO DEAL DEATH, AND TO GAIN THE KNOWLEDGE TO DEAL MORE. YOU ARE NOT

WELCOME HERE. IF YOU CHOOSE TO LEAVE, NOW, YOU MAY DO SO WITH YOUR LIVES AND YOUR POSSESSIONS. IF YOU DO NOT, YOU SHALL BE FORCED UPON YOUR WAY WITH ALL THE POWER AT MY COMMAND.

"GO, NOW, OR FACE THE FULL POWER OF MY WRATH!"

The voice fell silent, the figure still, its awesome frame untouched by the howling storm. For minutes, no adversary south or west of the immense figure dared to move.

Then, from all directions, from the savannah or swooping down from orbit, came squadron after squadron of armed Ertainian landing craft. They circled the titanic form like vultures, their thrusters consuming the atmosphere for miles around. Then they opened fire, each ship blasting sizzling pulses of energy at the giant figure.

Their mighty bolts of coherent light did nothing but animate the Colossus. The massive arms rose, lightning flashed from the gigantic fingertips, and ship after ship exploded thousands of meters away and plunged in molten pieces to utter destruction on the tortured terrain below.

In moments, thirty of the most potent fighting ships ever developed by a race of warriors ceased to exist. The remaining ships frantically powered away in all directions.

"YOU HAVE CHOSEN YOUR COURSE. SO BE IT!"

From deep within the Colossus, like an extension of the awesome voice, thunder began to rumble and growl. Flashes and strings and globules of blinding light roiled through the inner essence of the Being and streaked in all directions, creating brilliant red starbursts, ragged golden threads, silver-tailed comets of raw energy just beneath the translucent ebon skin.

And as the rumbling thunder grew, so did the violent energies coalesce and solidify in the core of the mighty Sentience, like a silver-streaked dark star glowing from within that fed from the palpable fury without.

The Colossus again raised its hands. Above it the clouds boiled and shuddered, and blinding chains of fervid lightning blazed through the gray-green heavens to the mind-staggering accompaniment of raucous, pealing thunder. Abruptly a stupefying bolt slashed from the angry sky, and another, to strike among the pirates near the plateau.

Again the figure gestured, and streaking lances of inconceivable power smashed through the electrified air to crash among the ships to the west. At the plateau and in the mountain camp the pirates screamed and fled in mindless, useless, hopeless efforts to evade their purely random fate.

Again and again the lightning speared down, blasting the trembling terrain to furrows and chasms of smoking, smoldering brimstone. And overhead the thunder rolled without end, deafening the victims, shaking the ground with its deep-throated fury.

Another flock of landing craft thundered down, but these did not curve in to attack. Showing courage that could only come from the command of dominant authority, the shuttles braved the gales and lightning and settled onto the ridges south of the plateau. One by one they popped their hatches.

The troops on the ground needed no further urging. They dropped their weapons and equipment and fled through the smoking terrain, flooding into the ships in such numbers that the pilots were forced to flare their engines to drive them back when they reached capacity. Heavily burdened, the craft struggled back into the air and upward to find whatever fleet ship would take them in.

The Colossus raised both arms to the clouds and bade the awesome assault to lessen in intensity, allowing the heavily buffeted ships a better chance to escape. The thousands of pirates took the break in the weather to run, some south from the plateau and many more back toward the landing area to the west.

The Colossus looked down upon them as they fled past its feet and waved an arm to point toward the grounded ships, clearly inviting the fugitives to pass. With another gesture it invited the ships to the west to rise and approach, indicating a series of weathered ridges much closer to the battleground.

A few intrepid pilots lifted off and made the short hop, and almost immediately started onloading the troops rushing to meet them. Seeing that, many of the other landing craft followed suit.

The Colossus planted its fists on its hips and waited, impervious to lightning, hail and fiercely driven rain as it watched the nearby ridges slowly fill with the escape vehicles. One by one, the small ships took on their passengers and clawed into the sky. As they roared upward, other craft circling outside the worst of the storm bored in to collect more.

Deep in his cave, Orion breathed deeply and allowed his giant construct to rest. The Colossus was pure energy, literally a figment of his imagination, and became solid only when physical contact was necessary. Its holographic form was unaffected by the violent weather that buffeted everything else, yet it served as the focus of the huge planes of force he wielded to bring the atmosphere into turbulent conflict.

For now, however, he gave the gales back to themselves, keeping the conditions harsh but not adding to them. Despite the Ertainians' reasons for being there, he was willing to show them mercy. He was content to allow them to evacuate with limited casualties as long as they did not resume their assault.

So the Colossus, and Jander by way of his telepathic link to the *Angel*'s sensors through Vickie's eyes, simply stood and watched them go.

<*"Jander, can you hear me?"*> It was Vickie, speaking through Pavel huddled behind a trembling tiger on the plateau.

The Colossus looked up with its fiery eyes and

nodded once.

<"*There's a squadron of battleships heading your way. These guys are much larger than cruisers, with twice the guns. We can't pick up any chatter from them, but they look like they're coming down to land. I can see you're letting the ground troops go, so they might be coming in to pick them up. We can't be certain, though.*">

The Colossus nodded again, then turned toward the redoubt, crouched and leaped into the air. It sailed untouched through the storm, twisted in midair and came to a soundless landing facing south with its hundred-meter feet on either side of the rockfall. It crouched and made a sweeping magician's gesture toward the ground. Between its feet grew a dome of shimmering energy to protect the seven Corpsmen and five tigers in their retreat.

The stress of that maneuver almost broke Jander's concentration, but he gritted his teeth and fought to maintain his focus on both the dome and the giant hologram. He struggled back to full control, raised the Colossus from its crouch and redirected his point of view to see the pirates streaming to the south and west. There were several thousand still to be evacuated.

He shifted his perspective to the troposphere beyond the roiling clouds and found six flares in circle formation dropping down from right above him. As large as they were, he could see they would still account for only a fraction of the escaping pirates.

He spared a small portion of his protean mentality to tighten his connection to Kalanev. Through his mind, reinforced by a dozen other telepaths, he could see Vickie's. She was in the command chair on the Bridge of the *Angel*, which was now parked in the shadow of the fifth moon, currently the nearest of the seven to the battlefield.

Vickie, as well as maintaining a solid rapport with Yukio and Pavel, was shifting her focus between the forward monitor showing the big battleships sinking toward the surface and the smaller monitor beneath it showing an image of the Colossus. Jander's construct was clear enough that the sensors could follow its every move.

Through the link he saw that Vickie was aware of several other squadrons following the battleships down, coming from all directions to converge on the plateau.

Far too many to land safely.

Then it hit him. The circle formation of the battle-ships was not one designed for a landing.

The Colossus stood and raised its arms, palms up and pumping in a raise-the-roof gesture.

Vickie saw the signal and instantly deduced its meaning. "Scatter! Worm us in there for a clear shot from our north polar guns. Neamhain! Set up a nuclear triple-tap on each of those battleships, no visual. Lock on and wait for my order."

Lam broke orbit of the moon and zigzagged through the packed Ertainian cruisers. Neamhain,

Mealla O'Hearne at armaments, took command of the three north polar pulse guns plus three from alternating Cancer sections and targeted the battle-ships as they came to bear.

Jander was irritated that he had fallen into another trap of his own making. The Colossus had offered clemency to any who chose to leave, and the Ertainians had appeared to take advantage of that mercy. But the ruthless Head and his minions cared nothing for the lower ranks. The evacuations were only a diversion to bring larger ships within range. And six of the strongest were now within striking distance.

In the cave, Jander set aside his emotions, relaxed into lotus position and pulled up every ounce of strength within him. The dome protecting the rock-fall changed composition and texture, infused with every absorbent shielding factor he could think of to withstand the nucleonic detonation he knew was coming.

Through his link to his furiously anxious woman, he saw the six battleships rock on their retros to bring no fewer than twelve nucleonic cannons to bear. The Colossus stood tall and raised its open hands, inviting them to fire.

Each of the twelve cannons unleashed a double volley, through the atmosphere, through the clouds, precisely on target.

In his cave Jander bent double with a guttural scream, taking the psychic blow like a lightning strike to the brain. The dome shrank back against the stupendous pressure that struck its surface, reflecting a deadly wave of ionizing radiation from the plateau through the ridges and ravines and over the hapless thousands of pirates in a blistering blanket of fire none could escape.

The blinding flash subsided. The battleships hovered at eight hundred kilometers, holding fire to see their results. Nothing moved in a ten-kilometer radius save for shuttles falling from the sky with their dead crews and passengers.

The Colossus, a mere hologram and impervious to harm, stared upward at the murderous battleships while the rippling dome slowly recovered its shape beneath it. Then the Colossus raised its arms in a twisting gesture toward the squadron of six, and a silver nimbus of energy swirled upward toward them from its sweeping hands.

Vickie in the speeding *Angel* leaned forward in the command chair, hazel eyes flashing. "Ready..."

When Jander's silvery cyclone reached the energy screens of the battleships, she snapped, *"Fire!"*

O'Hearne slammed her keyboard. Three volleys of six invisible nuke-infused spheres erupted from the pulse cannons at half-second intervals. The battleships exploded into white-hot shards of nanosteel that sent meteorites of molten metal blazing through Arcadia's atmosphere.

A few of the squadrons on approach to the planet sheered off, but the majority kept course to make their own attempts.

The Colossus raised its arms again to the stormy skies. The clouds parted like the eye of a hurricane, the deep well of the storm illuminating the plateau with its lightning. The Colossus beckoned, and the billowing cyclone of clouds spiraled down and closed over it, embracing it from the heavens downward in almost palpable folds of natural force.

Then, with a peal of thunder that dwarfed all others, the clouds slammed together in a glittering cascade of ionized hail, and the Colossus was gone.

That was Vickie's cue. The *Angel* and her crew, driven by grief, wrath and righteous vengeance, set to work in earnest.

CHAPTER 26

Incensed by the Ertainians' double-cross, Lady Alpha hurled the *Angel* into furious action. The ship under Scatter's direction seemed to her gunners to be everywhere, yet to the frantically fleeing pirates she did not exist.

From intercepted communications it was clear that Steele's hopes were realized; most of the panicky captains attributed the carnage to the mighty, mysterious god that mauled the ground force, taken the full impact of a twenty-four shot nucleonic assault with no damage, then spectacularly blended into the most violent storm most had ever seen. A number with more stable minds knew it had to be a trick, but they were not about to hang around to find out how it was done.

To speed them on their way, Vickie unleashed all eleven Banshees to harass the pirates remaining on the ground. Flying supersonic and with the tracer coloration removed from their pounding pulse guns they seemed to the terrified pirates to be an invisible extension of the thundering Colossus.

Their zero-point gravity engines made them mechanically silent, but one of the crews found that if they weakened their collision shields enough to let air through, the deep cones of the retro drivers captured the air and swirled it back out in a piercing Banshee screech. He passed it on to his squadron mates and they gleefully reduced the Ertainians to utter panic.

The pirates abandoned their captured territory en masse to seek haven in any ship they could catch leaving orbit. Every surviving shuttle took off within hours, leaving the Banshees to rule the firmament over the planet and between the moons.

But even with that incentive, there was no escape. Unleashed at last, crewed by furiously determined warriors who were fed up with being held back from their vengeance, the *Angel* wrought terrible havoc.

Using her superior speed and agility as well as her teleportation shifts, she struck with undetectable weapons from behind her baffle screens to decimate squadron after squadron of the pirate fleets. Kurino found the most dense concentrations, Tsin conveyed it to his teammates, Pashkov found the most efficient route to intercept the fleeing pirates, Lam maneuvered them into the cutoff position, O'Hearne alerted her gunners to their targets, and Angela added their numbers to the growing score.

Vickie allowed fewer than forty ships out of over four hundred thirty to escape. Most of them were transports, making it nearly certain that each of the survivors had taken in boats from the surface. Thus each escaping raider had at least one set of eyewitnesses as they fled in all directions.

Meanwhile, a single Sprite slipped through the chaos of the icy mountain hurricane and landed on the plateau under Jander's shield. Jander had managed to fly himself out of his cave and into the protective dome, which he somehow maintained until the Sprite arrived despite being barely conscious.

The shuttle, with its crew of two plus a trauma doctor and a zootelepath, took in the eight Corpsmen and five tigers, a very tight squeeze, and protected them as the battle and the storm raged above.

Many hours later, the *Angel* finally came to rest. The mighty jewel squatted on her three towering struts at the edge of the savannah, having visited the plateau only long enough to pick up the Sprite. Vickie took a very quick look and ordered the ship to a place less ravaged; thus the *Angel*'s crew could enjoy their first new planetfall without having to wear radiation suits and hip boots.

Soon after the *Angel* touched down, Alpha sent ghosts, newly minted pathport teams, and slower but just as effective telepathic-telekinetic teams flitting through the forests between the savannah and the mountains to track down any Ertainians left behind.

The pirates fought to the death with no thought of surrender, which suited the Corpsmen just fine. None of them was in the mood to take prisoners.

Jander, after his supreme effort, lay in a near-coma in the sick bay, guarded by Cinnamon the cat and the stern aegis of Dr. Kirkland. Denny was there, too, his bruised, radiated, half-deafened, multiply wounded and nutritionally deprived poundage swiftly recovering under the medical staff's intensive care.

Beside him rested Richard, his stalwart heart aching from the damage but now healed. The teleporter was truly dead by the time he had reached the ship, but the magnificent surgical skill and transmutational magic of Chloe and her team managed to knit him back together and breathe new life into his brawny frame.

In another room was Chelsea. Although she was physically unhurt except for the squeeze from Meshzner and the gremlin bites, she had pushed herself to almost total exhaustion—or as one of the medics put it, "a permanent case of stiff upper lip". She was under sedation to guard against any nightmares that might trigger her spectrality.

The Chief Surgeon clamped an airtight seal around all four of her patients, even refusing Vickie admittance until she was overruled by The Look.

Sharon Gibson found herself camping with nearly five tons of ferocious felines in a specially equipped storeroom next to Hydroponics on Deck Six, working with a good portion of the science department to heal their wounds. After a few days, having eaten their way through a month's worth of protein from the ship's larder, all but one were returned to the surface and relocated to good hunting ground.

The one exception was Leyla, who became so bonded to her person that Sharon demanded to keep her.

For the others in the strike squad, no celebration was too extravagant. Cielo and Walter lacked nothing from their ebullient comrades, being royally wined, dined and entertained on the sole condition that they talk themselves hoarse about their adventures. And the high point: the erstwhile enemies, Pavel Kalanev and David Malloye, shared in a bone-crushing handshake. Vickie explained it thus: "You both shake, or I shake you both."

The two old warriors then split a bottle of vodka and soon proclaimed their undying comradeship birthed from back-to-back combat.

Jander was released the next day and given over to his devoted wife, who spirited him to their suite and forced him to rest.

Still, his tired mind spent hours in dark reflection on the cruel circumstances that had made his supreme effort so necessary. He issued directives to set things right.

THEY GATHERED IN A FAR CORNER of the newly christened Whitney-Soames Park on the seventeenth deck of the *Angel*, as many of her crew as could leave their stations standing shoulder to shoulder in silence. Those who could not attend, including the Corpsmen on Gaea hundreds of parsecs away, were watching Angela's broadcast. Never since the *Angel*'s launch from the hidden Montana shipyard had the entire

Corps assembled in such full numbers.

Lord Orion, in full dress uniform as were they all, stood facing them with Lady Alpha at his right shoulder. Behind them in that quiet corner of the Park was a fresh garden of flowers surrounding five short mounds of bare soil. At the head of each small excavation was a foot-high gravestone of Arcadian granite, slanted back from bottom to top so that the carved transcriptions could easily be read:

ZACHARIAH DUNBAR WHITNEY
PEREGRINE
OF THE OMEGA CORPS

FREDRIC ANTHONY SOAMES
JUMBUCK
OF THE OMEGA CORPS

SIMON LEE CRAWLEY
PECOS
OF THE OMEGA CORPS

ELGA LORENA DOMINIQUE MANÇON
DOMINIQUE
OF THE OMEGA CORPS

WILLIAM SWIFTFOOT WIZE
KOHANA
OF THE OMEGA CORPS

Jander took a deep breath and let it out slowly, steeling himself for the most difficult address of his young life. He felt Vickie's empathy flooding him with a soothing affirmation of life tinged with the sadness of their loss. He drank it in and took his strength from it as he faced the somber throng of Corpsmen.

"Friends, comrades... family. We are gathered today to dedicate this small parcel of Gaean soil to the memory of our fallen brothers and sister. The nature of their passing prevents us from honoring their corporeal forms, but within the small receptacles interred here we have placed a previously stored DNA sample of each of them, along with a small possession they each cherished in life. In this way, a part of them shall remain here as long as the *Angel* and the Omega Corps shall exist.

"I don't need to retell to you the actions that brought them to this place. Their heroic sacrifice in the line of duty is now part of the legend of the Omega Corps and will be retold countless times. Nor need I ask you to reinforce your courage and dedication from their example, for you would not be here if you did not already share those noble qualities. These virtues are inherent in the Corps and always shall be.

"Rather, I ask that you reflect on the short-sighted conceit that led to their passing, the mistakes that were made, the careless arrogance that led us to imagine we knew all the answers and could handle any circumstance with ease. It is so effortless for us to wield our so recently received gifts with no thought to the consequences, with no caveat that we are all, still, very human. We swept out into the universe with our enhanced minds and bodies and our unrivaled technology and expected to be unchallenged every time. We have now brutally learned that nothing could be further than the truth."

He reached out with his mind to touch theirs. Many were really starting to think in the direction he was leading them. He continued, his voice even but grim.

"For all our talents and increased intellect, for all our greater knowledge and skill, we have yet to grow into our newfound power. We are children who have tossed away our matches and started playing with dynamite. And if we don't wake up and reassess both ourselves and the risks we face from those who could become our adversaries, we will soon blunder ourselves out of existence."

He swept an arm behind him. "These five should not have paid the price of that reality. I take that upon myself, and no one will ever talk me out of that. It has forced me to reevaluate my abilities, my achievements, my commitment. I have vowed to myself that, from now forward, I will do my very best never to allow overconfidence to betray the better part of me, ever again.

"But I can't improve my performance without every one of you standing beside me."

He paused to allow that to capture them. In those

few seconds of silence he started to see the change in them, the set jaws, the level gazes, the touches of pride born of allegiance.

"I say that with the full understanding that the final decisions fall on my shoulders. It is you yourselves who have charged me with that duty, and I bear it with every intention of proving myself worthy. But I must and shall call upon you, each and every one of you, to keep me grounded.

"You each were selected for the Omega Corps for much more than your variant potential. You were chosen for your intelligence, your common sense and your strength of character, qualities that beyond doubt contribute to our chances of success. I charge each of you to fully utilize the strengths that I know you have.

"Now, most of us were raised from childhood with a deference to rank, position and expertise that can sometimes silence us. That conditioning is hard to shake. But in truth, we all have so much to learn, and so much to give. No answer is so perfect as to be worth forfeiting one's right to question. We all must be willing to listen and be just as ready to speak, whatever the circumstances and whoever takes the lead. Only in mutual respect will we succeed as a team. Only in unselfish solidarity can we take to heart the harsh lessons that have brought us here today."

He looked over at Ann Whitney, standing close and facing her husband's monument with tears glistening on her pallid face. Her chin rose as she looked up, and she met his eyes with a solemn gaze.

He could see as well as feel her grief, yet she projected no anger, no accusation. What he saw through the tears was the same as he felt from every other Corpsman, the sorrow of the loss of family and the determination to do their very best to prevent it from happening again.

He acknowledged her emotions with a slow nod. "Make no mistake, we will always mourn the loss of our teammates. Their example and their sacrifice will always be a part of us, and we must do our utmost to be the better for it. Let us direct our feelings of loss to rededicate our lives and our actions toward the fulfillment of our self-appointed duty, to our planet, our species and our galaxy, no matter the cost."

He paused, not knowing what else he could say. He wanted to leave them with an inspiration, a message of strength and unity, but nothing further came to mind. Then he felt a tweaking thought pass from his wife into the Corpsmen in front of them.

From near the center of the crowd, a female voice started to sing. Softly at first, then with more confidence, the tune was caught and echoed by other voices, and spread throughout the assembly and across the parsecs to Gaea, growing in volume, in harmony, in strength.

As one, the entire Omega Corps clasped hands with those around them and said farewell to their comrades with a profoundly heartfelt song of hope and reassurance: Amanda McBroom's "The Rose."

EPILOGUE

Terry's other patients were released from the sick bay two days later. Jander left his quarters secretly, remaining invisible until he reached his office, then summoned Denny and Chelsea. He remained seated as they entered, the titan's massive paw carefully engulfing Chelsea's hand.

"You wanted to see us, Chief?"

"Yes." He leaned back and favored his friend with a look of contrition. "I want to apologize to you."

Denny shifted uncomfortably and shrugged his shoulders. "Hey, you don't have to do that, Jander. I've figured out what you were trying to do and I'm really…"

He waved the engineer to silence. "No, that's not what I'm talking about," he said. "After everyone in the ship slapped me down for second-guessing myself I decided I might as well let it slide. No, I wanted to apologize for digging into your department, ordering Hal Summers to do a job of special engineering."

Chelsea cocked her head and looked up at her man.

Denny, too, looked confused. "Gosh, Chief, that's your privilege," he stammered. "You're her designer, after all."

"No, you still don't understand. This was a job in the living quarters. I opened up one of the vacant family suites on Deck 14 and had Hal modify the gravity plates, so they can be controlled from within the room." He looked for a reaction.

Denny rocked back on his heels, obviously fogged. He could see that the otherwise brilliant engineer was still not with him. Chelsea, on the other hand, was almost glowing. Trying to keep his voice as businesslike as possible, he went on.

"The control is a rheostat, so you can adjust the internal gravity from two gravities all the way down to one tenth. That's so you can adjust it to bring your apparent weight down to, say, ninety-nine pounds..."

Denny swallowed hard, suddenly weak. He got it. White-faced, he stared down into the glittering eyes of his companion, who giggled under her breath and pressed her knee into his calf.

Jander cleared his throat. "Of course, you still have to watch your strength, but you're used to that. Oh, if it pleases you, don't forget that I have the authority as Captain to make damn anything official. Just say the word, and I can make this partnership as permanent as you both apparently want it to be."

He nodded once and flicked the back of his hand toward the hatch. "Go. Scoot. Dismissed."

Jander turned to his left-hand monitor that displayed his plans to find the Ertainian home world, effectively closing the discussion.

Denny leaned a step closer and tried to speak. Chelsea kicked him in the shin and tugged on his corded arm, struggling to guide him to the hatch. Denny showed the inevitable wisdom of agreeing with her and let himself be led. Hand in hand, the giant and the ghost headed for their next adventure.

ABOUT THE AUTHOR

Keith Huntsman moved from Maine to Texas as a teenager and never left. After the University of Texas and a stint in hotel management, he took a temporary job in government civil service for food money while trying to make it as an author. The temp job became permanent and he's been there ever since, rising from the mailroom to project management and legislative analysis. But *The Omega Corps* was always there, waiting forty years to mature with him and find its way to print.

An inveterate reader, Keith lives in Austin with a tortie named Rita and her two daughters, and an enormous media library touching every subject.